# *End of* ILLUSIONS

## ANNIE JOCOBY

**BOOKS**

## By Annie Jocoby

Illusions

*Beautiful Illusions*
*Deeper Illusions*
*End of Illusions*

Vinci Books

vinci-books.com

Published by Vinci Books Ltd in 2025

1

A CIP catalogue record for this book is available from the British Library.
Paperback ISBN: 9781036707286

The EU GPSR authorised representative is Logos Europe, 9 rue Nicolas Poussion, 17000 La Rochelle, France
contact@logoseurope.eu

# Chapter One

## IRIS

*Your husband is dead. We're sorry, we did all we could, but there was too much internal bleeding.*

I stared blankly at the doctor who was standing above me in a white coat, looking very serious. He had just appeared in the waiting room where I sat, alone, except for the female cop who was staying there with me. I guess that there was a fear that I would fall apart. I said nothing, just stared at the floor. I planned, in my head, the way that I would join him. Some way that wasn't too messy and wouldn't be too traumatizing for the people who loved me.

There was no way that I could live without him.

"I, I, I have to call somebody," I said in a monotone voice. I got out my phone, and proceeded to dial some numbers. They were random numbers. I had no idea about anybody's phone numbers at this point. There was just no way that I could possibly call anybody.

"Excuse me," I said. "I need to take this in the bathroom."

The doctor nodded, and the police woman looked at me sympathetically and shook her head.

On the way to the bathroom, I was thinking about finding a razor somewhere and slashing my wrists. Or busting into a drug storage room and swallowing a handful of whatever I could find.

Dead. There was no way this was true. My mind couldn't even start to comprehend it.

The image of Ryan lying on the floor, with blood squirting out from God-knows-where, was flashing through my mind like a neon sign that I just couldn't shut off. I took several clumps of hair in my hands, and pulled. I got into the bathroom, and started banging my head against the mirror, over and over again, and started screaming at the top of my lungs.

Then I collapsed.

## Chapter Two

I was woken up by a kindly gentleman who was gently nudging me in my chair. "Mrs. Gallagher. Mrs. Gallagher," the voice said, shaking me gently.

I looked at him. He was the man who just informed me about my husband's passing.

I just shook my head. Go away. I don't want to talk to you. Leave me alone.

"Mrs. Gallagher, I wanted to keep you updated on your husband's progress in surgery."

"My husband's progress in surgery? I don't understand."

"Your husband has been in surgery for the past 10 hours. You must have nodded off in your chair for a few minutes."

I was still foggy. Was this a dream? Or was I dreaming before? I prayed that this was the real scene, and that the other was just a horrible, horrible, horrible nightmare.

"Surgery?" I put my head in my hands. Why was it so

difficult to comprehend anything? I just shook my head. I felt the lady cop put her arm around my back.

"She's still in shock," she said. "Why don't you tell me what's going on with her husband, and I'll tell her when she's a bit more coherent?"

"Well, this has been a very delicate surgery, very touch and go. The bullet went through his abdomen and lodged near his spine. The spinal cord was not injured, but there is some swelling. Mr. Gallagher might be paralyzed for awhile, but hopefully that will only be temporary. He's still not out of the woods, but we are making progress."

"You hear that?" lady cop said. "Sounds like your husband is going to make it through surgery."

I nodded and said nothing. I had an Indian blanket wrapped around my shoulders, and I wrapped it around me tighter, clutching it for dear life.

"Do you mind if I look at your cell phone?" lady cop asked.

I just shook my head mutely, then pointed to my bag.

Lady cop dug through my bag and found my cell phone. "Now, Mrs. Gallagher, if you don't mind, I'd like to look through your contacts. Is there anybody on here that I can call to come and be with you?"

I nodded my head. "Nick. Call Nick."

Then she dialed the phone. "Hello," she said. "Is this Nick?...this is Officer Cecelia White....I'm sorry to wake you...Mrs. Gallagher is here at the Emergency Room at the hospital...she asked me to call you. Can you come and keep her company?..I'm sorry I didn't call earlier. Mrs. Gallagher has been in too much shock to give me permission to use her phone until just now....the doctor will have to explain... ok, see you then."

"He's on his way now, Mrs. Gallagher. He said that he'll be here in about 20 minutes or so."

I said nothing, just stared at the floor and wrapped my blanket around me even tighter.

Sometime after police lady got off the phone with Nick, I heard his familiar voice. "Hi, I'm Nick O'Hara. You must be Officer White."

"Good to meet you, Mr. O'Hara."

"What's going on?"

"The doctor will be out in a few more minutes."

"No, tell me now. What's going on?"

"Mr. Gallagher was shot. In front of Mrs. Gallagher. Mrs. Gallagher stabbed an intruder, but not before he shot Mr. Gallagher."

"Holy Christ." Then he was sitting right next to me, putting his arm around me. "Iris, Iris, are you there? Talk to me, Iris."

I looked at him, and then the tears started gushing. He wrapped his arms around me while I sobbed, my hands still clutching my blanket tightly. He gently put his hand in my hair, and I immediately felt comforted.

It felt just like Ryan's touch.

Then I remembered that Ryan was in surgery, and he might not make it, and, even if he does make it, he might be paralyzed.

"Shhhhh, Iris, it's going to be ok. Ryan's tough. He's survived this long, in the most messed up scenarios imaginable. Shhhhh, it's ok. It's going to be ok."

I just shook my head. "Dalilah," was all I said.

"Where is Dalilah?" he asked.

"Daniel. Daniel has her. Please call him, I need to see her."

At that, he whipped out his phone. "Daniel, it's Nick...I know what time it is...you have Dalilah there...could you bring her to the hospital?...Ryan was shot..........he's in surgery.......good point." At that he looked at me. "Uh, Daniel's ok with watching her. I'm not sure if it's a good idea to have her here in the waiting room."

"Is she ok? I need to talk to her."

"Is Dalilah ok?" Nick asked. "She's sleeping? Of course, of course, it's like 4:30 in the morning."

I pleaded with Nick, tugging on his shirtsleeve "Dalilah doesn't have anything there. No diapers, no toys, no breast milk, no nothing. I just gave her to him without anything at all. Please tell him to go by the house and get what she needs. Everything is in her room. There's a diaper bag with everything she needs, and the fridge is full of bottled breast milk."

I was amazed at how much just having Nick here was helping clear up my mental fog.

Nick said "Iris says to go by the house and get Dalilah's things. A diaper bag in her room, bottled breast milk in the fridge and..." Then he looked at me. Addressing me he said "She got any favorite toys that Daniel should pick up?"

I nodded. "A Winnie the Pooh stuffed bear, her Etch-A-Sketch, and some puzzles. Everything's in her room."

Nick turned back to the phone "You get all that?....ok, great, thanks...bye."

Addressing me again, Nick said "Daniel's on his way back to the house, and he'll call if anything is going wrong. Right now, he said that it's not a problem to take care of her."

I nodded. "Thanks."

He sat down. "Now, do you feel like talking about what happened?"

I didn't feel that I could talk without breaking down and crying, so I just shook my head.

"Ok, then, I'll ask Cecelia." Cecelia had stepped out, and was back in the waiting room with us. She talked into the receiver on her shoulder.

"So, Officer White, what happened?"

"We arrived at 6:07 PM to the Gallagher household. A neighbor who was walking his dog by the house called 911 after hearing a gunshot go off. We arrived and Mr. Gallagher was lying on the floor after having been shot. Mrs. Gallagher was with him. We rushed Mr. Gallagher to the hospital, and trailed behind them in a squad car. Mr. Gallagher was brought into surgery at 6:17, and has been in there ever since."

"Crap," Nick said. It was like the news just now hit him. He went pale, and sat down next to me. He was shaking. He put his head in his hands, his entire body visibly quivering.

I couldn't comfort him the way that he comforted me. I still felt numb, like my limbs simply wouldn't move. I cursed myself silently for my impotence.

We sat next to one another, silently, with Cecelia the lady cop still hanging around and talking into her receiver. I wondered why she was still there. Probably she wants to talk to Ryan when he gets out of surgery, but I wouldn't imagine that he would be in any shape to talk to anyone at that point.

Finally, Nick looked at me. "How are you holding up?"

I shrugged my shoulders and said nothing. I didn't want to talk. Dalilah was safe, and Ryan was still in surgery. There wasn't much more I could say at that point.

Then I was crying uncontrollably again. "Oh, Nick, what would happen if we lose him? I think that I would want to join him. I don't see myself living without him."

"Quit talking like that. We aren't going to lose him, so you don't have to worry about that. Now, stop. Just stop." But I saw his face, and it was clear that he, too, was afraid of what would happen to both of us if Ryan, God forbid, didn't make it out of surgery. He and Ryan had been friends since elementary school. His loss would be even more acutely felt than would mine.

To take my mind off of my horror, I decided to find out a little bit more about Ryan and Nick's friendship. "How did you and Ryan meet?" I asked him.

"It was kinda funny," he said. "It was in kindergarten. We didn't have home room together, or nothing, so we didn't see each other that much. But Ryan was on a tricycle, hogging it if I can recall, and I knocked him off it. He hit his head. I laughed at him, and he came after me. We got into a fight on the playground, and both of us ended up in the principal's office. We became friends waiting there for the principal to come out and scold us." He chuckled. "Both of us got in trouble at home, of course, him more than me. Goddamn, his dad sure was a bastard back then."

"What happened to Ryan?"

"He got beat, of course. But that was nothing new. He was always being beat by Benjamin. Maggie was just too much of an ethereal hippy to stand up to Benjamin and his tyrannical ways." He shook his head. "Poor Ryan. It seems that fate just never lets him catch a break. He meets you, the love of his life, but he can't be happy because something is always waiting in the wings to snatch it away."

"What about you? What's going on in your life?"

"Eh, same old same old. I'm just about ready to give Rielle every piece of property I own, in exchange for her leaving me the hell alone. It's not worth it. Love isn't worth it. No offense."

"Sometimes it is. Love. Sometimes it's worth it."

"Well, you guys got lucky in finding each other."

"Yeah. I just hope that…" I trailed off, not wanting to finish that sentence. To think that Ryan wouldn't make it through surgery was just too horrible.

"Listen, Ryan is a tough guy. He's in amazing shape. He's gonna pull through."

I just nodded my head mutely, then stared at my hands. I felt awful. This was yet more agony. Everything that had happened up until this point felt like the end of the world – Rochelle's attack, Andrew's rape, Natalie's pregnancy. It all chipped away at my soul, little by little. I bounced back after all of it, but there was a part of me that felt like I was permanently damaged.

Now this. This was far worse than anything else that had happened. Would I recover if he doesn't make it? Would I want to? Would I be able to get out of bed in the morning without seeing his beautiful face? What would happen to Dalilah if I just fall apart? What would happen to Dalilah if I didn't make it either?

She would be an orphan.

"Uh, Nick, I hate to bring this up. But, with Ryan in there, it is a reminder that life might be fleeting. If he doesn't make it, God forbid, and something happens to me – would you take Dalilah?"

Nick just stared at me. "Don't bring this up now. Nothing is going to happen to either one of you. Now stop it. Stop with the fatalistic bullshit."

I sighed. Who would take Dalilah? My parents were way too old, my sister way too unstable. Nick was so good with her - he would be the obvious choice. But he was right, I shouldn't be talking like this. It would just jinx everything.

We sat in silence some more, and were sitting there

quietly like that when the doctor came out into the waiting room. His face was non-committal. My heart was in my throat, trying to read his expression.

"We're through with surgery," he said. "Your husband has been taken to the ICU."

I started hyperventilating and shaking all over. I took Nick's hand and gripped it tightly.

"However, there is still a great deal of swelling around the spinal cord. Hopefully when the swelling goes down, your husband will regain use of his lower extremities. But, for now, Mr. Gallagher is paralyzed from the waist down."

"But he's alive? He, he, he's going to make it?" I gripped Nick's hand even tighter.

"Barring any kind of further issue, such as infection or an embolism, there is a good chance that your husband will be able to go home in a matter of weeks."

At that, Nick and I hugged each other tightly. We both were shaking, and I was crying uncontrollably again.

"When, when, when can I see him?" I asked.

"He's in the ICU. You can see him now, but he's not conscious."

"Can Nick come too?"

"I'm terribly sorry. Only members of the immediate family can see him right now."

I felt awful about that. If ever there was somebody who should be considered family to Ryan, it was Nick.

I looked at Nick, who looked pissed. But he nodded at me as I got up out of my chair to follow the doctor into the ICU.

Ryan was lying in the hospital bed, hooked up to a variety of scary-looking machines. His vitals seemed to be doing well, though, as I noticed that his heart rate was a steady 54 bpm, and his blood pressure was 105/64. He wasn't on a ventilator. He appeared to be resting comfortably.

I went over to the bed, and took his hand. I smiled. "My turn now, huh? You were by my side 24/7 when I was recovering from Rochelle's attack, now it's my turn to be there for you. I hope that you can hear me. I love you more than I ever thought possible. I love you, Ryan Gallagher. You're a part of me. And I'm going to help you get through this, just like you helped me get through Rochelle's attack. We're a team now."

I smoothed back his dark hair, and touched his face. His skin felt cool and clammy, which somewhat startled me. He also looked deathly pale. I so wanted him to open those beautiful eyes and let me drown in their depths, as was usual. But he just laid there, breathing in and out laboriously. A nurse stood by with a chart, ready to come and take his vitals.

I sat there for as long as I could, just talking away to him. I couldn't stop touching him. I thought that I would never again be able to touch him, never again be able to stroke him. Never again be able to run my fingers through his amazing mane. I was eternally grateful that I was given a second chance with him.

Finally, visiting hours were over. A nurse gently came up to me, putting her hands on my shoulders. "Mrs. Gallagher, visiting hours are over," she said. "Let me help you back to the waiting room."

I touched my fingers to my lips one last time, and placed them on his cheek. "I love you," I told him. "I love you."

I got back, and Nick was still there, reading something on his iPhone. He looked up at me. "How is he?"

"Resting comfortably," I said. "Thank God. What time is it? I'm starving."

"It's just about 10 o'clock. Ryan was in surgery for some 14 hours."

"Let's get breakfast, huh?"

# Chapter Three

Nick and I left the hospital and headed out to a local Denny's. I dug into my scrambled eggs and bacon hungrily. I had no idea why I was so famished. I guess because I hadn't eaten since...I couldn't remember. I skipped lunch because of the stress of the deposition, then, of course, didn't have dinner because, well, Andrew was there waiting for me when I got home from the courthouse.

Nick, for his part, got a Grand Slam with everything – bacon, eggs, hashed browns, pancakes and juice. Looking at his lean frame, I wondered where he put everything.

I didn't feel like talking still. I was completely wrapped up in my own head.

"How are you holding up?" Nick asked.

"I don't really know. I need to process everything, and it's just impossible right now. Just impossible. It doesn't even seem real. But Ryan made it through surgery, that's what's most important." I didn't want to think about Derrick Thomas, the defensive star for the Kansas City Chiefs, who made it through his surgery, was paralyzed, and died not a month later from an embolism, which was somewhat common in paralyzed patients. I also didn't want to entertain the possibility that Ryan might acquire a drug resistant infection and not make it out of the hospital. Right now, I had to concentrate on the fact that he was alive. He wasn't out of the woods, but he wasn't dead, either.

"Do you want to tell me what happened?"

At first I shook my head, staring at my shaking hands that were gripping my glass of water. I wanted to throw up.

But Nick just stared at me, not talking. He didn't try to fill the silence, so I hesitantly began my story.

"Andrew, he was uh, he was in my house. He was in my house, holding, holding, uh, Dalilah. He had, uh, a, a, g-g-g-un." Now I was trembling wildly. "He had a gun, and he thought that I was his ex-wife, Cherry. Cherry. She-she-she's dead, Cherry, she's dead. Dead. He thought I was her, and he-he-he-he threatened me. As her. He threatened me, thinking I was her. And Ryan came in and s-s-sacrificed himself for me. He made it so that Andrew wanted to kill him, not me."

"I'm not sure I'm following you."

"Ryan came in, and he basically told A-A-A-ndrew th-th-at Andrew wanted him, not me. Cherry was cheating on A-A-An, the bad man, and the bad man wanted to kill me, because he thought I was Cherry. Ryan came in and told the bad man that he-he-he was the one who was cheating with Cherry, so the bad man wanted him, not me."

Somehow, someway, Nick managed to follow the story, even with my stuttering and stumbling around. "So, cray-cray Andrew came in, thought you were his ex-wife, threatened you because he thought that you were cheating on him with somebody, and Ryan came in and posed as that somebody so that Andrew would kill him and not you?"

I nodded. "You managed to understand perfectly." Nick was apparently no dummy.

Nick just shook his head. "He said that he would give his life for you. I guess that he meant it."

I just nodded my head, then reacted to his statement several minutes later. "Uh, he said he would give his life for me?"

"Several times. It's probably 10% his guilt over putting you in those situations and 90% that boy's overwhelming love for you." He shook his head. "I've never met a woman that I felt that strongly for. Ever. I couldn't imagine taking a bullet for Rielle or Alexis. For my kids, sure, definitely. Would take 100 bullets for them. But the women in my life? Not a chance."

I felt badly for him, never experiencing that kind of unconditional love. Then I looked at my glass again. "I'd give my life for him as well. I love him so much, Nick. I'm still so scared about what might happen with him. He's not out of the woods yet. And he might be paralyzed. How will he deal with that?"

Nick just shook his head. "Listen, Iris, I don't think that you know Ryan as well as you might think. How much he has been through. You know the surface stuff about what happened, but you don't know the deeper stuff about him. How he thinks. What he has seen and done. Trust, he has been through far worse than not being able to have the use of his legs for a few months. Hell, he's been through far worse than not being able to have the use of his legs permanently. He's a tough guy. He'll get through this, like he has gotten through everything before."

I wondered what he meant by his words. That I didn't know the whole story of his life before me. I guess that I only knew the "highlights" – or low-lights, really. Nick had known Ryan virtually Ryan's entire life, so he knew Ryan better than anyone.

"I guess I don't understand," I said. "What do you mean that I don't know everything about Ryan's past?"

"You do," he said. "In a sense. It's like this – you like a certain band because of what you hear on the radio. Like Muse – you like them, right? Or the Silver Sun Pickups?"

"Yes, yes, of course," I said. Those were two of my favorite bands.

"What if all you knew about the Silver Sun Pickups was Lazy Eye? Or all you knew about Muse was Uprising or Resistance? Or, for that matter, all you knew about any band was their hits? You may think that you love Bruno Mars, but if you don't listen to him cover to cover, then you don't really know him."

"So, basically, I've gotten to know Ryan through his greatest hits, so to speak?"

"Yeah, something like that. All those other songs, the B sides and the unreleased, they all go into an artist's repertoire, but most people only know the bands by what they hear on the radio. Sometimes the deeper cuts are the most important ones of all."

"Well, we're here, talking. Maybe you can clue me in on some of the deeper cuts, so to speak."

Nick shook his head. "I'm not sure how much Ryan wants you to know. He's a complex guy. He has a dark side that he has managed to control for many years, and it doesn't entirely have to do with his drug use."

I nodded, encouraging him to go on.

"You might think that, because he's rich, he would just have access to whatever he wants, whenever he wants. Which is generally true, but there were times when he went off the grid, just like you did. I mean, not for weeks at a time, but he would hang out with some rough characters for days. Drug dealers, underworld guys, wrong-track junkies. He stayed in school through a combination of Alexis' charms and his father's money - otherwise he would've been thrown out for missing too many classes. Still, he always managed to get straight As. A lot of guys hated him for that reason alone."

"Alexis' charms?"

"Yeah. She's pretty talented in certain ways. She managed to wrap most of the Deans around her little finger. Professors, too. Ryan's absences were largely overlooked. Didn't hurt that Benjamin was one of the college's greatest benefactors."

"Why did he hang out with those types of guys? I mean, he's rich, he could just get his drugs through some kind of safe connection, right?"

"Yeah," Nick said. "But the guy had a death wish. Besides, Nate and I were constantly on his ass about quitting. Interventions, rehab, more interventions. I even restrained him for a three day period, like in that movie The Basketball Diaries. Had a puke bucket by the side of the bed, and I handcuffed him while he detoxed. I never had seen him so enraged as he was for those three days, then, when that was over, he disappeared for several days and ended up getting shot."

I examined my eggs and said little. I somehow knew all of what Nick was telling me about his friend.

"That shot, and another time he was shot weren't life-threatening – these shots were in the shoulder and the leg. He used to get involved with turf wars, so he was locked in a car trunk for two days, while the dealers threatened to set the car on fire. As I said," Nick said, shaking his head, "you may have an image of a rich kid getting his drugs the Upper West Side pristine way, but that's not how it was."

"How did he get away from all that?" I knew Ryan so well, yet I still didn't know the answer to this question of how he finally walked away from his drug addiction after being so heavily involved in it for so many years.

"It was him being locked in a car trunk that did it. He suddenly realized that he wanted to live, because he was so close to dying, with those thugs outside the trunk, threatening to douse the car in gasoline and light a match. They tormented him like that the whole time he was in there, but they really weren't serious. They just wanted to scare him. After all, the trunk had air holes in it, so they really didn't want to kill him. After he got out of that, he decided to seek intensive therapy. It took years for him to feel somewhat normal, but he finally started to come out of his dark place."

"So, he's survived some pretty tough situations, even more than I even knew about."

"Yeah. And he'll survive this, come what may. I honestly think that he's so happy to be alive, after all he went through, that, whatever his life throws at him, he takes it, because he's still above ground, instead of below it."

"That's certainly a good way to approach life."

"What about you? How will you handle it if Ryan is confined to a wheelchair, with a catheter and colostomy bag?"

"In sickness and in health, remember? No way I would cut and run. No.way."

Nick shook his head. "Easier said than done. There's going to be an emotional fallout. He might survive it, but that doesn't mean that he won't return to a dark place. He's difficult to handle when he gets severely depressed. Fair warning."

"We'll get through it. As you said, as long as he's breathing and not pushing daisies, then there isn't a thing that we can't handle together. Besides, look at all we've been through already. God knows that we've been tested, but we always come out stronger."

We ate a little bit more, then got a dessert to share. A fudge brownie sundae.

"Let's change the subject, shall we?" I asked. "There's no point in speculating about how much of a basket case Ryan will be, or myself, for that matter. Let's talk about you. What's going on with you and Alexis?"

"I thought we wanted to avoid depressing subjects," Nick said, his eyebrow raised. "Anyhow, she's in a treatment facility again. A familiar place for her. She's lost her job, and, I might as well tell you, because Ryan will at some point, but, Ryan's going to have to financially support her for the time being."

"The time being?"

"Yeah. As in, probably for the rest of Alexis' life."

"I see," I said. "Why is that?"

"Alexis has become unemployable."

"What does that mean?"

"She's done so much crazy shit that she probably won't be able to find another job. And, since she's broke, Ryan is the only game in town for her."

"How is she broke? I thought she was rich?"

"Her family is loaded. She, herself, was doing well because her job paid her anywhere from a half million to three-quarters of a million a year – it depended upon her bonuses year to year. Her family has long since cut her off, her job has fired her, and she has so many debts that any severance package she gets is going to be gone. Ryan has to support her."

I felt my mouth flatten out in a grimace, but I shrugged my shoulders. "Oh, well," I said. "If the worst thing that happens to us is that Ryan supports his mentally ill ex-wife, then I'd say we're doing pretty damned good."

Nick smiled. "I knew you would say something like that."

"Bi-polar disorder sucks," I said. "I wouldn't wish it on my worst enemy. Ryan is a great guy for doing that for her, to tell you the truth."

I noticed something different flashing in Nick's eyes, and it made me feel uncomfortable. There was a hint of the feelings that I got from Ryan. When I drowned in the depths of Ryan's eyes, and there was a look of overwhelming love for me, I saw, just a split flicker, of the same look in Nick's eyes.

I drew a breath, hoping that I only imagined it.

I tapped my glass impatiently and looked at my watch. "Uh, do you have to be somewhere today? I mean, it is a work day."

"No, I'm ok. I'm a partner, I can take off when I want, as long as I get my work done. As long as there are no meetings or anything going on."

"Must be nice," I said, still feeling that I needed to be somewhere. My entire life, I always had to be somewhere during the day, it seemed. It was still strange trying to adjust to the feeling that I literally didn't have to be anywhere at all. Except, of course, I had to pick up Dalilah.

"Listen, Iris," Nick said. "You're going to have to be at the hospital a lot. I don't have any major meetings coming up this month, so I can work from home. I need a breather from the Alexis situation. Maybe I could come and stay at your house and take care of Dalilah while you stay with Ryan?"

I looked at him, feeling my mouth gape open. This was arrogant, insensitive Nick? Sacrificing his time to watch my daughter while I tended to my husband in the hospital?

I suddenly started to understand why Ryan felt so strongly for the guy.

"That's wonderful for you to offer," I started. "But I can't ask you-"

"Don't be stupid. I want to do it. Somebody's going to have to watch her, because she can't be hanging around the hospital with you. I'm pretty good with kids, and she trusts me. This is going to be a weird enough time for her without her having to be in the care of a stranger."

"If you're sure…"

"Done."

"Well, ok, then. There is one thing, though."

"What's that?"

"I'm not at all sure I can return home. I mean, last I knew, the place was marked as a crime scene. I think…" Then I shuddered, not wanting to remember the fact that there was a dead body in the living room, the last I knew.

At least, I assumed that Andrew died.

That was my hope, anyhow.

Nick seemed to know the dilemma. "Of course. Andrew died in that house, presumably. And Ryan almost died. Not sure how that works, as far as how long the house will be inaccessible. You and Dalilah might have to stay with me."

I sighed. It looked like Ryan and I would be moving again. That was our lives – going from one new house to another, trying to escape the vestige of Andrew. It didn't seem right that one 5'7" man could wreak so much havoc, but he somehow managed to.

I blinked. "Well, thank you. You're a godsend. I also have to get ready for Rochelle's trial, although I would imagine that will be postponed once again, as Ryan is the star witness there."

I felt uncomfortable, though. I knew that Nick's house was, no doubt, gorgeous and spacious. There would be plenty of room for Dalilah and me to stay there while Ryan was in the ICU. Then, when Ryan moved into a regular room, I could probably just stay at the hospital with him. At least I hoped. But I might be staying with Nick for at least a little while, and I was getting a strange vibe from him that was definitely different than before.

My gut told me that the guy was developing feelings for me.

# Chapter Four

After breakfast, I went and got Dalilah from Daniel's house. As I was picking her up, I asked Daniel about mine and Ryan's home.

"Were the police still there when you went to the house?" I asked.

"Yeah," he said. "It still had yellow crime scene tape around it. They hassled me, but I finally managed to convince them to let me in to get Dalilah's things. I guess because Dalilah's room wasn't involved."

I went into the spare bedroom, where Dalilah was sitting in her playpen, busily working a puzzle. She had graduated from the simple infant puzzles to more complex ones with smaller pieces, and she delighted in them.

I had to remind myself that she was just over eight months old.

"Momma!" she shouted excitedly, her little hands going up and down. "We go home?"

"Baby," I said. "Uncle Nick is here, in the car. He's going to take you to his home for a little while." At that, I heard Nick come in the door with some boxes for Dalilah's things.

Nick, Daniel and I worked on loading Ryan's Escalade with her things, then went back over to the house, where the police were still working, and, after some convincing, we were able to get more of Dalilah's things, and about a month's worth of clothing for myself and Ryan. We then loaded up Maximus and Brutus in two enormous carriers, and Maddy in a small carrier, and put them all into the car.

Then we headed back over to Nick's to set up Dalilah's room in one of Nick's spare bedrooms.

Nick's home was a Provincial French style mansion, with a brick façade and enormous pitched roofs. It had several wings, a private drive, and was set several hundred feet behind brick gates. Inside was a marble foyer, with an elegant marble staircase that wound its way to the second story. Off to the side was a formal dining room, an enormous kitchen, and an entrance to the next wing, where there was a formal living room, den and movie theater.

Nick led me upstairs, motioning to one of the spare bedrooms. The bedroom had its own enormous bathroom with a sunken Jacuzzi tub in blue granite, with a matching sink and brass fixtures. As with my house with Ryan, most of the rooms had a fireplace. This room was no exception.

"Thanks," I said, putting down my bag of clothing, and heading to the enormous walk-in closet to hang everything up. Then we set up Dalilah's room right next to mine. The two rooms were actually connected, which made it very convenient. "We put the kids in these rooms when they were young," Nick explained. "They wanted connecting rooms, so we had it retrofitted that way."

"This is very nice," I said, setting up the baby monitor in my room. "I think that I could live here just fine, at least for awhile," I said with a smile. There was no reason not to smile right then – Ryan was out of surgery, so life was good.

Nick nodded, then motioned to Sheila, who was the live-in housekeeper, to help him bring in Dalilah's furniture. Then the three of us worked together to assemble everything while Dalilah watched us from the playpen.

By then, it was five o'clock, and the ICU visiting hours were starting again. "Uh, thanks Nick, for putting us up. We might be staying here for awhile, until we can get another house. I'd imagine that Ryan has no desire to return to that other house. I don't, either."

"You guys can stay here as long as you need. To tell you the truth, I'm jazzed about you guys being here. It was getting pretty lonely, which is part of the reason why I had Alexis move in. That obviously isn't gonna work out anymore, so I'm happy to have you guys here."

"You're ok with Dalilah?" I asked. I had already given him the bottles to feed her, and she was now sitting in her swing reading. She had already outgrown the most basic books, and had graduated to slightly harder children's books.

I thought about Ryan, who read *The Wind in the Willows* by his second birthday, realizing that Dalilah might even surpass that. Her progress was scary.

"Of course," he said. "I'm an old pro. Besides, I can have Sheila help me out if I get into trouble. She's certainly changed her share of diapers, even if she's not exactly considered to be a nanny."

"Well, thanks again," I said, heading out the door to go and see my husband.

# Chapter Five

I approached the ICU with a certain dread, as well as a certain lightness. Just being around Ryan comforted me. At the same time, it devastated me to see him the way that he was, helpless in a bed. I stopped in the chapel in the hospital to pray a bit before going to see him.

The chapel was lit up with candles, and there was a statue of the Virgin Mary at the altar. I genuflected as I walked into the pew, a habit formed during my Catholic upbringing. I wasn't Catholic anymore, though. I wasn't really anything, but I still believed in a higher power and angels. And I still prayed when I really needed to.

"God? Uh, I know that I don't talk to you much. It probably seems that I only talk to you when I really need you. Sorry about that. Anyhow, I really need you now. The sweetest, most generous and kind-hearted man is lying in a bed in this hospital, and it's going to be a struggle to recover. I just want you to watch over him and make sure he's safe." Then I thought about making a bargain with God, that if He allowed Ryan to recover, then I would gladly give my life in return. But I wasn't certain if that would accomplish much of anything, really. I didn't think that God worked like that. Trading lives, as if people were fungible.

Then I walked to the receptionist to ask how to get to the ICU. She gave me a map, which was difficult for me to read – maps are always hard for me, for some reason – but I figured it out after walking through the maze of hallways, and getting lost several times along the way. I also had to stop and ask several different people, several different times, about how to get there.

But I finally found it. When I got there, he was still lying there, but he was out from under the anesthesia, so he was conscious. His face lit up when I entered the room.

"Beautiful," he said weakly. "Thank God you're here."

"Thank God you're here," I said, rushing to his bedside. I brushed the hair off of his face, and took his hand gently.

"I got some great news," he said said haltingly and softly, between breaths. "The doctors were afraid that I might be paralyzed because of the swelling on my spine. The swelling has gone down, and I have feeling in my lower extremities."

My heart did backflips with joy upon hearing that news. "That's probably the greatest thing I've ever heard in my life," I said, gripping his hand harder.

"I mean, I don't necessarily think that I can walk again," he continued. "At least not yet. But at least I'm not paralyzed."

I tried valiantly to hide my tears, but he noticed them right away. "Hey," he said. "Those are happy tears, right?"

I nodded my head. The tears were happy, but they were also emotional. The tears had been threatening all through this ordeal, hidden behind a dam. The dam was always threatening to break, and it took all my efforts to keep the dam intact.

But I had to be strong, for him. I couldn't fall apart. He needed me. Dalilah needed me too. Even Nick needed me, as I suspected he was having a harder time, emotionally, than he ever led on. Crazy girlfriend, crazy ex-wife, and now his one solid source of support lay helpless in a hospital bed. There was only so much one person could take, and I suspected that Nick was also close to breaking down. I now considered the guy to be a friend, so I felt that I needed to be strong for him, as well.

I had my turn being stupid and weak, and it affected Ryan greatly. It was now my turn to have some strength. So, I lied and told Ryan "Yes, yes, these are happy tears. God, they are very happy tears."

He smiled weakly, then gripped my hand again. "I love you, beautiful," he said. "More than you will ever know."

"I love you, too," I said. "I feel that if I lost you that I would literally die."

"You're not going to get rid of me yet," he said. "Not like this, anyhow. Two ninety-year olds in the rocking chair, remember?"

"Of course I remember," I said, trying my hardest to put aside the fear of an embolism or an infection. God, why was I so apocalyptic all the time about things? Then I remembered all that I had gone through up until this point. Being apocalyptic came with the territory at that point.

He reached his hand up to my hair and smoothed it back, looking at me longingly. Then he asked "how's our genius girl?"

"Fine, fine," I said. "She's with Nick. I'm going to be staying there as well. Obviously, I can't go back to our home anytime soon."

"Yeah," Ryan said with another weak smile. "Looks like we're gonna have to move again, huh?"

I nodded. "But, the good news is, my love, I don't think we have to worry about Andrew anymore." I was sure that I would have to answer questions at the police headquarters soon, probably that day. I would then find out the fate of my stalker and rapist.

I was alarmed at how much I wanted Andrew dead. Me, the woman who literally wouldn't kill a bug, and I would rejoice at the death of another human being. That thought disturbed me just a little.

Then, the fact that it disturbed me only a little, disturbed me even more.

"Hey, listen," Ryan said. "Nick, he, uh, are you okay being alone with him?"

"Yeah, why?" I asked.

"No reason."

I narrowed my eyes. It was a peculiar question to ask, considering that I spent an entire week alone with Nick while Ryan was on a business trip.

But I let it go.

Then Ryan gripped my hand again. His eyelids were starting to close. "Beautiful, I want you to stay here," he said. "If you want. But I really need a little rest."

"Of course," I said. Then he was asleep almost immediately. I sighed and checked my phone messages, looking to see if there was anybody from the police force who was wanting to talk to me. Sure enough, there was a message from a Detective Branson. He was asking me to call him back ASAP.

"Detective Branson," a gruff voice answered when I called the number that was left on my voice mail.

"Hello," I said. "This is Iris Gallagher. You left a message for me to call you."

"Yes, yes," he said. "When can you come to the station?"

I looked at my beautiful husband, who was resting comfortably and breathing heavily in a deep sleep. A nurse had just entered the room, and she took his vitals.

"Just a second, Detective Branson," I said. "I think that I can come down today sometime, but I want to find out something about my husband first."

"Sure," he said. "I'll wait on the line if you want."

"Thanks," I said, muting the phone. Then I turned to the nurse. "Hi, uh, my husband – do you think he's going to be asleep for long? I mean, how much rest does he need?"

"Mr. Gallagher went through a great amount of trauma, so he needs to heal. He needs all the rest and sleep that he can get so that he can recover. Patients who have gone through as much physical trauma as he has typically sleep around 12 to 14 hours a day."

I nodded, knowing that Ryan probably would be unconscious for awhile. Then I turned back to my phone. "Detective Branson, are you still there?" I asked.

"I'm still here," he answered.

"I can be there within the hour. Would that work for you?"

"See you then."

Then I smoothed back Ryan's beautiful dark hair and whispered "I love you honey. I'm going to be talking to a detective, but I'll be back as soon as I can." I thought I saw a faint smile cross his face, but I was probably imagining it.

Then I grabbed my purse and prepared to head down to the station to talk to Detective Branson.

# Chapter Six

RYAN

Iris had just left, and I missed her already. But I really didn't have the energy to really talk with her. All I wanted to do was sleep. And try to forget about the feeling that I had when Andrew had ahold of her. When I walked through the door and saw him with his hand on his gun, jabbed into her back – I knew that I would do absolutely anything to make sure that she was safe. Anything.

Then the familiar feeling of being shot.

Now all I could do was try not to think about the other times when I was shot. Because to think about those other times would mean that I would have to revisit a past that I was constantly trying to run from. But I couldn't help it. I had to sit and ruminate, because being shot by Andrew brought it all back.

God, that weekend. It was the year 2000, and I had been a dope addict for three years running at that time. Nick had finally had enough. All the interventions, and subsequent rehabs, had failed miserably. I would spend just about every break from school in one treatment facility or another, only to get out even worse than before. There were more drugs available in the treatment center than there was on the street. I went in hooked on heroin, and came out having tried meth, ecstasy and crack. I didn't get hooked on those other drugs, though. The point was, those treatment facilities didn't help me even one bit.

I resented Nick and everybody in my life who didn't accept me the way I was. If I wanted to get high every day, that was my right, you know? Free country and all that.

I had come home from school that day at 1:30 in the afternoon. I was looking forward to the weekend just because it meant that I could have some uninterrupted time with my smack needle. Classes were a bother – they only got in the way of my having a good time. Yet I did manage to make it to class most days. Thank God school was always a breeze for me. I never cracked a book, ever, until the last second, then crammed everything in right before the exams with the help of my good friend blow, and I never got a grade lower than an A-. So, I figured, what's the problem? I was a functioning drug addict, and my life wasn't affected by it, so everybody needed to get off my ass about it.

So, when I got home that day and Nick ambushed me and tackled me with the help of three of his friends on crew, I literally wanted to kill him.....

On that day, I walked into the house that I shared with Nick, and, variously, different guys who crashed from time to time. Maybe they were trying to get away from their girlfriends. Maybe they were passing through. At any rate, there were usually at least a couple of guys who were hanging around mine and Nick's house at any given time. I figured that this weekend would be no different.

"Nick?" I said, looking around the four bedroom Cape Cod style Cambridge house with the cherry hardwood floors and exposed brick walls. Nobody answered. Huh, that's funny. His car is here.

Then, out of nowhere, I felt Nick tackle me to the ground. He had a handcuff in his hand, and he slapped it on one of my wrists.

"What the fuck?" I asked him. I shivered, remembering vaguely the times that I was handcuffed to a bed and not allowed to leave. *But who did that to me?* At any rate, the feeling was of panic, and I could feel my fight or flight impulse kick in.

It was then that I realized that Nick was not alone. Jonah, Jeff and Caleb, three guys on Nick's crew team, were also standing in the living room.

"Oh, Christ, not again! Not another goddamned intervention. Alright, let's get this over with."

"Nope, buddy, this isn't another intervention," Nick said.

"Then what is this?"

"You're going to fucking detox right here, whether you like it or not."

*Oh, no. No. He wouldn't dare. Wouldn't fucking dare.*

"Fuck you!" I shouted futilely, as Nick and the three guys literally dragged me, kicking and screaming, into my bedroom. The bed was lined with a shower curtain, and there was a puke bucket on the floor next to it. Before I could've reacted, I was literally chained to the bed, lying on my side. I started to panic, knowing what was in store for me with this planned cold turkey detox process.

"Listen, buddy," Nick was saying. "I know that you won't believe me when I tell you this, but this is for your own good. You have to get off this shit, somehow, someway, and interventions and rehab don't seem to be doing the trick for you."

"And you think this will?" I asked. "How fucking naïve are you? You think that you can just watch me puke, shiver and shake for three days, and then I'm gonna magically be ok?" I was incredulous. Nick was never stupid like this. Anyhow, I was a functioning user. As long as I made it through my classes with top grades, I was ok. He needed to just leave me the fuck alone about it. Quit harassing me. Accept me for who I am, or stop being my friend.

"I don't know what else to try. You're going to end up dead like Kurt Cobain, and I don't want to see that happen."

"Kurt Cobain suffered from severe depression and shot himself. He didn't die from his drug use."

"Kurt Cobain had a death wish. So do you. I really don't know what I can do to halt your death wish."

"This isn't a place to start."

"I know that, but I'm at the end of my rope. I'm the only one who's got your back in this world, so I wish that you would just listen to me for once in your fucking life."

Deep down, I knew he was right. Nobody else ever had my back for long. But that didn't stop me from hating him with the passion of a thousand operatic arias right at that moment.

And that weekend went just as I knew that it would. Every second I wanted to die. Every second I thought that I was dying. I'd seen movies where people were burning at the stake, and my suffering was much worse than that. Because their suffering was over in a matter of minutes. I was being flayed alive for two and a half days. It was if somebody had poured gasoline on me and lit a match, and I burned like that the entire time I was in that bed. And, for three days, I screamed at the top of my lungs every single obscenity known to man. I could hear Nick and the guys downstairs, playing video games, and Rielle came to visit, and I heard the two of them going at it.

What I didn't hear was any word as to when I was going to be released from this prison.

Nick checked on me at least once an hour, to his credit, and every time he peeked his head in, I bit it off with more obscenities. It was like the movie *The Exorcist*, except my puke wasn't quite green, and my head didn't do a 360 degree turn.

I think I might have even told him that his mother sucks cocks in hell, even though his mother was still alive.

Still, he kept checking on me.

Finally, Monday morning came, and I was released. Nick wasn't interested in me missing more classes, so he let me go. "I don't know if you are detoxed yet," he said. "But you have to get to class if you don't want to get booted out of this place. So, I'm letting you go," he said as he loaded up his backpack and prepared his walk to his morning class.

"Thanks, buddy," I said sarcastically, then flipped him off the second his back was turned. I waited for him to leave, then I got my car keys and headed to a seedy area of Boston. I had to get away from Nick and his bullshit and find some people who understood me more. I had some friends I had made on the street, so I went to hunt them down.

I arrived at a street where there were people standing around a lit garbage can, drinking out of a paper bag. The men and women here were passing around a pipe that had some kind of unknown substance. When I got a little closer, I realized that the substance in that pipe was crack. I knew the smell anywhere. One of the men looked at me with a funny expression. I supposed that I didn't really fit in here - I was young and fit and had all my teeth. I had brought my non-descript car, however – it was a hoopdie Toyota that I drove whenever I wanted to fit in with some of the non-rich kids at school. I was constantly finding that those kids made better companions than the privileged ones.

Of course my best friends and my girlfriend were privileged, so I guess I didn't try too hard to make friends with the poor kids.

I had my hands shoved in my pockets. I hadn't shaved or showered in three days, and I didn't bother to comb my hair before coming down here, so I hoped that I didn't look too out of place.

"Hey there rich boy," one of the men said. "What's up?"

So much for my trying to fit in. "Yeah," I said. "I'm looking for somebody. You might know him. His name is Seth. Short guy, around 5'5", tightly curled black hair. He stays around here sometimes."

"Yeah, I know him," the man said. "He staying at a house around the corner," he said, gesturing to a small blue house with peeled siding and a hole in the roof.

"Thanks man," I said, before jogging away towards the blue house. I arrived there and knocked on the door. A Hispanic guy with a goatee and beer belly opened the door.

"Yeah?" he inquired, his voice thickly accented.

"Looking for Seth," I said.

"Seth!" he called behind him, then turned to me. Seth appeared behind him.

"Ryan," he said. "Good to see you."

"Can I come in? I need someplace to stay for a couple of days."

"Sure, come on in," he said, standing aside to let me come in.

I went in the house and looked around uncomfortably. I

didn't want other people to be hanging around if I didn't trust them. Call me crazy, but I didn't want to end up in jail or in the hospital.

I didn't entirely mind if I ended up dead, though.

In fact, I found myself wanting that.

I gestured to the Hispanic guy. "He ok?" I asked Seth.

"Yeah," he nodded. "He's actually just leaving."

I understood. The guy was a customer. Not a biggie, then.

The guy left, then I asked "You got any stuff?"

"Does a junkie have a needle? What a stupid question to ask."

"Fucking A," I said. "My asshole roommate literally held me hostage over the weekend. I'm dying here."

Seth left and came back in a short time with the bag of smack in his hand. I could feel the absolute relief when I saw the drugs. I almost started salivating.

I ended up staying there for three days, crashed out on his couch, high the entire time.

Then was awakened, rudely, by a hulking guy with multiple tattoos and piercings. He was yelling at the top of his lungs, and was flashing around a .45 pistol.

I was still barely coherent, but was soon brought to my senses when a bullet pierced my leg.

"Fuck!" Seth said. Then he addressed the hulking guy with the gun. "Get the fuck out of here, Jared. I gave you the stuff you needed."

There was more of a scuffle, but the hulking Jared ended up leaving. I was vaguely aware that I was bleeding profusely.

I wondered if this was it – that I'd bleed out in this shit-hole house. Not that I minded. I welcomed it, in fact.

But I didn't die, of course. Seth ended up putting a

tourniquet on my leg, and dug into my leg with a knife and tweezers to get the bullet out, then poured rubbing alcohol in the wound. Then he stitched up the wound. I was glad I was still pretty high when he was doing this, otherwise it would've been unbearably painful.

"Dude," I said. "Where did you learn how to do all this?" I examined the stitched up wound carefully. It looked pretty professional.

He shrugged. "I was an EMT for a little while before I got into dealing."

I nodded. "Thanks, man. You did a good job."

At some point I drove home, limping into the house. I couldn't stay away forever, I knew. I just wanted to make a point to Nick – that he would drive me out of the house if he didn't allow me to do my drugs at home.

"What the fuck?" he asked when I dragged myself home.

"What? You drove me out of the house, you mother-fucker. Drove me right out. Your little stunt back there, keeping me chained up while I sweated and puked, was the height of not-cool."

"So, where did you go?"

"Nunya. I'll tell you this, though. You pull that shit one more time, and I'm moving out. I got a place to stay where nobody is going to judge me about what I do with my own time. You got that? I'll pack my bags and get the hell out of here so fast if you even try something like that again. No more interventions, either. Got that?" I stood there looking at him, both of my fists balled up tight. I was in no mood for his bullshit, and I was ready to haul off and hit him.

He looked chastened, which was an unusual look for him, even then. One thing about Nick – the guy was always cocky. Guess he had a right to be. Studly, popular, got straight As, always had the girls dripping all over him. And guys, of course. But at this moment he actually looked… fearful. Fearful at my words. He knew that I was dead serious.

Then that look of fear vanished. The cocky wall was back on his face. "Yeah? You're bluffing. You ain't gonna live with your junky friends."

I was in no mood for his crap. I was weaning myself off the drugs after my three day bender with Seth, and my leg was hurting like hell. My head was pounding like a snare drum, and my hands were shaking like I had the DTs.

So, just like that, I punched him in the face. Hard. He wasn't prepared for my onslaught, so he fell backwards onto the coffee table, striking his head on the corner. He looked at me, stunned, holding the back of his head, then he looked at his hand. It was covered in blood, because there was an open wound on his head, where it struck the coffee table.

I just smirked at him, not even bothering to go to the bathroom to get something to dress his head. I raised an eyebrow, then went into my bedroom to play some video games, before taking a well-needed nap.

That plan didn't last long, of course. Nick stormed into my bedroom, and tackled me.

And we were off to the races.

I punched him hard in the stomach, and he punched me harder across my face. I responded with an upper cut on his chin, and he pummeled me more on the side of my head. I put him into a headlock and punched him several times on the top of his head. He got out of the headlock and pinned me on the floor, beating me over and over again on the face.

"You fucking junkie!" he was screaming over and over again. "You want to die so badly, maybe I should just fucking let you, you mother fucker! Go live on the streets, go find your smack buddies, drop out of school, become a waste! I'm through with you! I'm through trying to help you! You can just rot on the streets, you mother fucker! YOU'RE NO BETTER THAN YOUR FUCKING FATHER!"

That was hitting below the belt. Bringing my father into the fight brought my adrenaline back to full force, and, with a bellow that came from the deepest part of my soul, I pushed him off of me and pummeled him over and over and over. My fists were on his face, on his ear, in his chest and abdomen. I kneed him in the groin, then, when he collapsed in agony, I kicked him in his back, over and over again.

I was frenzied, a rabid animal. After awhile I was blinded, completely blinded. I didn't even see Nick anymore. He was a blur. On and on and on I punched and kicked, while he lay completely immobilized.

"Hey! What the fuck is going on here?" Caleb was in the doorway, having let himself in, as he usually does. He was immediately on top of me, but I barely felt him. It was as if I was on PCP – I had the strength of ten men, and I was in a blind rage. Then, not five seconds later, I felt a baseball bat whack me hard on my arm. I turned to face Caleb, and he had the bat at the ready, brandishing it. I was breathing heavily and sweating profusely. I felt like I had just rowed 100 miles on my own. I was going to take Caleb on next, but the way he held that bat told me that I probably should leave well enough alone.

By then, I had calmed down a little. Which meant that I no longer was in my rage-induced altered state. I was still extremely angry, and was in serious need of a fix, but I was no longer blinded by my hatred.

Caleb had his cell phone in his hand, calling 911. I looked at Nick. He wasn't moving. I wondered if he was still breathing. Then I saw his chest heaving up and down.

I felt like Ivan Drago in *Rocky IV,* muttering under my breath "if he dies, he dies."

Then I got up, went into Nick's room, and locked the door. As I heard the paramedics outside the door load up Nick to take him into the hospital, I already had my tourniquet on my arm, chasing the dragon. I played a CD of my go-to band for getting high, The Smiths, and as Morrissey wailed, I soared. I heard the paramedics leave, and then Caleb was pounding on the door. "Open up, you piece of shit! You might have killed your roommate and best friend. Open up you mother fucker! You fucking junkie, get your ass out of that room right now!"

I simply flipped him off from behind the door, then laid down on Nick's bed and felt the rush. When Caleb burst through the door, after having kicked it in, I was already in an extreme euphoric state, and I wasn't going anywhere. I just looked at him and smiled, while he screamed at me at the top of his lungs, his face centimeters away from mine. He pulled me off the bed, then brandished the bat while I laid on the ground.

I didn't care. I could barely hear him – it was like he was at the end of a long tunnel.

Turned out Nick was in the hospital for a week. He started out in critical condition, and it was touch and go for awhile, but he made it through surgery.

I never once visited him in the hospital. That was a lost week for me, as I spent every minute of every day getting high. I was usually a functioning user – I used just enough to get me through the day, but not so much that I was incoherent. I had to still go to class, as much as I could. But that week was different – I was completely stoned the entire week.

I was never even questioned by the cops about this incident. My dad was out of my life, yet always in my life, because his unseen hand was always there, getting me out of trouble.

When Nick came home, things were different between us for awhile. He didn't talk to me much for months, and I didn't have much to say to him, either.

But my goal in disappearing for those three days was accomplished – Nick never hassled me again about my drug use. The interventions stopped, there were no more home detox events, and he quit trying to force me into rehab.

Now, I laid in my hospital bed, exhausted and trying to sleep, but the memories of that time at Harvard haunted my mind. I still felt so ashamed of how I behaved back then. I was such a different person at that time. I would've sold Iris to the highest bidder back then, if I had known her then, just to get my junk. I treated everybody like shit. Why Nick still stuck around was beyond me. I don't know, to this day, why he kept me as a friend.

I'm only glad that he did.

A nurse came by to take my vitals. I haltingly asked her "where is my wife?"

"She went to see a detective about something. A Detective Branson."

I nodded weakly. I really missed her. I always missed her when I wasn't with her. When she left me, after Natalie got pregnant, it took an absolutely heroic effort on my part not to get back into the smack. I wanted to, every day. Every.single.day. Every minute of every day. So, I spent all my time in my art studio, painting feverishly. The main things I painted were portraits of her, created from the photos I had taken of her. Some of the portraits I made of her were abstractions, and those were the ones that I created out of my memory.

I wondered if she would be freaked out if she saw how many portraits I painted of her during her absence. But I absolutely had to do it, because it was the only thing that kept me sane and off of drugs.

I sighed, and felt myself drifting off to sleep. Iris would come back after she talked to that detective, and I knew that she had to talk to him about what happened to me and to Andrew. I was anxious to hear from her, anyhow, about all that. I assumed that Andrew was dead – I vaguely remember him crashing to the floor right after he shot me. I'm not sure exactly what happened to him – I think that Iris did him in somehow.

If she did, then good for her. She finally got a sense of sweet justice for all that man took from us.

# Chapter Seven

## IRIS

I was heading down to see Detective Branson, at the police headquarters in the downtown area. I was excited and nervous for this visit, all at once.

The main reason why I was excited was because I would find out, once and for all, if that bastard Andrew was dead.

I got to the bullet-proof window where an African-American lady with cornrows was sitting. "Can I help you?" the lady, whose name was apparently Kadesha, asked me.

"I'm here to see Detective Branson," I told her.

"Just a second, I'll call him for you," she said, dialing her telephone. "Detective Branson? A lady is here to see you." She looked at me. "What did you say that your name was again?"

"Iris. Iris Gallagher."

"Iris Gallagher." She nodded, looking at me. "I'll tell her." Then she hung up the phone. "Detective Branson will be right out to meet you and escort you back to his office."

I nodded, then took a seat. It wasn't five minutes before a nebbish looking man with a hunched over posture and a cheap suit came out to greet me. "Mrs. Gallagher," he said, holding out his hand. "I'm Detective Branson."

"Iris," I said, shaking his hand. "You can call me Iris."

"Come on back," he said with a nod. "Follow me."

He buzzed both of us through the building, then led me to the elevator and onto the main floor. There were police men and women answering phones everywhere throughout the floor, and he led me to his office towards the back. He cleared off his desk, then got a pen and paper out to make notes.

I took a seat in a small red gingham-covered chair.

"So, Mrs. Gallagher, I mean Iris. I wanted to get some information from you about Andrew Stout."

I nodded. "He's dead, I presume?"

"Yes, very much so," he said, looking at me quizzically. "You killed him. How do you not know this?"

I felt an overwhelming sense of peace and relief at the words that Andrew was dead. I felt an enormous smile creep up on my face at Detective Branson's words.

But he was still looking at me with a perplexed look on his face. I killed Andrew, how did I not know that he was dead?

"Well, Detective Branson, it's really very simple. I don't remember much about the incident. I mean, I remember putting the butcher knife into the bastard, I mean Mr. Stout's back, but I don't remember a whole lot after that. My husband was shot, and I kinda went into shock after that."

Detective Branson nodded. "That makes sense, then. Anyhow, I wanted to get your statement about what happened."

I drew a breath. I fought down the sense of panic that inevitably welled up whenever I talked about what had happened to me. *You're ok, Iris, you're ok. Andrew is dead, and he can't hurt you anymore. So go ahead and talk about it.*

"Andrew was my bodyguard for a short time," I said after a few minutes' pause. "He, uh, actually ended up r-r-raping me in my home. He disappeared for a long time, but then he ended up breaking into my home. I came home from the courthouse – I was being deposed for another case that I am involved in – and he was there in my living room, holding my daughter Dalilah, with a gun in his hand." I shivered, then looked down at my hands. As much as I tried to get that vision out of my head – seeing my daughter endangered like that – I just couldn't. I saw it constantly, every time I closed my eyes.

"Why was he in your home?"

"He was obsessed with me, mainly because he had a psychotic break and thought that I was his wife. He came to my house with the intent to kill me, I think."

Detective Branson was carefully taking notes about everything I was saying to him. "Go on," he said.

"He threatened me with his gun. My husband came in and pretended that he was the person that Andrew really wanted, so Andrew shot my husband. And I must've gotten a butcher knife out of the kitchen drawer and plunged it into his back. That part is kinda hazy right now," I said, with another shiver. The only scene that was replaying in my mind, in an endless loop, of the moment that I killed Andrew, was Ryan being shot and falling to the floor. I closed my eyes, and that was what I saw. Ryan being shot and falling to the floor, and the awful sight of Ryan's blood on my hands as I futilely attempted to stop the bleeding.

"So, you say that this man, Andrew Stout, was obsessed with you. What signs were there that he felt this way about you?"

"Just second-hand information. My husband's father was keeping tabs on Andrew, and he reported to my husband and me about Andrew's whereabouts and state of mind."

The questions continued from there, for several hours. Detective Branson was very thorough, asking question after question about the incident and my history with Andrew.

About 2 PM, he finally seemed ready to quit and let me leave. "I'm terribly sorry to make you have to relive all this, Mrs. Gallagher. I'll have my team check out your story, and I'll get back with you."

It just then occurred to me that there was a slight possibility that I could be in some kind of trouble. Of course, it was both self-defense and defense of others, but I hoped that there wouldn't be any charges pressed against me if Detective Branson didn't believe my story.

"Um, I'm not in trouble, am I?" I asked Detective Branson tentatively.

"Well, any time there is a homicide, there has to be an investigation as to whether the self-defense story is going to hold up. But I'll be honest with you – considering the fact that this man shot your husband, I would say that there is almost no chance that you will have charges pressed against you. Your story about self-defense seems pretty airtight. But no promises."

I nodded my head. "Thank you, Detective Branson, for your time."

We said our goodbyes, and I was on my way.

# Chapter Eight

## RYAN

I was wide awake, waiting for Iris to return. I impatiently looked at the clock – it read 3 PM. She had been gone that entire afternoon. I was half conscious when she was here last, but now I'm awake, and on pins and needles. I needed to know what happened to Andrew. I also needed her here, because I was spinning into dark, negative thoughts. This shooting was bringing up so much crap up for me, things that had never even crossed my mind for many a year. I guess it was because I almost died, again. In fact, I did, briefly, die. I knew that I had flatlined on the table. I knew it, because it was just like in the movies – I suddenly was floating above the table and watching down below, while the doctors and nurses were using their paddles and shouting "clear!" Then, just as suddenly, I was pulled back down, and I don't remember much after that.

Having this near-death experience was bringing up other times when my life was endangered. Things that haunt me to this day.

I was obsessing right then about the three days I spent in

the car trunk, thinking for sure I was about to meet my end. I had cheated death with the suicide attempt and the shooting at Seth's, and it seemed that fate had finally caught up to me....

It was right after I had a talk with one of my professors. He summoned me into his office on a warm October day. Fall was always my favorite time of the year – it brought back memories of football games and homecoming parades and bonfires with friends. The air was crisp, and the leaves were changing into their brilliant red and yellow colors. Alexis and I were getting along during this time, and we were going to take a drive that weekend to the country to see all the leaves changing and buy warm apple cider at a roadside diner we loved so well. The trip would include our usual rations of drugs, of course, so that was a bonus for me.

So, I actually was in a good mood as I approached his office in one of the ivy-covered administration buildings.

"You wanted to see me?" I inquired as I lightly rapped on the open door to his office. Professor Warren was a slight man, balding and bespectacled. He wore bow ties and cardigan sweaters and vests, and his pants were always slightly too short. He was definitely not an intimidating sort, so I wasn't feeling threatened as I sat down to talk to him.

"Yes, Mr. Gallagher. Have a seat."

I obeyed, putting my hands on my lap.

"I'm just finishing up a little bit of paperwork. I hope you don't mind. Just give me a few minutes."

I nodded. I felt uncomfortable, because I didn't know what he wanted. I hadn't been summoned to a professor's office before. However, this office was a nice one – it was lined with wood panels, and the carpet was red, so the room had a definite cozy, yet masculine, air to it. He had an entire wall of books. Dostoyevsky, Proust, Tolstoy, Fitzgerald, Hemingway, and many non-fiction books. He had candles burning on the desk. Outside the window, I saw leaves falling to the ground.

My mind drifted to the coming weekend and the Christmas holidays that were just around the corner. I always loved Christmas. Nick's family always tried to make it special, especially for me, since I was essentially an orphan. And, when I was a small child, my mother went out of her way to make sure that I got everything I wanted for Christmas. I got to pick out the tree, and she got ornaments just for me, and special ornaments for Sarah as well. Even my father tried to be civil on Christmas Day, although there was at least one occasion when I got smacked across the face so hard that there was a large mark on my cheek. The mark could still be seen in the Christmas home videos they made of me riding my tricycle.

Finally, Professor Warren was finished with what he was doing, and he turned his attention to me. "Uh, Mr. Gallagher, I wanted to talk to you about something very important to me," he said. "I wanted to talk to you about your absences."

Uh oh. No other professor had called me on this. I think that my father's unseen hand had a lot to do with this, coupled with the fact that I was carrying a 3.9 GPA, and was on track to graduate *magna cum laude*.

"My absences, sir?"

"Yes, your absences. Now, I know that your other professors don't seem to care that you continually violate their absences policies, but I do."

"Yes, sir. I'll do better, sir."

"There's another thing," he said, fiddling with his paper weight on his desk, and not looking me in the eye. "I don't want to offend, but at the same time, I can't keep silent about this. I kept silent about my suspicions with my son, and that had tragic consequences." He took a deep breath, and I watched him expectantly. What came out of his mouth was something that surprised me completely. "I suspect that you are a drug user."

Now how did he know that? If there was one thing that I was an absolute expert at, it was hiding the fact that I was a junkie. I never went to class completely high – I only did enough to take the edge off in the morning, and I saved my heavy drug use for the weekends.

"I'm sorry, sir, I don't know why you would say that."

"My son died of a drug overdose. I know the signs. They're subtle, but I see them in you. I can't even put my finger on it – it's just something that I know in my gut. Anyhow, I wanted you to know that I'm here to talk if you need me."

"Well, I thank you for that, sir, but you are mistaken. I am very sorry to hear about your son. But I'm not a drug user and never have been." I looked him right in the eye as I said this. I was well-trained on how to lie to people about this subject. Sometimes I felt that I deserved an Academy Award for my incredible acting abilities. *And the winner of the Best Actor award, for his role in My Life on Smack, is Ryan Gallagher!!!!!*

He looked pensive and sad for a few moments, then he raised his eyebrows in a way that said *I'm calling bullshit.* But he said nothing more about it. "Anyhow," he said, "You need to watch your absences in my class. Now, I know that you are on track to graduate as a magna, but that doesn't mean that you are deserving of special treatment from my class or any other class."

"Yes sir," I said, glad that it was the weekend and I

didn't have to worry about missing his class the next day. "I'll be sure that I'm there every Tuesday and Thursday, right on time."

"Thank you for coming by. And remember, if you need somebody to talk to, I'm here. I don't want to lose another promising young life to that junk."

I nodded. "Well, again, I thank you, but trust me, I don't do drugs." I chuckled. "Well, I mean, unless you count an occasional beer."

And I made my goodbyes and left.

But his talk gnawed at me. It was one thing for Nick and the guys to be constantly badgering me about the drug use. It was another for this man, whom I barely knew, to do the same. I felt ashamed, more ashamed than I had ever felt, and that shame was like a 1,000 pound weight on me. It was dragging me down as I walked along the tree-lined path towards my car.

And I handled my shame the same way I handled every other negative emotion in my life.

I immediately headed down to Boston to see Seth.

I got to Seth's house, and got into the usual routine. Shoot up and lay incoherently on his couch the entire weekend. I blew off Alexis, of course, ignoring the phone and the constant missed calls from her. The changing leaves and cozy roadside diner would have to wait until next weekend. This weekend would be saved for one thing – getting high.

But I got a rude awakening, ruder than even the rude awakening I got with the hulking Jared. I came out of my stupor and saw three guys standing in the living room with semi-automatic weapons, aimed at Seth.

"We understand that you have been poaching some of Jack Haley's most lucrative clients," one of the men accused Seth. He was well-dressed in a three-piece suit and expensive shoes which were buffed to an impeccable sheen. His pants were perfectly tailored, as was his jacket. He, like the other two men, was wearing a Halloween mask. The other men were not dressed as well, as they were in white t-shirts and black shoes and pants. Both of them were dressed the same. All of the men were slightly built and under the height of six foot.

"I don't know what you're talking about," Seth protested, his hands in the air.

One of the guys gestured at me with his semi-automatic. "Who is this pretty boy?" he asked.

I spoke up. "I'm just here. I've got nothing to do with Seth's deals."

"Well, Mr. Just Here, looks like you are in the wrong place at the wrong time," the leader in the three-piece suit said to me. "Too bad for you."

Seth was talking again. "I'm serious here, I have no idea what you are talking about. What clients am I poaching?"

"You want me to give you a list?" three piece suit asked. Then all three men started laughing. "Nah, we can't give you a list. We ain't that organized."

Seth looked over at me and shrugged. He seemed strangely unperturbed by this entire scenario. I, myself, also wasn't too freaked out, simply because I was still extremely high when these guys came in.

There was an inner voice that was screaming at me, though.

"Well, now, you, Seth, and your pretty-boy friend Mr. Just Here, obviously need to be taught a lesson." Then he put a bag over Seth's head and mine, and jerked me off the couch. They roughly led me over to a car that was apparently parked in an alley, and I was startled by the rat-a-tat-tat sound of a semi-automatic weapon being fired.

Now I was finally freaking out. Did they just kill Seth? Was I next?

Then I realized that the sound of the weapon was not the sound of bullets hitting a body. It was the sound of bullets hitting something metal.

I soon found out what the sound was – the bullets were making air-holes in a car trunk. I heard the trunk opening, and I was shoved into it. My hands were not bound, so, after the trunk lid was shut, I was able to take off the bag over my head and breathe.

I tried not to panic. I had never been claustrophobic, thank God, but I still felt extremely uncomfortable in this trunk. I could hear the men talking, just outside the trunk. One of them was talking on a cell phone.

"Yeah, Jackie. I got a guy in the trunk. His name is Just Here," he said with a laugh. "What do you want me to do with him?" Then he paused. "Ok, you want to set the car on fire with him in it? That can be arranged. That can definitely be arranged."

I started to breathe heavily. I was sobering up with every word I heard from them. My blood ran cold when I heard what the men were saying. They're going to set the car on fire with me in it. I never feared death. I always wanted it. But not like this. Not burned up like some kind of a low-life. Not burned up, period. That seemed to me to be the single worst way to die, and that was the only thing that scared me at this point.

"You hear that, Mr. Just Here? We're going to set the car on fire with you in it. Ty, give me that can of gasoline." Then I heard the sound of gasoline being poured outside.

Then another guy said "let's not do this now. Why don't we let pretty boy in there suffer."

So, for a time that seemed like an eternity, but was really

actually two entire days, I lay in that car trunk. I heard the men outside laughing, talking and joking around the entire time. From time to time I heard one of them say "you wanna do it now and get it over with?" Or "come on, I'm tired of hanging around here. Let's just set the car on fire and be done with it."

While I was in the car trunk, I started to come down off my high. I was convinced that I wouldn't make it out of this alive, so I silently prayed for death. I wanted to die before they set the car on fire, so I didn't have to endure the agony of burning to death. I had the usual feelings that I got whenever I had to go cold turkey for a matter of days, but the headaches and extreme nausea were not as bad as usual, because my mind was more focused upon what was going to happen to me at the hands of these three men.

Then, out of the blue, after I had given up all hope of ever seeing the outside of this car trunk, I heard a voice.

A female voice.

"Well, you really got yourself into it now, huh, Ryan?"

Her voice was unfamiliar, yet she appeared to know my name. "What? Who is this?"

"Don't worry, you're not going to get burned up in this car. It's not your time. It's not your destiny. Besides, there's somebody who needs you to live."

"Who? Who needs me to live?"

"Your daughter. She needs you to live."

"What daughter? I don't have a daughter." At least I hoped that I didn't have a daughter. Who knows? It was certainly possible that I had a daughter somewhere out there, with as many women as I had been sleeping with, during the times that Alexis and I had broken up.

"She ain't been born yet. But her destiny is tied with

yours. If you die, she can't live. And she's going to be important."

I sighed, but, at the same time, an overwhelming sense of peace came over me.

And I knew that I was going to make it out of that trunk.

Then I heard the sound of the three men coming back to the car. "Who the fuck are you?" asked one of the men.

"Name's Rosemary, who the fuck are you? Why don't you get the hell out of here?"

Then one of the men started speaking in Spanish, which was a language that I had always known well. He was saying "Man, something ain't right with this woman. I think she's a witch."

One of the other men started laughing, then the third man said, also in Spanish, "a witch. Whatever. Anyhow, let's get the fuck out of here. This scene is played." Then I heard the three of them running away.

Then the trunk popped open. I was blinded completely by the light, then, when my eyes adjusted, I saw the three men down the street, running at top speed. Just above me was a woman. She was about 80 years old, dressed in rags and missing most of her teeth. Her white hair was loosely held back, with several large strands loose around her neck. She outstretched her bony hand, and I took it. She pulled me out of the trunk.

I was confused, to say the least. "Who are you?"

She just smiled and said "I told you you'd get out of that trunk."

"What were you saying about my daughter? I don't understand."

"You'll see," she said.

I just stood there, trying to clear my head. I was just

about to invite her to have lunch with me, so that I could find out how I could set her up, and get her off the street, when a truck passed by me a little too close. I was brushed back a little, startled, then the truck stopped and the driver yelled "watch where you're going!" I turned my attention briefly to the truck driver, then turned back to address Rosemary.

But she was already gone.

I looked for her in that vicinity for over an hour, before giving up.

*Well, that was weird.*

And I felt guilty that I never got to thank my benefactor properly.

As I laid in my hospital bed waiting for Iris to return, and that memory flooded through me, I felt further shame. Even after that incident, I continued to use for several years, although my drug use was not nearly as heavy as before. One thing did change for me, though – even though I continued to use, I no longer wanted to die. Rosemary's words were like an epiphany. I had felt, up until that point, that I had nothing to live for. I had felt that I was contributing nothing to the world. However, Rosemary let me know that I did have a purpose in the world, a destiny that was uniquely mine. I was going to father a child who was going to be important.

It just dawned on me who that child was.

She was finally here.

My special daughter Dalilah.

## Chapter Nine

IRIS

I was finally finished talking with Detective Branson, and I headed over to see Ryan. As usual, I was feeling mixed emotions about seeing him. I was happy, so happy, that he was alive and he made it through surgery.

At the same time, there was a dark sense of foreboding that I just couldn't shake. I wanted him to come home, and I wanted him to get past the point of danger. He was still in danger, and this is what occupied my mind. Post-surgical complications were what I was obsessing about.

Still, he had feelings in his lower extremities, so that was extremely encouraging.

I stopped by the gift shop and picked up a little Winnie the Pooh bear. It was silly, and it was mainly for me – I always loved Pooh. But I wanted Ryan to have a little something to cuddle up with for times when I couldn't be around.

I arrived at his room on the ICU floor, and felt somewhat relieved to see that he was wide awake and sitting up.

His entire face lit up as I pulled up to his bedside, and little tears formed when I gave him the bear.

"Thanks for this," he said, hugging the bear tightly to him. He put his head down into the bear, like a little boy, then took my hand and squeezed it tightly. "I'm really glad you're here. It's uh, been difficult without you."

I looked into his eyes, and I saw a great amount of emotional pain behind them. I wondered if he was spiraling into negative thoughts, as I remembered Nick's words about how Ryan had conquered darkness. I guess I didn't really think about Ryan's dark side as much as I should've, because he had always been so light with me.

Always the strong one.

"Are you ok?" I asked, staring into his beautiful eyes that shone even brighter than usual, because they were set against such pale skin. I cleared his hair away from his face, feeling extremely concerned about his color, but not wanting to address it. I hated seeing him like this, so pale and wan, and seeing the darkness behind his eyes scared me even more.

He nodded. "I've just been thinking about things lately. Things that I've wished to forget." He looked ashamed. "You know so much about me, but I think that you'd be surprised to hear what an asshole I was to Nick."

"Well, you had a difficult life."

He shook his head. "No excuse. I wonder if this is all karma for me. Biting me on the ass for how I treated Nick for so many years."

I narrowed my eyes. "Was Nick the only person who you treated poorly?"

"Pretty much. It's ironic, but I abused him just because he was the only one who cared enough about me to try to save my life continually. Nobody else cared enough about me to do some of the things he did for me, so he was really the only person I abused. As long as everybody else stayed off my back about my drug use, I didn't get in their face. But with him – I treated him so shitty. I'm so filled with shame about that."

I gripped his hand harder. He continued.

"We got into a massive fight one time, and I sent him to the hospital with broken ribs, bruised kidneys, a ruptured spleen and a concussion. It was touch and go for a few days, and he stayed in the hospital for an entire week. I never visited him. I was never sober enough to do so."

"What happened that you would do that?"

He shook his head. "He told me that I was no better than my dad. He was right, you know. That's what enraged me. I was a waste, just like my dad. And I was always so scared that I would turn out like him. Raping, molesting, abusing. Nick tapped into my fear of being like my dad, and it just came out of me. I almost killed him, and, what's worse, I didn't care."

I just sat there looking at him, gripping his hand and stroking his arm. "Shhh, let's not think about that right now. You have to think of your recovery. That's what is most important."

He just shook his head. "I never apologized for that incident. And I don't think that I ever properly thanked him for saving me from my hell. I feel like such a low-life right now."

I put his head in my chest and stroked his hair. "Please try to think of more positive thoughts. Nick has forgiven you, obviously. He loves you. He's not angry with you. That was many years ago."

But, by looking into his eyes, I knew that what happened with Nick was not in the past with him. It was consuming him. Why it was consuming him right at that moment, I didn't know.

I only knew that it was.

"Please don't leave me," he said.

"What? Why-"

"I'm not a shitty person. I'm not. I'm not like my father. I could never be like him."

"Of course you aren't." I looked at him quizzically, wondering why he was talking like this.

"I'm so scared," he said. "I don't ever want to be abusive with you or with Dalilah. I love you both so much."

"Of course, I know. Why are you saying these things?"

There were tears that were pouring down his left cheek. "I was like him, once. Violent, full of rage. It's in me, still. It's just buried. I don't want to excavate it."

"And you won't."

He said nothing, just dropped my hand and looked away. His face was filled with shame.

"Ryan," I said, my voice forceful, "you're not your father. You're not like him. Even he realizes that. I mean, remember the letter he wrote you – he was frustrated because you're not like him, and he wanted you to be. Please don't go down this road. You need a positive frame of mind if you're going to recover completely."

I brushed back his hair, but he still wasn't looking at me. Then he finally faced me. "You always felt that you weren't good enough for me. That isn't true. That's never been true." Then he took my hand again, and looked at me with pleading eyes. "The truth is, I'm not good enough for you."

*Where was this coming from?* "Honey, you can't think that about yourself. You have the tops of everything – intelligence, looks, kindness, everything." I smiled lightly. "You're a catch."

He just shook his head. "Damaged. Damaged goods." Then he looked at me again. "Uh, Iris, I really need my rest. I hope you don't mind."

I felt a little bemused, then recovered. "Sure, of course. You have to get your sleep. I'll be back later, for visiting hours, ok?"

"Ok," he said, without enthusiasm. "But maybe you should stay home this evening. Dalilah needs you, and I'm not much company."

"I want to come back."

"I know, but I sleep a lot. I don't want to be rude."

I felt tears threatening, but I just nodded my head. "Then I'll be back tomorrow morning for visiting hours at nine."

"Sure," he said, again without enthusiasm. Then he wrapped his arms tighter around the Pooh Bear, and looked up at me. He looked just like a little boy at that moment. "Bye, Iris. I love you."

I smiled, but inwardly cringed at the use of my given name. "I love you too."

He was acting so strangely.

I shook my head as I left the room. I was feeling concerned, but it was such a vague feeling. I had no idea what I was supposed to be concerned about.

# Chapter Ten

I arrived at Nick's house, feeling forlorn and confused. Ryan seemed like a different guy just now in his bed. What was up with all that talk about how worthless he was, and how he feared being like his father?

When I walked through Nick's door, I saw Nick and Dalilah sitting at his grand piano. Nick had concert-level piano skills, to my surprise. I mean, I knew that he was a good piano player, because he played the piano at my own house while he stayed with Dalilah and me. But he was so much more highly skilled than I had anticipated. He was playing a complicated piece that sounded like Rachmaninoff, one my own favorite composers, closing his eyes and swaying his head.

Dalilah was sitting beside him, in a specially made seat, quietly studying him. And when I say that she was studying him, that's what I mean – she wasn't like most infants, who would be busy with toys or something else to distract them. No, she was watching him intently, studying his hands, which were flying across the keys rapidly, as the music was hitting a crescendo. Her gaze never left Nick's hands. Her little eight-month-old head was going back and forth, following Nick's movements precisely.

Needless to say, neither of them even noticed me standing there in the foyer.

I stood there watching the two of them for a little while, fascinated. Fascinated by how talented and passionate Nick was at the piano, and by how entranced my little daughter was by it all. I wondered if she would be like Sarah, playing the piano at age 3. And it struck me that Nick had a sensitivity to the music, and it's nuances and phrasing. Sensitivity that always seemed to be lacking in his everyday interactions with people.

Nick was finally done with his piece, and Dalilah clapped her little hands appreciatively. "Bravo," she said, giggling.

*Bravo?* How does she know that word? I mean, I'm sure that she heard it somewhere, but it boggled my mind that she was able to use it in context the way that she just did.

Just then, Dalilah finally noticed me. "Mama!" she shouted to me, reaching for me out of her specially made seat. "Come here, mama, come here!"

I rushed over to her, and picked her up. She clung to me tightly. "Uncle Nick play the piano!" she said excitedly. "He's really good!"

I laughed a little, and looked at Nick, who was sitting at the piano bench. He looked like he just had a workout, as a little bit of sweat beaded his forehead and he was breathing slightly heavily. I supposed that playing the piano, with as much force and passion as he was playing it, could take something out of a person.

Nick smiled. "Hey, good to see you home. How's my boy?"

I shook my head, and motioned to Dalilah. I knew that she could understand my words, so I didn't want to say too much in front of her.

Nick understood. I mouthed the words "we'll talk later," and he nodded his head.

"How's daddy?" Dalilah asked me, her little hands clutching my hair and examining it.

"Daddy's fine," I said. "He loves you and misses you."

"Daddy hurt?"

"Yes, baby, but he'll be home before you know it."

"I miss daddy," she said, her face looking crestfallen as she continued to play with locks of my hair.

"So do I, baby. So do I."

That night, after dinner, I tried to call Ryan. His phone rang and rang, and the attendant came back on the phone to tell me that he was resting comfortably.

Then I put Dalilah to bed, and Nick and I shared some Scotch and had our talk.

"I'm worried about him, Nick. I mean, I know that he went through major trauma, so he isn't 100%. But he's talking more negatively than I have ever heard him."

"What's he saying?"

"He keeps trying to convince me that he's not like his father. That he's a good guy. But he also said that he wasn't good enough for me, and that he was, quote, damaged goods."

Nick shook his head. "I was afraid of this happening."

"What?"

"He's apparently taking stock of his life. As people tend to do when they've come out of a life or death situation. His is one life that should never be examined."

"What do you mean?"

"He had to work through a lot of shame. Shame about

ANNIE JOCOBY

what happened to him as a kid, but also shame about how he acted when he was an adult. How wasted he was. I suppose he never told you about how he almost killed me."

"Almost killed you?" I was extremely startled by this revelation.

"Yeah. In a fight. I was in critical condition."

"He told me that he sent you to the hospital with bruised kidneys, a ruptured spleen, cracked ribs and a concussion. I didn't know you were in critical condition."

Then Nick proceeded to tell me the story.

"Fuck," I said. "That doesn't sound like him at all."

Nick nodded. "Yeah. And he was a man whore. Never when he was in a relationship with Alexis, though. But when they were broken up...." Nick shook his head. "Geezus Christ, that man could get the women. He would just walk into a bar, and they would be dripping off of him five seconds later. He'd have all these one-night stands, and the women would get obsessed with him. It got to the point where he could never bring a woman home, because she would stalk him for months afterwards. They would key his car, put sugar in his gas tank, bash in the windows of the house. They did everything but boil a bunny, but if we had a bunny, that probably would've happened too."

"So, he stopped having one-night stands?"

"Nope. He just took them to a hotel or went to their place. Gave them fake phone numbers to call him. That stopped the fatal attraction chicks, except for the most enterprising ones who still managed to find his address and would come by. That didn't go over well when Ryan and Alexis got back together and these random women would just show up, let me tell you."

"I see. So why are you telling me all this?"

"Because that's a part of his issues now. He treated those

66

women extremely carelessly. He knew that they always got attached to them, yet he played them like this grand piano here. That's a part of this shame."

"But he had a rotation of women going right before he met me."

"That was a bit different. He dated those women. He didn't just fuck them. In college, he was a user of women. He was pretty flagrant about it, too."

"And what does all of this have to do with what he's going through right now?"

"I'm not sure. I haven't seen him yet. But I would suspect that he's taking stock of his life, and not liking what he's seeing about himself. About how he was."

"Was is the operative word, here. Was. Not is. Was."

"Yes, but do your actions ever really leave you? Or do they become ingrained, a part of your identity? Think about it."

I knew he was right. I still looked upon some of my actions with a great deal of shame, even though those actions were also long in the past.

That night, I was tossing and turning in bed, when I got a phone call at about 2:30 in the morning.

"Hello?" I said, not recognizing the number, but feeling apprehensive because the call came so late at night. I tried to shut off the fear that the voice on the other end of the line would tell me that my husband threw a clot and was dead.

"Mrs. Gallagher?" a female voice said inquiringly.

My blood ran icy cold, and I started breathing heavily. "Yes?"

"This is Joelle Krueger, the head nurse at the hospital."

Now I was hyperventilating, and feeling like I was going

to pass out. Trying hard to conceal my panic, I just said "yes?"

"It's your husband. You need to come down here right away."

*Breathe, Iris, breathe.* My head started swimming. "Why? Why? He isn't.."

"No, he's alive."

"Why, what happened?"

"You need to come down here."

"No, tell me now. I want to know right now. Right now."

A long pause. Then - "Mr. Gallagher attempted suicide."

# Chapter Eleven

Attempted suicide? My mind wasn't comprehending her words. How was that even possible in the ICU?

"I'm sorry, Ms. Krueger, I guess I don't understand. My husband is in the ICU. I know that people watch him around the clock there. How is it possible that he attempted suicide?"

"Mr. Gallagher was transferred to a regular room about three hours ago. I'm very sorry. I thought that somebody would've contacted you by now about that."

"No, nobody contacted me," I said, feeling irrational anger building up. "Why can't you people get your shit together?"

"I'm very sorry, Mrs. Gallagher. I'll find the person who was responsible for contacting you about transferring Mr. Gallagher to a regular room, and that person will be reprimanded."

"Whatever. That's not important. I'm sorry for snapping at you. Now, please, tell me what happened?"

"Mr. Gallagher broke a mirror in his private bathroom, and used the jagged edge of the mirror to slash his wrists."

My hyperventilating started anew. *Breathe, Iris, breathe. But don't hyperventilate.* I started taking deep breaths in through my nose, expelling the air through my mouth. I felt hot tears flowing down my cheeks.

"Ok, um, ok." That was all I could think to say at that point. "How did he get to his bathroom?" I knew that Ryan wasn't able to walk, so I didn't know how he could do that.

"Mr. Gallagher is regaining use of his lower extremities. He can walk now. Is that what you were asking?"

"Yes, that's what I was asking," I said. I was stalling, trying to calm down before getting behind the wheel to see Ryan. I considered calling Daniel to drive me. I even considered getting Nick to drive me. But I wanted to see if I could drive myself first.

"Are those all the questions you have, Mrs. Gallagher?"

"Um, yes. Yes. I, I will be down there in about a half hour."

"Thank you, Mrs. Gallagher. We were going to wait until later this morning to call you, but felt that this was an emergency."

"No, I'm glad you called."

At that, I hung up the phone, and sat on the edge of the bed. I was getting the familiar feeling that everything was surreal, like a Dali painting, and I had a difficult time discerning if any of this was reality. Was I dreaming? Did I dream up everything, including dreaming up Ryan himself? I had been through so much in these past few years that nothing seemed real to me anymore.

I guess that was my mind's way of coping with all the trauma.

I went down the hall and knocked on Nick's door. To

my surprise, a drop-dead gorgeous woman in a baby-doll nightgown answered his door. The woman was around 5'8", slender with enormous natural breasts, with luxurious chestnut hair that curled down her back. Through full lips, she asked me what I needed.

"Uh, I'm so sorry. I need to talk to Nick."

Nick appeared directly behind her, wrapped only in a towel. His body rivaled Ryan's, as it was just as sinewy, muscular and lean. I felt immediately uncomfortable seeing him like this. *Stop, Iris, this is Ryan's best friend.* Yeah, Nick was man-candy, but he was like a Jaguar car – if you don't own it, you can look, but never touch. Besides, if Nick was a Jaguar, Ryan was a Lamborghini. Both of them beautiful, sleek and top-of-the-line, but one of them was the absolute cream of the crop, and that was Ryan.

"Yeah, Iris, what do you need?"

I looked at the girl, then to him, wondering if he would introduce me. But Nick made no move to do so.

He still stared at me expectantly.

I took a deep breath. "Uh, I need to talk to you. Privately."

Rack girl just gave me a disgusted look, then made her way back into the bedroom. Through the crack I could see that the bed was outfitted with handcuffs on the bedposts, and there was a riding crop in the corner.

I wondered who used that riding crop on whom.

"Just a sec, Iris. I need to put on some clothes." At that, he went back into the bedroom and shut the door behind him. He emerged a few minutes later in shorts and t-shirt.

"Now, what's up?"

"I need to go to the hospital."

Nick looked alarmed. "What? Why?"

"Ryan, he…"

"What? Ryan what?"

"He tried to kill himself."

At that, Nick's eyes got huge and he started shaking. "Oh, shit, shit, shit. I was afraid of this."

"So, could you care for Dalilah while I'm gone?"

"Yes, yes, yes, of course, of course." Then he shook his head ruefully. "I need to get rid of Tessa in there. Can't be too distracted when you have an infant in the house."

"May I bring you the baby monitor?"

"Sure, please do. Remind me to buy one for my room as well. Just in case I need it."

"Sheila's around, right?"

"Well, yeah, she lives here. She helps with Dalilah while I'm around, but I don't expect her to get up in the middle of the night to help."

"You don't have to get rid of your guest. I could always take Dalilah down to the hospital with me."

Nick rolled his eyes. "Don't be stupid. I'll get rid of Tessa. She's kinda a rando anyhow."

I inwardly smiled, remembering how Nick was talking about Ryan being a man whore earlier. Nick still held the title of the biggest man whore around, especially since he didn't limit himself to just one sex.

"Thanks Nick," I said, suddenly feeling irritated, "but Dalilah doesn't need to be exposed to your randos." At that, I went to Dalilah's room to wake her up, Nick right behind me. I turned to Nick and said "besides, seeing Dalilah might be just the thing to bring Ryan out of his depression."

As I started to open up Dalilah's door, Nick slammed it shut. "Listen to me. An attempted suicide is not simply depression. You can't take this lightly, like you seem to have done with everything else. There's no going to a drug house or to San Francisco to try to avoid this. You have to be his rock. Be his rock or get out of his life."

I looked at him like *what the fuck?* I didn't have time to think about how Nick was absolutely right about me and my avoidance and running tendencies. I also didn't have the patience for the lecture. I needed to get to the hospital, and quick.

"Are you going to let me get Dalilah, or aren't you?"

"I'm not. The hospital is not a place for an eight-month-old, and you can't drag her out in the middle of the night."

"Listen, I don't have time to argue with your ass. I need to get to the hospital, and you appear to be busy, so I need to get my daughter and get the hell out of here pronto. Capiche?"

He stood there, in front of Dalilah's door, his arms crossed. "Iris, you make really poor decisions. Really poor ones. Sometimes I think that you don't have a brain in your head, and this is one of those times. You're leaving her here, and that's that. End of discussion."

I felt like hauling off and hitting him, or howling like a beagle. How dare he make decisions for me like that?

God, he was such a controlling silverback.

I half expected him to start beating his chest and roaring.

I found myself glad that I was married to such a sweet guy. I wouldn't last two seconds with a guy like Nick ordering me around.

What could I do? Nick obviously wasn't going to let me take her, and the bimbo in the bedroom had yet to emerge out of Nick's bedroom and into her car. Sheila was asleep in the guest cottage out back, which is where she lived. I didn't trust Nick with my daughter, not with rack rando girl in there. It seemed that she was getting ready to handcuff him and whip him. What would he do if Dalilah needed him and he couldn't get to her because he was literally tied up?

*Catch more bees with honey than vinegar.* I had to try a different tact. "Nick, please. I think that Ryan needs to see his daughter. I think he's spiraling into depression because he feels that he doesn't have much to live for, and taking Dalilah over there will remind him that he does."

"Iris. It's 3:30 in the fucking morning. You're a moron. That's all."

At that, rando girl finally peeked her head out the door. "Are you coming back, or aren't you?"

I shot her a look, as did Nick. "Tessa, I'm sorry. I think it's best that you leave. I have to care for my friend Ryan's daughter while her mother goes to the hospital."

Tessa rolled her eyes. "Fine. You won't see me again. Asshole."

At that, Nick turned back to me and said "leave her here. Now get the fuck out. Now!"

I wanted to see Tessa leaving with my own eyes. But I didn't have time. I had to get out of there to see my husband.

So I left, without another word.

# Chapter Twelve

I felt irrational hatred for Nick as I made my way to the hospital. My nerves were raw, absolutely raw, and he was getting on my last one. I was shaking, and the road was almost a blur in front of me. I prayed that a cop wouldn't pull me over. It was too much, all too much. I didn't know how much more I could take.

I finally arrived at the hospital and went to the front desk to find out what room Ryan was in now. I was still angry that nobody had informed me that he was moved to a regular room. I was his fucking wife. I needed to be in the loop on my husband's progress, goddammit.

I didn't really have time to figure out what, or whom, I was really angry with. Perhaps Nick for being such an ass and a man whore. Perhaps the doctors and the attendants for not keeping an eye on Ryan.

No, I was angry with Ryan. How could he do this to us? Why would he ever think about leaving me and his daughter behind? He made it through surgery, which was a godsend. Now he was trying to do himself in anyhow.

A part of me didn't even want to see him. But a bigger part of me wanted to take his beautiful dark hair and put it on my chest and stroke it while he cried it out. Whatever it is that he had to cry out, I wanted him to do it with me by his side.

"I'm here to see my husband, Ryan Gallagher," I told the front desk attendant. I felt a bit breathless, and very anxious.

"Mr. Gallagher," the attendant said. "1002. That's the psych ward. Do you have a patient code for him?"

He was transferred to the psych ward already? Now, why didn't the lady on the phone tell me this? And give me a patient code while she was at it?

"No, I don't have a flipping patient code for him. I didn't even know that he was transferred to the psych ward." I couldn't hide my impatience, frustration and fury at this whole situation.

They best get their act together, because I was ready to cut a bitch.

"Could I please see your ID?"

With shaking hands, I fumbled around in my purse for my wallet. Crap, where is my wallet? I gradually realized that the wallet wasn't in my purse, for whatever reason. Then I remembered that I ordered something online earlier, and got the wallet out to place my order, and failed to put it back. Which meant that I not only was going to have problems seeing my husband, but I also best be careful to not get pulled over on the way home.

"Listen, uh, Vicki," I began, reading her name tag. "My husband was shot and almost killed. He made it through surgery, and now he has tried to kill himself. And you wouldn't believe the stuff that I've been through these past couple of years. It would boggle your fucking mind. Now I don't have a patient code, because I had no friggin idea that I needed one. Last I heard, Ryan was in the ICU. The lady who called me told me after the fact that Ryan had been transferred to a regular room. She never said a flipping word about having to have a patient code. Now, I get here, and all I want is to see my husband, and you're saying that I can't see him because I don't have a code that I never knew that I had to have."

The lady actually looked sympathetic to my plight. I looked down, not meeting her eyes, because I was just too afraid that she was going to turn me away. In which case, I imagined myself getting in my car and driving it through the front door of this place. I could now see why people did things like that in real life. Dealing with incompetents would drive anybody crazy.

She finally took a deep breath. "I'm not supposed to let anybody through who doesn't have a patient code." I continued to look at her, because I saw that there was the word "but" soon to come.

I wasn't disappointed. "But I'm going to make an exception. You really need either a patient code or ID when you come back, preferably both. So get the code from your husband when you see him."

I sighed with relief, as she directed me to the door where I would be buzzed through to the elevators, which would lead to the psych ward.

I got to the room where my husband was, and I saw him lying in the bed, staring at the ceiling. Both of his wrists were bound in heavy gauze.

I rushed to him, and he just looked at me. I wasn't at all sure if he was doped up, or simply in a different world at that time.

What I did know was that the person who was staring at me was not my husband.

"Ryan," I said, tentatively. "I'm here."

He blinked his eyes dully, then looked away.

The night nurse came in to check on him, and I got up to ask her what was going on. "Ryan. What's wrong with him? Is he on painkillers? Some kind of heavy duty anti-psychotic meds? What's going on?"

"Of course, he's been on painkillers since his surgery. And it looks like he has now been prescribed Seroquel," she said, examining her chart.

Seroquel. Might as well induce a coma and get it over with.

"Why Seroquel? My husband isn't bipolar, nor is he schizophrenic. He's apparently depressed. I'm not sure why he was prescribed something that is going to make him catatonic. And how high of a dose was he given?"

"You'll have to talk to the doctor about that."

"Get him in here right now. And I mean right now."

In about five minutes, a Dr. Hahn appeared in his white coat, looking all official. I bit my tongue, not wanting to rip into him like I was tempted to. "Hello, Dr. Hahn," I said as pleasantly as I could. "I'm Iris Gallagher. Ryan's wife."

He reached out his hand to shake mine. "Mrs. Gallagher, I understand that you have some questions about your husband."

"Yes. My husband isn't bipolar. He's never been bipolar. He's depressed because he went through major trauma and major surgery. Now you have him drugged up like he's a circus elephant who's recently charged his keeper. I'm not sure why this happened. I only know that I want it to stop."

"Your husband had an acute manic episode."

"Meaning?"

"Meaning that he smashed the television in his room, tore the shower curtain off the rod in his bathroom and broke a mirror. He used the mirror shards to cut his wrists."

I drew a deep breath, concentrating on breathing through my nose and expelling through my mouth. *You aren't going to get upset. You aren't going to go Dexter on this asshole. You are going to resist the urge to shove him out this window.* "Dr. Hahn. My husband is dealing with severe trauma right now. He went through major surgery and a near-death experience, which made him take stock of his life. Trust me, his life hasn't been pretty. He apparently hasn't always been the nicest guy in the world. He's dealt with things that you couldn't imagine in your pristine little suburban world. Or maybe you can, but only if you're a huge fucking pervert. He doesn't have a chemical imbalance in his brain, and he never has, to my knowledge. He doesn't need meds. He needs me, he needs time to heal, and he probably needs to talk to his therapist. He doesn't need horse tranquilizers."

Dr. Hahn simply continued to examine his chart, his eyes not meeting mine. I slammed my hand down on his chart, and forcefully brought his chin up so that his eyes were squarely aligned with mine. "No horse tranquilizers. That's not helping him. I'm his wife, his next of kin, and I can't imagine that he consented to being drugged like this. He's got shit to deal with, but he needs to deal with it and feel it. Own it. Drugging him with fucking Seroquel is only delaying this process. I can't believe that I have to tell you this, but here we are."

Dr. Hahn simply stood there, smugly smiling at me. "I'm Mr. Gallagher's attending physician, Mrs. Gallagher, so I think I know what he needs."

"Listen to me, and I mean listen to me good. My husband's father is extremely wealthy. Which means that he can hire a team of lawyers who will live for nothing more than to make your life a living fucking hell. This might be malpractice. It might not be malpractice. I suspect that it is malpractice, simply because I suspect that you gave him way too high of a dose, because Seroquel will make you somewhat out of it, but not catatonic. Malpractice or not, what's certain is that they will drag your ass through litigation for years, because that's what they do. They live for that shit. They won't even care if they win, because they'll be getting paid a king's ransom for chasing you all over town from one deposition to another, win or lose. Now, either you take my husband off of this fucking Seroquel, or you'll be hearing from the best attorneys in the country in the morning. Your choice."

That's all I needed to say – the "m" word. As with every doctor, Dr. Hahn lived in fear of the dreaded malpractice suit. "Well, uh, Mrs. Gallagher, I guess we could wean him off these meds and see what happens. I'll taper his medication down immediately."

"No tapering. He just had his first dose this evening, apparently. There's no reason to taper him off. He doesn't need any more of these drugs, period."

I faced him, engaging him in a staring contest. Turned out that having a bipolar sister came in handy for me, because I knew my shit when it came to anti-psychotic drugs.

"You're right, Mrs. Gallagher. He doesn't need to taper. Well, I have other patients to see so…"

I nodded my head. *Don't let the door hit your ass on the way out.*

And, just like that, he was gone.

I sat down next to my incoherent husband, and took his hand. To my surprise, he was able to grip my hand, although his expression was still blank. "We have to get you out of here. These people are a bunch of assclowns." Then I sighed. Get him out of here? How would I ever do that? He was in the psych ward after trying to kill himself, and he apparently just got out of the ICU. I didn't know the first thing about how to get him out of there. I only knew that I wanted him out of that hospital.

I supposed if some money changed hands, then that might facilitate things. But probably not even then.

I needed to have some type of influence. It was kinda like a politician. Nobody dances unless there is some huge benefactor making them do so.

Then I got an idea. Benjamin Whitney was known for his charitable work around town. I wondered if his work included hospital charities. This hospital in particular.

I quickly grabbed my iPhone out of my purse, and Googled Benjamin Whitney, adding in the words "hospital charities." To my delight, it turned out that hospitals were among his pet causes. He had donated $1.1 million dollars to this very hospital, and there was a wing that was named in his honor. He had donated money to many other hospitals around town, as well, as I found out through my Google search, but this was the only hospital that I was concerned about.

With shaking hands, I looked through my contact list to find Benjamin's phone number. What time was it? My iPhone indicated that it was presently 4:50 AM. I couldn't remember if Benjamin was still in his Rhode Island home, but I hoped that he was. That way, it would be close to 6 AM there, and not too early to call. Presumably.

It didn't matter, I was going to call him anyhow. Then find some home health nurses who could live with us while Ryan recovers.

I had to have Ryan come home with me. I didn't trust these people any further then I could throw them. They weren't keeping me in the loop about anything, and they overmedicated my poor husband so that he was practically a drooling idiot.

I sat down on a chair and dialed Benjamin's number. It was his personal cell number, so I hoped that one of his help didn't answer it.

"Hello?" a rather robust-sounding voice inquired.

"Yes, Mr. Whitney?"

"Yes? Who is this?"

"Iris. Iris Gallagher. I have to talk to you. It's a serious emergency."

"Iris. Good to hear from you. What emergency are you calling about?"

I explained everything to him, while he interjected outraged phrases such as "how dare they?" and "what a bunch of incompetents," and "my son has to get out of that place."

"Yes, Mr. Whitney. So, you see, we have to get him out of here and bring him home. I don't think that they'll release him. This is where you come in. I need for you to use your influence to make it happen. Also, I was hoping that you could get some home health workers to come home with us while Ryan recovers."

"I'll make some phone calls," he said.

Within a half hour, a nurse arrived in the room. "Mr. Gallagher has been released. He's free to go home."

I nodded my head. "Thanks. I just need a wheelchair to get him to his car. I don't think he can leave on his own two feet right now," I said, feeling outraged again at the over-prescribing doctor.

Oh, how I wanted to go Dexter on his ass.

If I ever saw his smug face again....

I got the wheelchair, wheeled him down to the lobby, then brought the Escalade around and loaded him into the front seat.

Then, with a flip of my middle finger out the window, I drove off.

While I was in the car, I dialed Benjamin again. When he answered, I said "hello, Benjamin. It's Iris again. Thank you for making the phone calls to have Ryan released."

"Of course. Is there anything more I can do for you?"

"The home health workers? Did you contact them?"

"They'll be waiting for you when you get home."

"Uh, Mr. Whitney, I appreciate that. But we don't live in the same place anymore."

"I know. You're living at Nick O'Hara's home."

How did he know that? Benjamin certainly does have a way to keep tabs on all of us.

"Right. Well, thanks again."

I soon arrived at Nick's mansion to find that there was a team of people who were getting out of cars and going into the house. Nick came out to greet us himself. I felt bad, because it was five in the morning, and I had no idea if Nick was ambushed with these people, or if Benjamin called him to give him a heads up. I also felt a little bit scared that Nick might think that this was all a horrible idea. I wasn't looking forward to him yelling at me and berating me for pulling yet another rash action.

It was entirely possible that, after I had calmed down and contemplated everything, I, myself, would also find this entire scenario to be stupid and not in Ryan's best interest. But I went with my gut, and I was feeling good about my decision to bring Ryan home.

I got out of the car. "Nick, I need help with Ryan. He's not coherent right now."

Nick's face was indiscernible. I couldn't tell if he was pissed or impressed.

Maybe he was a combination of both.

Nick opened the passenger door and stood Ryan up, putting his arm around him and Ryan's arm around his shoulder. Ryan could barely walk, but Nick managed to get him into the house and into a lower-level bedroom that was being outfitted with a hospital bed by two men. The hospital bed was set up in record time, and Nick laid Ryan down on it.

Nick looked at me. "I don't even know what to say to you right now. I don't know yet if I want to kill you or kiss you. What I do know is that I need to figure out what is going on with these workers, and find out who does what."

At that, Nick left and summoned the leader of the home health worker team. "George, get everybody together here in the foyer. I need to get a handle on who everybody is and what their function is. Also, I'd imagine that I'm gonna need at least two workers to move in here for the time being. They can stay in the guest cottage with Sheila out back behind the pool."

As everybody started streaming into the massive foyer, I hung back and sat with Ryan. This was a gorgeous room, with brand-new cherry hardwood floors and a huge stained glass window that streamed primary colors. There were orchids everywhere in this room, which was my favorite flower and Ryan's as well. The walls were a relaxing shade of faux finish yellow, and the room was attached to a massive bathroom with marble countertops and brass fixtures. There was an enormous plasma screen that was mounted on the wall, and there was soft music playing through some surround-sound speakers. All in all, this was a peaceful room, so much better for Ryan's recovery then the sterile white hospital room with the tiny bathroom and old-school television that was mounted on the ceiling.

I climbed into bed with Ryan, as there was more than enough room for two, and put my head on his chest. He didn't react, but I could hear his heart pounding, and it was soothing to me.

After a few minutes, I fell asleep.

# Chapter Thirteen

I woke up several hours later. There was a young nurse who was standing by the bed, taking Ryan's vital signs. There were various machines that were brought into the room while I was unconscious, and I recognized that these were the same machines as those that were in the hospital.

I looked at Ryan's face. It seemed that he was becoming more coherent, for he looked at me and his eyes showed recognition. He still looked dreamy, but not quite as catatonic as he was before.

"Ryan," I said softly. "Are you there?"

He nodded imperceptibly. "The Pooh Bear. Did you get him?"

*Crap. The Pooh Bear.* I didn't even see Pooh in Ryan's room when I hustled him out of there. "Oh, no, honey, I didn't get him. I didn't see him when I got you out of the hospital. I'm so sorry." I wondered if I could call somebody to get that bear and bring him home to be with Ryan. It obviously meant so much to him.

He said nothing more, turning his face away from mine. I could see tears forming in the corner of his eyes.

At that, I silently got out of the bed and went into the bathroom to make a phone call to the hospital. When the attendant answered the phone, I asked if there was a Pooh Bear in the lost and found. The attendant went to look, then came back and confirmed that there was a Pooh Bear there. Then I called Daniel and asked him to pick up Pooh and bring him to Nick's house. He readily agreed.

"Good news, honey. Pooh is coming home to be with you."

He didn't say anything, just looked at me blankly. "Um, Iris, I'm pretty tired right now. I need my rest. I was wondering if you could give me some space for a little while."

I nodded. It was peculiar that he didn't even question how he got out of the hospital, or tell me how he managed to get out of his hospital bed in the first place to ransack his room. Last I knew he couldn't walk. But yet he suddenly got up to go berserk in his room. I was starting to want answers from him, but I didn't push.

"Honey," I said, "do you want Max and Brut in here to keep you company? I could put their beds next to yours if you like."

Ryan half-smiled at this suggestion. "Yes, that would be great, Iris. Please bring them in."

At that, I walked to the door and whistled for the dogs. They came bounding in, and started nudging Ryan while they whined and tried to lick his face. He smiled wanly, then looked at me with his now-familiar blank expression. "Thank you, Iris. And thank you for giving me my space. Be sure to check on me in a couple of hours, ok?"

I only nodded, then silently left, shutting the door behind me.

# Chapter Fourteen

## RYAN

I was shutting out the most important person in my life, and I really didn't know why.

I only knew that I really didn't want to be around her anymore.

But it wasn't just her. I didn't want to be around anybody anymore. Yet, there I was, in the house with not just her, but also Nick and Dalilah. Inevitably Alexis was going to join the party, because she was going to need a place to stay after she got out of her own treatment center.

This scenario was exactly what I didn't want. I loved Iris for doing this, though. Her heart certainly was in the right place, even if her brain necessarily wasn't. It was bullshit that Dr. Hahn chose to drug me up past the point of coherence. But, then again, I probably deserved it. I pretty much went ape shit in that hospital room. It was a reaction from the self-loathing that began the moment I started spinning into my negative thoughts about the actions I had taken during my life.

And I just couldn't seem to stop those dark thoughts from crowding my headspace. It wasn't just Nick that I treated like crap during my college days. It was also Natalie and all the random women who shared my bed. I don't think that I even remember most of their first names, let alone their last ones.

I'm not sure if I knew their names then.

I only knew that getting women was something that was never a problem for me. I'd roll into a bar, find the hottest girl there and, before I knew it, we were making out on the dance floor. An hour or so later, it was back to her place or to a hotel, where we'd fuck and I'd make an excuse to high-tail it out of there immediately afterwards. It was always a game for me. I couldn't care less about any of those women.

As for Natalie, she was always a great friend. I'd call her in the middle of the night, booty call her, and she always let me come over. We'd screw, I'd crash, then leave the next morning while she was still sawing logs. Then she'd invite me over to watch movies or something, and I always found an excuse not to. Because I never wanted anything from her. I never wanted anything from any of the women I bedded.

To tell the absolute truth, I really never wanted anything from Alexis either, although she was always the most steady girl in my life during this period. Which wasn't saying much, considering we were broken up far more than we were together. Alexis was my drug buddy more than anything else. Sid and Nancy she called us, and that's who we were. Completely destructive for one another. But, we were mutually destructive, so it worked for us. Symbiotically destroying each other, like two parasites devouring each other alive. To think that I always thought that I was in love with her. Now, I know that it was never love, but more like a kind of obsession that both of us had for one another.

Now, since I was obsessed with examining my past, I was feeling the need to examine the using of women thing as well. I still needed to get to the bottom of who I was and why I was the way that I was. All those years of therapy really hadn't helped me do this. The therapy helped me overcome trauma about the abuse from my father and from losing my mother at such a young age. Recently it had helped me move past the trauma from the sex parties and Rochelle, and it had also helped cement the fact that I had forgiven my father for putting me through everything that he had.

But all my years of therapy hasn't really touched upon the shame I felt for how I treated the people in my life for so many years. Nick was the only one I physically abused, and, I'm ashamed to say, mentally abused as well. But the women were also victims of my narcissism. And I needed to come to terms with that.

And I was obsessing about Rachael Smyth. I needed to find a way to make amends for what I did to her. Find some kind of closure and peace about that.

So, I was obsessing about Rachael, when I really should've been obsessing about my wife, because she thought that I attempted suicide, when it wasn't that at all. When I broke the mirror in the bathroom, I accidentally put both of my arms on the counter, and the shards of glass cut into my wrists. I was bleeding pretty badly − I guess I really didn't know what I was doing, because I was in such a blind rage about my life. I didn't even realize that the mirror shards were cutting deep into my skin.

Then, the next thing I knew, I was being injected with something and I don't remember much after that.

Now, Iris thought that I was suicidal again. She no doubt was angry with me for wanting to kill myself, when she and Dalilah were in my life. But I just didn't have the energy to talk to her about what was going on with me.

# Chapter Fifteen

## IRIS

I just left Ryan's room, and I ran into Nick, who was standing just outside the room, wanting to go in to talk to Ryan.

"Ryan wants to be alone right now," I said to Nick.

Nick just nodded and shrugged his shoulders. "Sure, sure. But he shouldn't be alone too much. So, I'm going to make him join us for dinner. He obviously isn't having too much trouble using his legs if he was able to ransack the hospital room like he did."

"Yeah, about that. Is that something that he used to do?"

"No, never. He never was a property damage kind of guy. Aside from kicking the living shit out of me that one time, and just generally being a pain in the ass junkie, there was always a part of him that was very polite and respectful. I know, it seems weird, but he always seemed to have two distinct sides to him. So, no, he would never have been disrespectful enough to destroy property back then."

"Wonder what made him do it this time?"

"Dunno. I'm sure we'll find out in time."

I certainly hoped so. I didn't want to examine my feelings about this new turn of events. Ryan was treating me like a stranger, not the love of his life. I tried not to take that personally, how weird he was acting just now. Calling me Iris, instead of his usual nicknames for me, and generally acting like I was somebody whom he barely knew. The one good thing was that he was seemingly desperate to get the Pooh Bear back. Considering that he was not that fond of Pooh – I was the one who was crazy about the bear – I presumed that there was still a part of him that was very much in love with me. The bear somehow represented those feelings.

At least I hoped that was the case. Maybe he just wanted the bear back because it was soft and fun to cuddle with. Kinda like how he used to feel about me.

I had been replaced by a bear.

That evening, Ryan refused to join us for dinner. Sheila had made a beautiful roast chicken with all the trimmings. She seemed to be an amazing cook. I was salivating as she brought the bird to the table. I had talked to Ryan earlier in the evening about coming to dinner, and he was non-committal about it.

"I don't know, Iris. I really don't want to be around a lot of people right now."

By "a lot of people" he meant "anybody," I was finding out. He didn't even want Dalilah to come and visit him in his room. "She doesn't need to see me like this. It might traumatize her," he said.

"But honey, she's desperate to see you. She's been talking about you all day. She even made a beautiful little watercolor painting just for you." And by watercolor painting, I didn't mean rudimentary dogs and stick people. She had painted a little cottage in the woods, with purple exterior walls and a real thatched roof. There was a light that shone through the window. It wasn't Thomas Kinkaid, but, considering her age, it was very good. It resembled a painting that an older child would paint, perhaps a five-year-old painting in kindergarten.

"I know, honey, but I don't have the energy to see her. And she might be haunted by the sight of her dad with his wrists bandaged up for the rest of her life. You have no idea how that sort of thing affects a child." Then he looked out the window with a faraway expression. "It happened to my mom, you know. She cut herself on a window that she broke when she got into a fight with my dad. It was extremely scary for me. I think that I was permanently scarred by seeing her bandaged up like that."

Fair enough. "Ok, then, I won't force you to see her. I can bring food into your room, though. You need to eat. I don't think that you've eaten all day."

"I'm not hungry."

"Listen, just like you forced me to eat when I was attacked by Rochelle, I need to do the same for you. Now, Sheila has made a wonderfully juicy roasted chicken with new potatoes and green beans. She seems to be an amazing cook. I need for you to eat."

"I'm not hungry, goddammit, now leave me the fuck alone!" Ryan's eyes got wide and a little vein was popping out of his forehead.

I had never, ever seen him get this angry. Well, maybe that one time when he threw me out of his house when I first started living with him, but that was over something that was kinda major. This fury was coming over roasted chicken. And the anger came on so suddenly, seemingly out of nowhere.

"Ok, ok, ok. I'll just go and eat dinner and I'll be back to see you afterwards."

"Don't bother," he said with a hard-edged tone. Then he softened some. "I mean, I'm really, really tired. These painkillers are doing a number on me. I'll be ok, just see me in the morning, ok?"

I nodded my head. It was going to be very difficult to know how to treat him. One thing was for sure, he was going to need to see his therapist, soon. He was spiraling, and I had no idea how to reach him.

Over dinner, I felt uncomfortable. Sheila had joined us, along with the two live-in nurses. One was named Gercon. He was a French immigrant, with black tightly curled hair and a lean and trim body. He spoke perfect English, but with a very thick accent. The other nurse who stayed with us was Tammy, a willowy blonde who had eyes for my husband. I could see the way that she looked at him. But, then again, it wasn't any different from how any other woman looked at him, so I wasn't offended.

But Dalilah was pretty upset about the fact that her father was in the next room and refused to see her. "I wanna see daddy now!" she had screamed earlier, her little face getting as red as her hair, her hands balled up into tiny little fists. "Why can't I see daddy?"

"Baby, daddy's tired. He wants to see you, but he needs his rest."

Dalilah looked unconvinced. "Give me painting. Daddy's painting."

I went into the other room and brought the painting to her.

She promptly tore it up in tiny little pieces.

*Oh, boy, she's going to be a handful.*

"Dalilah, why would you do something like that? You worked so hard on it."

"Daddy make me mad. Daddy don't love me."

"Baby, please. Daddy loves you very much. He's just very tired right now, that's all. He needs his rest."

I was amazed at how perceptive she was about the situation. She clearly wasn't satisfied with my explanation of why her daddy wouldn't see her.

So, dinner was uncomfortable. Dalilah sat in her high chair, eating her chicken and fixins, clearly still very angry. She usually was quite chatty, but tonight, she ate in a sullen silence. Combine Dalilah's attitude with the fact that I was sharing dinner with three strangers and Nick, while my husband was in the same home, and I felt that the entire affair felt surreal.

My life was, once again, like a Dali painting. Nothing made sense.

Nick kept shooting me meaningful glances, but I just shook my head. We would have to discuss everything later.

After dinner, I helped Sheila clean up, while Gercon and Tammy went to check on Ryan before retiring for the evening. Then I joined Nick in the den, where he was playing with Dalilah. He was showing her an Old Maid game, which seemed to cheer her up some. She was quite good at the game, and laughed at the different characters on the cards. Then she saw me, and she started pouting again.

Ignoring me, she asked Nick if they could play Chutes and Ladders next.

"No, Dalilah," Nick said. "You have to get ready for

bed. Your mother's here to give you your bath and tuck you into bed."

"NO," she said. "You to give me bath and tuck me into bed."

I just shook my head. My daughter, entering her terrible twos already, before she even had her first birthday.

I didn't want to deal with it. "Nick, do you mind doing that for me?"

"Sure," he said, "but don't make a habit of it. You're the parent, not me."

"I know," I said. "I just really need a glass of wine right now. I know it sounds selfish, but I'm at my wits end right now." And Dalilah wasn't helping one bit.

"Ok," he said, picking her up. "Say night night to mommy."

Dalilah just shook her head and stuck her thumb in her mouth.

If she had the power to flip me off, she would have.

About an hour later, Nick joined me in front of the fire. I was on my second glass of wine, staring at the fire pensively.

"Do you want to talk about it?" Nick asked.

I just looked at him. He was so hard to figure out sometimes. He could be such a controlling, insensitive jerk. But there was also a sensitive side, and I was seeing this more and more.

"I don't know what to do about Ryan," I began. "I mean, I know I need to give him time and space and everything. I understand that. But it's so hard for me to figure out what I need to do to help him. I'm not good at this kind of thing. A part of me wants to force myself on him – go in there, whether he wants me to or not, and force feed him and sleep in the bed with him. Hold him and tell him that everything is going to be ok. Then there's another part of me that says to give him his space, and he'll come around. What should I do?"

"Give him time and space. He'll come around and let you know when he's ready for your help. In the meantime, take your cues from him. Trust me, I know what he's like when he's forced to do something he doesn't want to do. That's what almost got me killed, when I pushed too far. So I suggest that you tread lightly."

I sighed. I knew that he would say something like that.

"What about his therapist? He should see Dr. Halder."

"You can't force him to go. He'll go willingly when he's ready. Iris, I've known this guy almost my entire life. I know him very well. No offense, but you've known him for just a few years. Please listen to me when I tell you what you should do. I'm a Ryan expert if ever there was one."

I took another sip of my wine. I wondered if I should even go and see Ryan and tell him good night. Even that small gesture might be somehow intruding on his space.

Nick changed the subject. "So, what's going on with the Rochelle thing?"

I shrugged. "I don't know. Ryan needs to be a part of that. He needs to be deposed. The trial has been rescheduled for next month, but I don't imagine that Ryan can be a part of that so soon. So, I would imagine that it would be drug out some more. That's the least of my worries, now, though."

"Yeah," Nick said. "Ryan is the star witness for the prosecution. I would imagine that the entire case will hinge upon his testimony."

I nodded my head. "You know, it's strange. Before all this other stuff happened to myself and Ryan – the shooting, the rape, etc., etc., I was obsessed with Rochelle and what she did. Now, it's like a distant memory. I really don't care what happens to her, to tell you the truth."

"That's understandable. I would imagine that all your mental energy is focused on that guy in the bed in the next room."

"That's an understatement. He's all I think about. That's probably why Dalilah is mad at me – I don't think I've been giving her enough of my attention, because I've been so fixated on Ryan. I hope she's not scarred about all this."

"Well, you are unfortunate in that Dalilah is probably the brightest child I've ever met. Which means she probably won't forget about whatever it is she's angry about, like other children would. You might be stuck with a pouty little girl for awhile."

"Ugh. One stressor at a time. I can't even think about the fact that she's going to be uncontrollable for me. I've never dealt with a genius in my life. Well, except for my husband. I wonder if he gave his parents the same type of attitude?"

"No, he didn't. Sarah did, though. From the stories I have heard from Maggie, Sarah was a lot like Dalilah when she was little. Ryan never gave his parents grief, though. They gave him a lot of grief, but not the other way around. At least that's what Sarah and Maggie tell me."

We stayed up talking for a little while later before I begged off and went to bed. "It's been nice talking with you, Nick. But I really need some shut-eye."

"Sure, see you tomorrow."

Then I went to my huge empty bed, and cried myself to sleep.

The next morning, I crept into Ryan's room. I had prepared breakfast for him – I was energetic the previous evening and made a cheese strata that was refrigerated overnight. That was one of his favorite breakfast meals. I went to the market to buy some Challah bread, which was a Jewish egg bread, and some special imported cheeses. Then I layered the Challah bread with the cheese in a heavy baking dish, and poured an egg mixture over all of it. I added some spices and refrigerated it overnight so that the bread could soak up the egg mixture, then put it in the oven that morning. Cheese strata was always a favorite of us both, and it was what he had made for me on our first breakfast together, so it had a special meaning for us.

My mouth was watering as I brought it out of the oven. It smelled divine, and I couldn't wait to share it with him. I made some Mimosas and Bloody Marys to go with it, and some chicken breakfast sausage. I actually made the sausage myself in Nick's meat grinder – I simply ground up some chicken breast, added apple, fennel and spices, and made it in to patties. Then I went into Nick's garden to prune a few roses, with Nick's permission, of course.

"Nick," I had said. "Do you mind if I prune a couple of roses from the garden?"

"No, of course not," he said. "What do you need them for, though?"

"I'm going to bring Ryan breakfast in bed this morning. I know how much he loves roses, so I thought it would be nice to have some on the tray in a little vase."

Nick said nothing at first. Then he said "ok, but please don't get your hopes up. It might not go the way you'd hope."

"Meaning?"

"Meaning nothing, maybe. But if he doesn't react with hugs and kisses, don't take it personally. Just sayin'."

I thought about Ryan's sudden bout of temper yesterday

when I tried to get him to eat the chicken, and felt a little bit apprehensive.

But I had to try.

So, I prepared a little tray with the goodies. I even baked chocolate chunk cookies, which were his favorite treat. I found a little crystal vase and put the flowers in that, and made a plate with the strata, the sausage, and a couple of cookies. The Mimosa and Bloody Mary rounded out the breakfast. Then I made a tray for myself as well.

"Knock, knock," I said, as I opened up the door to Ryan's new room.

Ryan was sitting there on the bed, watching television. It was some kind of History Channel show, I surmised.

Ryan looked at me, said nothing, then turned his attention back to his show.

I took a deep breath, feeling daunted. Then I set the tray up on his lap. "I made you all your favorites. I even pruned some roses for you."

Ryan still said nothing. He just continued to stare at the television set.

"Can I scoot in next to you? We can eat together."

Ryan said nothing, and made no move for me to get into the bed with him.

"Ok, then, I won't eat in bed with you," I said. "I'll just eat at this little table here," I said, gesturing to the small table and chairs that were next to the bed.

I started eating, and I was talking nervously, trying hard to fill the silence. Ryan wasn't eating any of the food, nor was he reacting to anything I was saying. Still, I kept talking.

"I see you have a World War II show on. What is the exact subject?"

Ryan said nothing.

"Dalilah made you another picture. I hope I get a

chance to give it to you. Looks like she's really going to be a prodigy. Might even have a musical ear, too. She sure is mesmerized by Nick when he's playing the piano."

Still nothing.

"This strata is really good, if I do say so myself. I found some really nice imported cheeses at Dean and Deluca. There's Cantal and St. Nectaire in there, both imported from France. I also added some Camembert, and a little Gruyere. The bread's very nice, too – I got that at Whole Foods. Take a bite. I think you'll be in heaven."

Ryan still said nothing, his eyes glued to the television set.

I started to feel depressed, but the food was so good, it cheered me up some. Then I immediately started to worry – food used to be the way I drowned my sorrows, before I met Ryan. I could polish off an entire log of cookie dough – not the actual cookies, mind you, just the dough – in one sitting, and top it off with an entire bag of Kettle Chips. I was overweight when Ryan and I had met, then lost a ton through being in a three-month long coma after Rochelle's attack. Then lost even more in the aftermath. I had since maintained my smaller weight, through great diligence on my part.

Now I was, once again, using food as a way to cope with rejection. Because I felt happy, even though Ryan was completely shutting me out. The happiness was coming through eating this really delicious and rich meal. I'd have to stifle the urge to eat the rest of it after I left the room. I'd made an entire baking dish full of it, and I figured I could feed Nick, Dalilah, Sheila and the workers with it. But there was a voice in my head that was telling me to eat all of it before anybody even knew it existed.

I soldiered on, determined to engage Ryan some.

"Here," I said, putting some strata on a fork and putting it close to his mouth. "Here's some. Taste it. It's pretty divine, really. I could get on a cooking competition with this one."

He said nothing, but turned his face away, his mouth closed, his face in a grimace. It was obvious he didn't want to try my delicious strata.

Should I just give up? Nick's warning was ringing in my ears – don't get my hopes up. Ryan doesn't like to be pushed. I tried not to take it personally – I hated him for several weeks after my rape. It wasn't rational for me to feel that way – he was just a convenient target for my rage. I imagined that Ryan was going through something similar. So maybe it was a good idea just to leave it alone right now.

So, I finished my breakfast and got up. "I'm going to go right now, honey. I want to leave the food there for you, though, so if you get hungry, you can eat it."

He said nothing, but handed me back his tray of food.

I took the hint, and left his room without another word.

I brought Ryan's tray of food back to the kitchen, then devoured everything he didn't eat. I rationalized doing this because it wouldn't be sanitary to serve it to the other people in the house, and I certainly didn't want to waste it. I drank his Mimosa and Bloody Mary as well.

I saw Nick sitting outside on the back patio. "Um, I'm going to get Dalilah, and maybe we could all eat together?" How badly I wanted some companionship. I didn't like to eat alone, and that was what I just did. I ate two breakfasts alone, and I was about to eat a third with Nick and Dalilah.

I had to stop myself before I binge-ate my way to *The Biggest Loser* competition.

"That sounds great, Iris. I saw that strata you made, it smells really good. Do you mind if Sheila, Gercon and Tammy joins us?"

"Of course not. I made enough for everybody."

So, all of us feasted on my cheese strata, chicken sausage and cookies.

"This was delicious," Sheila told me. "You have to give me your recipe."

"Oh, it was a little of this, a little of that, and some spices. But I could write it down if you like."

"Please do."

"I'm happy you liked it. I'm just glad that somebody appreciates me."

Nick gave me a look when I said that. Then, later, he cornered me alone and said "Ryan shut you out during breakfast, didn't he?"

To my surprise, I started crying. I nodded my head.

To my bigger surprise, Nick wrapped his arms around me and let me cry on his chest. He gently stroked my hair. "Shhhh, it's going to be ok. He won't be like this forever, but you have to give him his space. Shhhh, don't cry. You're going to be ok."

Then he lightly kissed my forehead. "Let me get you a Kleenex," he said. Then he left and gave me a box of tissues. "Here. Now, go and wash your face and meet me on the patio."

I nodded my head, and blew my nose. Then I went to the bathroom to splash some cold water on my face. "God, Iris, you look like hell," I said to my reflection. Blotchy cheeks, swollen eyes, the whole nine. My hair was ratty as well, so I got a pony-tail holder and put it up. Then I went to the patio to meet Nick.

Nick was waiting for me with another Mimosa. "You feeling better, hon?" he asked me, and put his arm around me.

"Yeah, a little. Thanks, though. You've uh, been a good

friend lately. Thanks for that."

"Well, I know what it feels like to be on the other side of Ryan's brick wall. It ain't fun, I'll tell you that."

"I'll be ok. I'm just kinda overwhelmed. I just need to stay away from the cookie dough and Kettle Chips, though. I might have had a drug problem after my rape, but food has always been my main addiction."

"Well, I'll make sure that you don't binge eat."

"Thanks."

"Where's Dalilah?" he asked me.

"I put her down for a little afternoon nap. She usually doesn't nap very long, though, so I should probably check on her in a few."

"Yeah, do, and bring her out here if you like. It's a nice day."

"I will." Then I looked at him hesitantly. "You, uh, you've been really nice to me lately. I, I, I, well…"

"You didn't think I had it in me to be sensitive and caring, huh?"

I said nothing, just shrugged.

"I'm not a bad guy," he said. "I just have a lot of armour, that's all."

I nodded. "I know about armour. I think everybody does."

"Not you," he said. "You're very transparent. You wear your heart on your sleeve more than anybody I've ever met."

"Yeah, I guess I do tend to be an emotional basket case."

"No. Alexis is an emotional basket case. You're just… transparent. Refreshing, really."

I blinked my eyes. He sure was in a good mood.

"Anyhow, you better check on your daughter. I just wanted to make sure you were holding up ok."

"I am, thanks," I said, getting up. I went to get Dalilah, and I brought her back out on the patio. Nick had stripped down to some swimming trunks, and was sitting in the hot tub.

"Hey," he called. "Why don't you girls get into your suits and join me?"

"Are hot tubs good for babies?" I asked.

"No," he said. "But you can take her into the pool here. I know it's kinda chilly, but the pool is heated."

So, that's what we did. It was May, so the weather was in the 70s, way too cold for a cold swimming pool. But Nick was right – the pool was heated, so the water felt very nice. Nick got out of the hot tub, and joined us. The two of us frolicked in the pool for a couple of hours, and I had to say that, by the end of our little play-session, I was feeling much better.

A week went by, then two. I managed to make Ryan eat just enough to sustain him, but he was rapidly losing weight and becoming a shell of himself. He refused to leave his room, and he continued to refuse to see Dalilah or even Nick. He was still shutting me out completely. Every day was like the day of the strata – he would be watching television when I would go in, and he wouldn't acknowledge I was there. He would just be staring at the TV, not saying a single word.

I really wanted him to keep up his strength, and I was worried about him losing too much weight and getting weaker because of malnutrition. So, I would leave trays of food for

him, in hopes that he would eat when I left the room. Sometimes, I would find that the food was gone. Other times, the
food was left untouched. There didn't seem to be any rhyme
or reason for this, either. It wasn't that he didn't like the food –
I brought him his favorites, such as roasted chicken, pan-fried
salmon, grass fed steak, and various pastas. Yet, he sometimes
would leave everything on the plate, without even a bite. I felt
heartened that other times he actually did eat everything.
That was a good sign, I decided, that he would be leaving the
dark place which had occupied him ever since the shooting.

I worriedly talked to Gercon and Tammy about how he
was doing.

"He doesn't talk much, but he's certainly not unpleas-
ant. And he seems to be showering regularly, which is a
good thing, because I don't think he gets out of that bed
much," Tammy told me.

Gercon didn't have much to add. "I don't think that Mr.
Gallagher has said three words to me the entire time I've
been here. What was he like before?"

"Well, he certainly has had his bad times," I said. "But
he handled them really well. I've never seen him even
remotely like this, although Nick has said that he has seen
Ryan like this before. So, I hope that this is something that
we can eventually overcome with some good therapy and a
lot of love and support from me."

I even tried to send a psychiatrist to see him a few times.
Ryan, unfortunately, didn't take well to this intrusion.

"What the fuck is going on here, Iris?" he asked when I
walked in with Dr. Ballast, who was a renowned psychiatrist
who specialized in PTSD.

"Mrs. Gallagher is very concerned about your mental
health," Dr. Ballast said. "She called me to come and see if
there was anything I could do."

"No, there's nothing that you can do except get the fuck out. Now!"

Dr. Ballast persisted for about a half hour, before finally leaving. "He's not ready," he told me. "The old saying is true – you can lead a horse to water, but you can't make them drink. You know where to find me when he is ready, though."

Other times, I would go into his room and see that his eyes were swollen and red. He would see me and immediately turn away.

I did notice that he was feverishly writing in a journal by the bed. He bookmarked the places where he left off, and I noticed that he was writing about twenty pages every day. I wished he would share them with me, but I knew this was just a dream. There was no way he would possibly do that right now.

Every evening, before I retired to bed, and after I put Dalilah into bed, Nick and I would sit around and chat. I found his presence to be the only comfort for me during this period of time. I was so hungry for information about Ryan, and Nick was definitely the one to go to for this. He knew Ryan better than anybody, bar none. He was truly the only person in Ryan's life who had been there with him through everything. He knew just what made Ryan tick, and how Ryan thought and felt about everything. He was very reassuring that Ryan would eventually come out of it and return to me.

"Are you sure, Nick?" I asked one night over a glass of wine. Wine was becoming my only friend these days, unless you counted Nick. I was drinking a little too much for my own comfort, but I rationalized this by saying to myself that I needed some kind of escape. And I did. Who wouldn't after what I went through, and was continuing to go through?

"For the thousandth time, Iris, yes. Yes, Ryan will come out of this. When, I don't know. What I do know is that he loves you. You are the first woman he has ever really loved. You're a part of him, so there is just no way that he won't return to you when he decides to come out of this. I know this is frustrating for you, but you have to have patience and persevere. For better or worse, remember."

And Dalilah, for her part, refused to stop being angry with me. It was as if she blamed me for her daddy refusing to see her.

Every day, she would create a new little picture for him. Every day she would rip it up when she couldn't see her daddy in person. And she was increasingly throwing tantrums in her room. She would scream and cry for hours. I had to keep breakable objects away from her, because she would throw them on the hardwood floor and smash them. She wasn't quite able to walk, but she would stand in her crib and cry. I would pick her up, and she would just cry some more, grabbing my hair in her little hands and pulling on it until I got a massive headache.

Nick was the only one who could calm her down. When I had enough and was ready to break down in hysterics myself, Nick would appear in our bedroom and sit down on the rocking chair with Dalilah on his lap and read her a story. She would sit with her head on his chest, her thumb in her mouth, and quietly listen to various tales about magic and far away lands.

"Ok, Dalilah," Nick said. "Let's continue our story about Charlie and the Chocolate Factory. Where were we? Oh, yes, I think we were just getting to know Augustus Gloop, the fat kid."

Dalilah giggled. "The fat kid," she said, obviously understanding it. "What next?"

I loved seeing them together, but I was getting depressed. Dalilah didn't want anything to do with me, and Ryan should be here reading her stories, not Nick.

While he was reading to Dalilah, I would exit the room and break down in tears.

This scenario happened far more than I wanted it to. I couldn't believe that my nine-month-old daughter hated me already.

Nick would come out of the room after he put Dalilah into bed and say "you have to get it together with your daughter in there. I love that little girl, but I have a life, too."

"I don't know what to do. I'm at my wit's end here. She hates me, Ryan hates me. Who likes me anymore?"

"Me. I like you." And he would look at me in the same way that made me uncomfortable all those weeks ago when Ryan was first out of surgery.

I studiously ignored the way that Nick looked at me sometimes. I had to. There was a part of me that actually was very drawn to him, especially now that I was seeing his more sensitive side. And the way he was with Dalilah was starting to make me melt.

But he wasn't Ryan. Ryan was the absolute love of my life, even if it seemed during this period that Ryan not only didn't love me, but he actively hated me.

But there was no way I would break down in a moment of weakness and give into my budding attraction to Nick. Even though my female intuition told me that Nick was having feelings for me that went beyond friendship.

I even noticed there were no more bimbo eruptions after the Tessa incident. "Hey, I've got an extremely intelligent and inquisitive little girl living under my roof. I have to have respect for that. I realized after I had Tessa here that I was being selfish and stupid. Dalilah shouldn't be exposed to this."

I accepted this explanation, although I suspected it was something else. I suspected that his feelings for me were stronger than I cared to admit.

And I was scared to death of this.

Nick even admitted to me that he had never been in love. "I thought I loved Rielle. Who knows? Maybe I did at one time. I guess it's hard to think about that in retrospect. After all she has hurt me, and I've hurt her, it's hard to believe that there was ever love there. But I've definitely never experienced the kind of all consuming passion that you and Ryan have."

"Had."

"What?"

"You said have. As if Ryan and I still have this all-consuming passion."

Then the old Nick was back. "Don't be a dumb-ass. Something like that doesn't just evaporate into thin air. God, sometimes you are so fucking stupid. Trust, that passion is still there for both of you. It's just dormant right now."

I hoped against hope he was right. But I had my serious doubts. With every day that went by and Ryan refused to even acknowledge my presence when I went to visit him, I had doubts. With every failed attempt to engage him in some kind of conversation, I had doubts.

What if Ryan never comes back to me? What if he falls in love with somebody else, like willowy Tammy, whose attraction to my husband was extremely obvious for all to see? It seemed she was kinda getting somewhere in talking to Ryan, in that he said a few words to her every time she attended to him. She would dutifully report back to me every word that he said, and I hung on to her reports like a life raft.

Ryan was there, somewhere. He was being reached. Not by me, which gave me great pain, but by somebody. That gave me hope that maybe someday I could reach him as well.

Then, one day, I went to his bedroom, I found that Ryan was gone.

# Chapter Sixteen

## RYAN

I snuck out of the house this morning around 5 AM, because there was no way that Iris would've let me leave without rightfully pitching a fit. After all, I was in the ICU not three weeks ago, and I still don't feel physically one-hundred percent. I hadn't been eating much these days, at all, so I was feeling pretty weak and nauseated. In other words, there was just no way that I should've been leaving my bed to do what it was that I was about to do.

Yet there also wasn't any way that I could've continued to lie in my bed and obsess about the event that had brought me the most shame and darkness in my life. I tried so hard to bury it, and, for years, I was able to do just that. It was easy to sweep my emotions about this event under the rug, because there was always something to occupy my headspace. However, it had become impossible for me not to dwell on this event these days.

After all, I almost died, again.

So it had become impossible for me to stop thinking

about the life that should still be in existence, and probably still would be, if not for me.

And now all I could think about was how I could address the problem and meet it head-on. Maybe if I could come to terms with what I did, and attempt to make amends, I could find peace. With some peace, I could go back to my beautiful wife and baby girl and give them both the love they deserve.

But, with all the self-loathing that I was feeling right at that moment, there was just no way that I could love them the way that they deserved.

So, I was taking a trip to try to apologize for what I did all those years ago, and, hopefully, bring some answers and peace to the family of the girl who died because of me.....

It was in the year 2000, shortly before I was locked in the trunk and had my epiphany about my life. So, at that point, I was still pretty bitter about my life, and was still constantly stoned. Rachael Smyth was a girl in one of my classes. It was obvious that she was into me, and, to tell the truth, I was kinda into her as well. She was very pretty, with dark hair and blue eyes and cheekbones that went for miles. When she smiled, her entire face lit up, and she never wore makeup. Nor did she need to.

She wasn't one of my usual types, though. I usually went for the typical bimbo types – all big hair and fake tits, the kind of girls who competed in beauty pageants and were extremely narcissistic. They'd whine if their father didn't buy them a new Lexus every year, and they expected no less pampering from the men they sought. They were the kind who would butter up a guy to get some drinks from him at the bar, then high-tail it the moment they were cut off by said guy, then move on to the next target.

I intentionally limited myself, sexually, to those kinds of girls. I figured that they deserved a slam and go, and I secretly delighted when they would stalk me, only to be ignored. I wanted them to feel the pain that they inflicted on their marks - all those men who tried, and failed, to please their voracious appetite for material goods. I felt I was taking one for the team.

But Rachael was definitely different. She was more the studious type and a natural beauty. She was pre-med, with dreams of becoming a heart surgeon. She was definitely the type of girl I would have brought home to my mother, if my mother wasn't locked up in a mental health facility at the time. She was good, intelligent and kind, and had more integrity than anyone I had ever known. She was also guile-less. There was just nothing artificial about her.

And she never did drugs, even once in her life.

So, I didn't pursue her, romantically. There would be no point. I wasn't good enough for anybody at that time, except for Alexis. And I only felt I was good enough for Alexis because Alexis and I shared both needles and deep self-loathing. Alexis and I were mirror images of one another, so Alexis was the only woman who I would hang out with on a regular basis.

And I really wasn't good enough for somebody like Rachael.

Yet, it was clear that Rachael was into me. She wrote a paper for me in a class when I was falling behind schedule in writing it. The reason why I was behind schedule was simple − I was busy getting high and crashing on Seth's couch, and just forgot to write the paper. She wrote it for me, without asking a single thing in return.

I felt I had to thank her for doing this for me, so I invited her to a party.

Unfortunately, this party was one of those wild affairs

where women rode men like horses in the living room. Not naked, though – they were fully clothed, but there was silliness like that all through the house. Men were being thrown through windows, and a blow-up doll made the rounds.

When Rachael and I arrived at this party on this unseasonably cool April evening, we were greeted with a whiskey bottle being offered by Shane, a buddy of mine. Shane had evidently been drinking extremely heavily, for he smelled like a brewery and hung on me like a cheap suit.

"Ryan, my boy," Shane said. Then he whispered in my ear "Rachael Smyth, huh? Classing up the bimbos, I see."

"It's not like that. We're just friends."

"Uh huh. Like you could ever be just friends with a chick. I'd like to see that."

I whispered back "as you said, Rachael isn't a bimbo. Therefore, there will be no action between us. I brought her here to thank her for saving my ass in Hadley's class. Girl wrote a 15- page paper on the possibility of common currency in the GCC countries in just under a day. Have to hand it to her – she's as brilliant as she is beautiful. But me looky and no touchy."

In the meantime, Rachael was standing in the threshold, looking around. She looked a little bit intimidated, and I wondered why.

"I, uh, have never really been to a party like this before," she explained. "I really haven't had much of a social life, I'm afraid."

"Well, then, you came to this party with the right tour guide," I said. "And you have to be initiated with a shot." At that, I handed her a shot from the whiskey bottle that was proffered by Shane when we walked through the door.

She reluctantly took it, making a face when the liquor

went down her throat. "Yuck!" she said. "How can anybody like the taste of that?"

"Nobody likes the taste," I said. "Well, most people don't dig the taste, anyhow. But the feeling you get is what's important. So take another one, and loosen up a bit. Let's have some fun."

Just then, Matt, another buddy of mine, pulled me aside. "Got some China White," he whispered. "You interested?"

I blinked. I really wasn't planning on doing the smack that evening, because I wanted to be somewhat coherent for Rachael. It wasn't fair to go to la-la land and just leave her stranded with a bunch of drunk and stoned fools that she didn't know.

But China White? How could I pass up heroin that pure?

"Where'd you get it?"

"My supplier got his hands on some. You won't find a higher grade. Period."

It had been so long since I was able to find China White, so I ended up in the bathroom with Matt and a few other guys, and I came out of the bathroom in a euphoric state such that I hadn't ever experienced.

I was so high that I hardly noticed that Rachael was in the middle of the room with some other kids doing what was called the Power Hour – taking a shot of beer every minute for an hour. I had no idea how she got involved with that group, but, I figured, if she was hanging with them, then I didn't have to entertain her after all.

So, I sat down on one of the couches and closed my eyes.

Rachael came up to me, evidently soused after doing

her power hour. "I need to go home, Ryan, please. I don't feel so good."

I just looked at her. There was no way we were going anywhere.

"We can't leave," I said, pouring another shot of whiskey for her to drink. "Take this, and you won't want to leave. Trust me on this."

"No. More alcohol is the last thing I need."

"Ok, then, be that way. But we aren't leaving, so I suggest you take this shot and relax with me."

She took the shot, not making a face this time. "There," she slurred. "You happy?"

"Yes, very. Now, take another one and then another and another until you feel okay to stay. Alright?"

So, Rachael took another shot, then several more in rapid succession. "Showed you, huh? You didn't think I could do it, huh?" she slurred.

"I knew you could. Now take some more."

Rachael took several more, then sat down on another couch next to me. I couldn't really see her all that well, but she seemed to be swaying and laying her head off the edge of the couch. "I need to go upstairs," she said. "Come with me, please?"

I shrugged. I was at the point where nothing bothered me, and I really didn't care what I did, as long as I didn't leave that house. "Sure," I said. "I'll go upstairs with you."

So, we headed up to one of the bedrooms that had about a hundred coats laying on top of the bed. Rachael lay down on top of the coats, and I lay down next to her. Within seconds, she was passed out.

I sat down on the floor, with my head and body against the bed, and just drifted off to my happy place. I could hear loud music downstairs, and louder talking and laughter.

Couples opened the door several times, thinking this would be a good place to screw, then quickly left again when they saw that the room was occupied.

"You can come in here," I said to one couple. "I don't mind watching."

At that, the girl just giggled and said "you join in, and we gotta deal."

I shrugged. "Nah, not in the mood. But, seriously, go ahead and fuck here, with the lights on. I totally groove on that."

The girl looked gung-ho about the prospect, but the guy, not so much. "Come on, Alecia, let's go find someplace else."

"But that guy is so cute!" she said. "Let's try to get him to join us."

"Three's a crowd," he said. "Let's find someplace else."

And so it went. I found it all so humorous.

The party went on until about four in the morning, at which point I was finally ready to leave. I was coming down a bit off my earlier high, so I felt ok to drive.

I stood up from my position on the floor and nudged Rachael to wake her.

"Rachael," I said. "Let's go."

But she didn't move.

I shook her, harder this time. "Come on, let's get out of here before they throw us out, Rachael."

Still, she didn't move.

It was then that I noticed that she wasn't breathing.

I felt a bit of panic, but I was still high, so the panic wasn't as acute as it should've been.

I felt for her pulse, and found none at all.

So, I went downstairs to find Brett, the party host. I found him, passed out on the couch, his hand on a whiskey bottle that was on the floor. I nudged him, and he woke with a start.

"Uh, Brett, you have to call 911. My date, uh, I think she's dead."

"What?"

"Go upstairs and see." I realized that I was being entirely too calm for the situation, but that's what high grade heroin does – it numbs the negative feelings.

Brett went upstairs, then came right back down and grabbed his cell phone and dialed 911.

The ambulance came within a few minutes, and brought Rachael downstairs on a stretcher, a sheet covering her head.

A cop questioned me, Brett, and the other stragglers who were at the party. All of us went to the station to answer intense questioning. But the whole thing was ruled as an accidental death from acute alcohol intoxication, and none of us got into any kind of trouble.

I never told anybody about what had happened. I was surprised Nick and Alexis never found out about it. I mean, the entire school knew about her death. Everybody was talking about it for a few days after it happened. But somehow Nick and Alexis never associated her dying with me, so I was relieved about that.

And, from that moment on, I tried not to think about what happened to her, and I never considered it to be my fault. I didn't force her to do a power hour, after all. She was a big girl, and she was responsible for herself, I reasoned.

I wasn't responsible for her dying.

But now I knew that wasn't true. A beautiful, intelligent and full of life girl was in the ground because of me. There was no escaping that fact. It had taken a near-death experience for me to finally experience that epiphany, and, ever since I had come to terms with this fact, I had been obsessed about my role in her death.

So, I was heading to Brooklyn, where Rachael's parents still lived. There really wasn't much that I could say to try to make things right at this point, so I didn't really know why I was going there. It was just something that I felt that I needed to do at that point. I needed to own up to what I did and try to apologize to them from the bottom of my heart, and then go from there. There wasn't anything that I could do to make things better for them, let alone bring their daughter back, so there was a part of me that felt this visit was futile.

Yet there was another part of me that felt that it was necessary and way, way, way overdue.

Still, I couldn't just leave Iris without letting her know where I was going. I remembered well when she went missing, and how much of an awful panic I was in because of that. I couldn't do that to her, so I left her a letter on her nightstand before I left.

The letter said:

My Dearest Beautiful Iris,

I needed to write this to you, because I don't want you to panic when you see I've left. I've not left for good, I promise you this. I could never, ever leave you for good. You've been the brightest spot of my entire existence, and what I feel for you is indescribable. Simply put, you brought me out of darkness and into the light, and there is no way that I would ever give that up.

But the darkness has returned, and it has nothing to do with you. It really doesn't have anything to do with the shooting, either, except for how the shooting has made me examine my life and what I've done. The people I've hurt.

And there is one episode in my life that shames me more than anything else that I have ever done.

There was a girl, around 13 years ago, who was put into the ground because of me. Because of my carelessness and drug habit, Rachael Smyth no longer exists. What kind of a life would she have led if I didn't take her to a party that fateful evening? With her brilliance, she could've been a surgeon, healing others. That was her dream. She probably also would be raising a brood of equally brilliant children, who might have grown up to change the world. But she never got to do any of it because of me.

For years, I swept my feelings about this event under the rug. I wasn't responsible for her death, I reasoned. She made her choices that evening, and she would've died with or without me.

No, that's not true. That's never been true. It's just a lie that I've been perpetually telling myself to avoid the truth, which is that I am directly responsible for her death. It's a long story, one that I don't want to explain in a letter, but I'll explain all to you when I get back.

And here's one thing that you really need to know – I'm still passionately and completely in love with you. My feelings for you have not dimmed, even one iota, despite the way that I've been treating you these past few weeks. I'm sorry for shutting you out, but I've been so filled with black self-loathing that I just can't bring myself to be with you and give you the love that you deserve from me. That's why I left – I need to seek forgiveness, redemption and peace. I need to find out if there is anything I can do for Rachael's family that might bring just a measure of happiness to them. There's no way I can bring Rachael back, of course. But I, at the very least, need to own up to what I did. I don't expect them to forgive me, but that is still my grandest hope.

At any rate, I hope to come back from Brooklyn and be the husband that you deserve. I love you, beautiful. You are my world, and you always will be.

I will see you soon.


Love always and forever,


Ryan


I prayed that Iris would see the letter and, hopefully, understand that I have to do this. I also prayed that she didn't worry about me too much. I had to admit I wasn't feeling entirely well, so I was slightly worried about my physical well-being. But I was hoping that by the time my plane touched down at La Guardia, I would be feeling strong enough to face the people who were devastated because of my actions.

At least that was my hope.

# Chapter Seventeen

## IRIS

"Nick! Nick! Nick!" I cried, upon seeing Ryan's bed empty. "Come here!"

"What is it?"

"Ryan. He-he-he-he's gone!"

"Calm down. He's probably around here somewhere. Maybe on the grounds. I'll go and ask everybody if they've seen him. He can only stay cooped up for so long, you know. It's good for him to get out and get some fresh air."

I just shook my head. "No, Nick. I think he's gone."

After about an hour of looking for him on the grounds, around the home and in the guest house, Nick concluded that Ryan had, in fact, left.

"Looks like you're right. He's gone."

Nick looked worried.

I knew what he was thinking. He was thinking of all the times that Ryan disappeared during the college years. He was always up to no good when that happened before.

"Well, I'm quite sure there is a logical explanation for this," Nick said.

ANNIE JOCOBY

"Yes," I said. "He doesn't love me anymore, and doesn't know how to tell me."

Nick just shook his head. "Listen, Iris. I'm sick and tired of having to reassure you about how Ryan feels about you. So, I'm just going to keep my mouth shut from now on. You can sit and stew and think what you want. I know the truth."

"Well, then, I'm just going to call him and see what he says."

"You do that."

"I will," I said, getting out my iPhone from my pocket. With shaking hands, I dialed.

"Hello?" Ryan said on the other end of the line. "Iris?"

I just started crying hysterically and couldn't speak. "Ryan, where are you? Where did you go?"

He was deathly silent for a matter of minutes. "I don't understand," he finally said. "Didn't you read my letter?"

"What letter?"

"I left a letter for you on your nightstand. I guess you didn't see it, huh?"

*Breathe, Iris, breathe.* That letter wasn't a goodbye letter. It was something else. It just had to be something else.

"What did the letter say?"

"It's a long story. Too long of a story for right now, because I have an appointment to keep."

"An appointment?"

"Yes. Uh, I'll explain later. Bye."

And he hung up.

Nick came out and saw me standing there, the phone at my side. My right hand was gripping the phone, and it was shaking like I had a tremor.

"Iris? Are you ok?"

I shook my head. "No, Nick. I'm not ok. That was

126

Ryan. He said he wrote me a letter telling me about where he was going, and that it was too difficult to explain. He also said that he had some kind of an appointment to keep." What I didn't tell Nick was that Ryan's voice and demeanor on the phone was business-like and cold. There wasn't any warmth or levity in his voice when he was talking to me.

It had been that way ever since the shooting, really. He was such a different person now. There wasn't the look of desire and love in his eyes anymore. Instead, there was either a blank stare or a look of outright hostility. There was no longer the playful tone of voice. His tone with me was cold, clipped and formal. Like I was his headmistress or something. That was when he would deign to even talk to me at all. Most of the times he treated me with an icy silence.

Everything I loved about him was missing these days.

Worst of all, I didn't know if it would ever come back. Any of it. I was trying so hard to be patient and under-standing. Trying to give him just what he needed, if I could ever figure out exactly what that was. Yet all I was getting was the literal cold shoulder and the feeling that I was living with a stranger.

Nick and I were still standing out in the garden, which is where I chose to make my call. I walked back into the house, and Nick followed me close behind.

Dalilah was waiting for us to come back in. She was standing up in her playpen.

She soon would be walking. Would Ryan be here to see it?

"Mama," she said, putting her arms out to me. I was a little bit startled, because she hadn't been coming to me lately. I always had to go to her, and she was still pouty with me. But she seemed to want my affection now, so I bent down and picked her up.

"Where's daddy?"

"Daddy isn't here, baby. He has something that he has to do."

Dalilah looked sad, and put her thumb in her mouth.

"Would you like to go in your walker?"

She said nothing, but nodded her head.

"Ok, then," I said, putting her in her little walker. She started walking all around the room, and started giggling when the dogs came up to her and tried to play. She was seeming to get back to normal.

Getting back to normal when everything was falling apart.

Well, Dalilah seemed not to hate me anymore. So that was one good thing in my life right now.

Nick came back inside about an hour later. I was sitting on the couch, a glass of wine in my hand. Dalilah was in her playpen working her Etch-A-Sketch. I was staring off into space, and I didn't hear him come in at first.

"Iris," he said, and I jumped, startled.

"Oh, sorry, Nick. I was zoned out."

"It's ok," he said. "How are you doing?"

I just shrugged. I was trying very hard not to spiral into depression, but it was getting increasingly difficult.

"You know, Nick," I said. "I never thought my life would be like this."

"Like what?"

"Chaotic. It's like I don't have any traction anywhere in my life, so it's really difficult getting some kind of forward momentum. And I don't even know where to begin to bring myself out of the ditch. I need a strong tow truck and chain, and I don't know what that would be."

Then I looked at little Dalilah. She was getting more beautiful by the day, and, as she grew, she resembled Sarah with Ryan's green eyes. And her intelligence was scaring me a little. At any rate, I should've been happy. Dalilah was everything that a mother could ask for in a little girl, aside from her occasional temper tantrums.

Yet even Dalilah brought me no joy.

"You want to talk about it?"

I just shook my head. "I'm losing hope, Nick. I'm losing hope that things are going to get better." I took another sip of my wine. "And there's not a light at the end of the tunnel. I mean, it's like I'm resigned again to be a single mother. Because I don't know what's going on with Ryan. He's changed, Nick. I don't know the person who has treated me like dog shit for the past few weeks, then left the house without so much as a goodbye. I never thought Ryan could be like this."

"Iris," Nick began. "This is a part of who he is. The darkness is in him. It always has been. You've been lucky that it hasn't come out before. You've....well, let's just say that his meeting you is what brought him into the light. He changed after he met you. But the man you're seeing now is who Ryan is, as much as the man that you married is. It's a facet of his, and it's something that you might always have to deal with. I'm not saying that Ryan is going to live in this darkness for the rest of his life. I'm just saying that the darkness is in his DNA. So, you need to come to terms with this."

"I know, Nick. I'm trying to come to terms with it." The tears started to come again. "It's just that I've lived with this sort of thing all my life. My sister was always like this. She'd hole up in her room and never come out for months, except to go to work. She attempted suicide several times, and was hospitalized for depression more times than I could count. She became addicted to crystal meth and used that for several years. She never left home."

Nick put his arm around me lightly. "Must've been tough, living with that all your life."

"Yeah, you might say that." I took another sip of my wine. "When I met Ryan, I never would've thought that his life was anything but grand. You know, he's drop dead gorgeous, intelligent, educated at the best schools, has megabucks. I was on the outside looking in all my life, like the little match girl. And Ryan was like a guy that I was looking in on all my life, thinking that he had it made, while my life was in the crapper. I never imagined that a guy like that would fall in love with me, and I really never imagined that a guy like that would have anything less than a perfect life. And I never could've imagined that loving a guy like him would be so difficult."

Nick's arm was still around my shoulder. I looked at him. His face was so close to mine. I felt my heart quicken, and my hand started shaking violently. I ended up spilling wine down his shirt.

"Oh, shit, I'm so sorry. Let me clean that up for you."

"No need," he said, as he took off his shirt. His muscles rippled, and I lost my breath looking at his naked torso. I could feel myself hyperventilating.

Nick got up to put his shirt into the washing machine, then left and came back in a few minutes in a new shirt. "Not a big deal, Iris. Spills happen."

I could say nothing, just nod my head.

Dalilah was in her playpen watching both of us intently. I could almost see her wheels spinning.

She didn't look happy.

"Mama," she said. "When's daddy coming home?" Her

sentences were becoming more and more perfect. Pretty soon she'll be reading *War and Peace* I thought, ruefully, translating it from the original Russian.

"Soon, baby," I said, hoping I wasn't lying to her.

She said nothing, just looked at Nick and me on the couch.

Nick's scent was intoxicating, and the sight of him with his shirt off was burned in my brain. I could feel my breath quicken.

He was so close to me.

Then I started to feel I couldn't breathe.

"Uh, I need to go outside for a little bit. Get some fresh air." I then picked up Dalilah. "You want to take a walk with me outside, baby? Go through the garden and smell all the pretty flowers?"

She nodded her head.

"Good." Then I went to get her stroller out of the closet.

"We'll be back," I called to Nick. "We're just going to go and take a little walk."

"Sure, I'll see you in a bit. Sheila's going to start making dinner in a few, too. Any special requests?"

"Surprise me."

I hadn't explored Nick's grounds yet. His house sat on at least an acre of land, which was difficult to find in the middle of the city. As I walked along, I saw prize roses lining the walkway. There were about a hundred different varieties. I knew Nick had a gardener who came in and maintained these beauties, and that gardener obviously knew his stuff. The roses were perfect. There were different shades of reds, yellows and oranges. There were also purples and even black roses.

In the middle of the garden was a stone bench. It had a

plaque on it, which I read. It said "Abrianna O'Hara. 2002-2009. Forever in our hearts." A little angel was in the middle of the plaque.

I wondered about that one. Did Nick also lose a child? Perhaps she was his niece.

I realized how little I knew about the guy living in that stately home, but I was starting to get to know him more. He no longer was strictly the insensitive, blunt jerk I thought he was. It was bluster, I guessed, because he had such a soft spot for my daughter and even myself these days.

I couldn't be more confused about my life than I was right at that moment. Somehow, Nick and Ryan managed to trade places. Now, Nick was the sensitive one (although he still had his moments of jerkitude), and Ryan was the ass.

Sitting there in the garden, I couldn't get the sight of Nick with his shirt off out of my brain. Nor could I stop thinking about his intoxicating scent. It was some kind of woodsy cologne. Then it occurred to me that he had no need to wear cologne, because he wasn't going anywhere. He was working from home, as he had been since Dalilah and I moved into his house.

Was he wearing that cologne because he wanted to impress me?

I turned Dalilah around to face me, then brought her onto my lap. I plucked a daisy that was growing by the bench, and gave it to her. She looked at it with wonder, then looked at me. "Thank you, mommy!" she said, beaming.

"You're welcome, baby."

I tried to stop my mind from wandering to different scenarios, each more horrible than the last. That Ryan had left me. That Ryan would somehow burn up in a plane crash. That Ryan was suddenly taken over by a Body Snatcher.

That scenario seemed as logical as any other at this point.

Then I had to stop my mind from wandering over to Nick, who my subconscious was regarding as Plan B.

Ryan dumps me, and I'll marry Nick.

Stop it, Iris. Stop, stop, stop, stop, stop. Stop!

Actually, the peacefulness of the garden reminded me of my wedding day with Ryan. Now that was a memory that I could savor. God, there was so much love between us that day. There had always been such pure, unadulterated love between us. No matter what happened, the love was always there. Nothing ever made it diminish. Not the episode with Nat, nor my stay in the drug house after having been raped, nor my leaving him for San Francisco and hiding his daughter from him for several months. Nothing ever made that burning lamp dim.

I had to hold onto that. Hold onto the hope that it could be like that again. We made it through horrible situations before. Situations that looked absolutely hopeless at first glance. Yet, we always found that we weren't broken, just bent.

And we always managed to find our way back.

We'll find our way back this time, too.

I can't give up hope.

But that night, Nick and I shared a couple of bottles of wine after Dalilah went to bed. I could feel my resolve lowering just being near him, and the wine wasn't helping matters any.

Nick had actually been drinking before we opened up the bottle of wine. I could tell that he was quite intoxicated.

"You know, Iris, having you and Dalilah here these past few weeks has been a godsend to me. I don't think I've told you this."

"Well, you taking us in has been a godsend to us, too. It goes both ways. If you didn't take us in, I literally don't know where we would be. I mean, we all couldn't have stayed at my mother's, which means that Ryan would probably still be at that hospital, which I don't want to think about." I shuddered my shoulders a little at that thought, then took another sip of wine. "And there really is no place for us to go, except for my parents' house. And God knows they don't have the room for us, even for just Dalilah and me. So, really, you are the one who saved us."

"Well, maybe we saved each other." He stoked the fire a little bit with his poker. "You know, about the hospital situation. Do you think that maybe you overreacted just a teensy, teensy bit?"

I laughed a little. "Maybe just a bit," I said, making a gesture with my thumb and index finger that was the universal symbol for "little bit." I looked at my wine glass, and Nick poured me another. "But I don't know, Nick. I was on autopilot when I did that. All I knew was that Ryan had attempted suicide, and I couldn't stand having him someplace other than right where I was. Looking back, I think that was the real reason why I had him pulled out of the hospital. I felt that I needed to protect him, like he had always protected me. I mean, I was angry with the hospital for not telling me things, and really angry with the doctor for overmedicating him, but that wasn't the real reason why I had him taken out of there."

Nick just stared at me for a few seconds, sipping his wine. My heart quickened a little. Then a lot. *Is it getting warm in here, or is it just me?*

Then he looked away and shook his head. I heard him mumbling a little under his breath, although I couldn't make out any words.

"What's wrong?" I asked, concerned.

"Nothing, nothing. It's just that, all my life, I've met exactly one kind of woman. The gold-digger. I don't think that I've ever been with a woman who could give a rat's ass about my well-being. The only thing that they've ever cared about was about was my black MasterCard. Do you know that I once dated a woman for about a month, and she already was pouting because I wouldn't buy her a Beemer. I bought her a new Toyota Camry. Good little car, sporty. She didn't have a car, because she was a grad student, so I figured I was doing a great thing." He shook his head. "When I gave it to her, she didn't say thank you. She just said 'that's great, but what I really wanted was a black BMW.'"

I had to suppress a smile. I didn't think it was funny that Nick had such bad luck with good women. But I did think that he was stupid if he kept falling for the same type every time, then get angry when it doesn't work out. He obviously hadn't heard the definition of insanity – doing the same thing over and over again, and expecting a different result.

"Nick, just out of curiosity. How do you choose these women?"

He looked at his glass, then looked at the wall. "I admit, I only date the hotties."

"Well, here is my theory about hot women. Do you want to hear it?"

"Sure, why not."

"There are nice hot women out there. I've met them. But they're all currently in a relationship. So, you're looking at hot women who are either not in a relationship or are willing to cheat on their current relationship. That narrows down your prospects right there."

"So, you're saying that all the good hot women are

already taken, so the ones that I meet are the bottom of the barrel."

"Something like that. They're the ones who are single for a reason, you know?"

He fingered his glass lightly, then looked up at me with those blue, blue eyes. "So, what do you suggest I do?"

I shrugged. "Broaden your horizons. Find some woman who's not a ten, and give her a chance. You got nothing to lose. Who knows? There might be chemistry there, and you'll be a very happy guy. The point is, if you are only looking at women who look like Alexis and Tessa, then you're limiting yourself."

Then he looked away. "Well, I've had my eye on a non-hot woman for awhile now, but I don't think she's interested. I mean, she's cute, but not a supermodel."

"There you go," I said, lightly punching his arm. "Go for it! She'll probably make you very happy."

"One problem. She's married to my best friend."

I wanted to say that I didn't quite understand what he was talking about. Perhaps he has another best friend? I felt extremely uncomfortable, suddenly, so I decided to change the subject. "I, uh, I always wanted to ask you something. I hope it isn't too personal."

"What's that?"

"How, when did you know that you were bisexual?"

"Geez, Iris, I don't know. When did you know that you were heterosexual?"

"I know, I know. Dumb question. Um…"

"No, no, it's ok. Actually, when I was 13. I was in the Boy Scouts, and an older boy of 17 sucked me off. And I liked it. It was very confusing for me, to be honest with you. I mean, I've always loved girls. Always. And I always had a ton of girlfriends. Yet, I found out that I also liked guys. For the longest time, I didn't quite know where I fit in. I wasn't quite gay, and I wasn't quite straight. Although I've always been more straight than gay. So, my adolescence and young adulthood was even more confusing than most people's were, I think."

"How did you learn to accept that part of yourself?"

"I don't know, exactly. I just woke up one day and decided that I had to live my life without giving a good goddamned about what people thought about me and my lifestyle. So, I decided to do just that. I thought for sure I would lose friends, but that didn't happen. And the funny thing is, I found that I wasn't alone. Not by a long shot. You'd be surprised to know how many men are just like me, even if they would never, ever admit to it."

"Oh, I would be less surprised than you might think," I said. "I did the research after finding out about you and Ryan, and it turns out that there are a good percentage of men who are into men and women. I've always known that there were lots of women like that – I met quite a few women like that in college, for instance. I never thought the same about men, though. Now, I know differently."

"What about you?" he asked. "Do you like girls?"

"Well, no. I mean, I've never experimented or anything like that. I've thought about it, though."

"And what keeps you from pursuing it?"

I shrugged. "The temptation was just never that strong with me."

He looked at the fire, then took a sip of his wine. Then he sighed.

"What's wrong?" I asked.

"Nothing," he said. "It's just…"

"Just what?"
And then he said something that stunned me.
"I think I'm falling in love with you."

# Chapter Eighteen

## RYAN

As I sat on my private plane, sipping a glass of Scotch, I tried my very hardest not to think about what was ahead. There was a nagging voice in my head that told me that this was all a huge mistake that was going to have bad consequences. Consequences that I could never comprehend. Why I thought this, I knew not. I thought that perhaps it had something to do with the fact that I just left Iris without a word. I mean, I did write her a letter explaining things, albeit in a very cryptic way. But would she understand? Could she? Why was I treating the most important person in my life in such a way?

I knew why I was treating her this way, deep down, however. It was the old cliché – you can't love somebody until you love yourself. And right then, because of all the negative thinking I had been doing as I have reviewed my life, I loathed myself. Despised myself. The way that I acted during my college years was beyond reprehensible. Why did Natalie and everybody always think that I was a great guy? I treated her like shit, along with many other people, yet she always had me up on a pedestal, as she does still today. Not to mention Nick, the faceless bimbos, and, especially, Rachael.

There was very little that I could do about a lot of my actions in the past. I mean, I could apologize to Nick profusely, as I never had really apologized to him before. That's one thing, and I will do that when I get back into town. I could go and see Natalie while I'm in the New York City area and do the same. The other people I hurt – the endless stream of women – I couldn't apologize to them even if I wanted to, because there was just no way that I could remember who all they were.

But Rachael's parents – that was another story. I could explain to them what happened, and hopefully help them find peace in her death. I could never be redeemed for what I did to Rachael, and for how much her parents were, no doubt, devastated by her death, but what I could do would be to try to help them come to terms with what happened to her. And maybe that would give them some modicum of closure.

But the nagging voice inside of me just wouldn't be quiet. The voice told me that I was only doing this for myself, not for them. That I was only doing this to make myself feel better, and, really, all that I would be doing for Rachael's parents, thirteen years after the fact, would be reopening old wounds that might have already healed. That was really the more likely scenario, but, then again, I would never know unless I tried.

So, the upshot of this was that I was finding myself on my plane heading to La Guardia early on a Thursday morning. I left when Iris and everybody was fast asleep. I knew that Iris would never let me go on this trip, because I had been out of the ICU for only a few weeks. There were

any number of things that could go wrong while I'm travel-
ing, and I researched all the risks. The biggest risk was that I
simply wasn't ready to be doing this. I wasn't taking care of
myself, I knew, because I wasn't eating right and getting
very little exercise. I spent all my days staring at the television set blankly, instead of trying to help myself get better.
So, I probably wasn't ready for this trip. And Iris would've
done everything in her power to prevent me from taking the
trip. Hell, she probably would've gotten the handcuffs out,
like Nick did all those years ago. She could be so strong-
willed when she really wants to be, and I knew that she
absolutely would've prevented me from leaving.

Yet, I was compelled to leave. I had to do it. I was spinning so much into my depression and negativity that I
became virtually obsessed with the issue of what could have
been. It became all that I thought about, once I allowed
myself to actually think about it. And what triggered it? It
was the journaling that I was doing, and it was the appear-
ance on television of somebody who resembled Rachael a
great deal. It was also, as trivial as this might sound, an
episode of one of the shows that came on – not sure which,
they all blended together after a little while – that dealt with
the issue of a college student who died from acute alcohol
poisoning. I was immediately tripped into what had
happened, and, once I journaled it out, the inescapable
conclusion was that I caused Rachael's death.

Me. Nobody else. Just me.

So, at the point when I came to terms with my absolute
role in her death – when I had my epiphany, if you will – I
knew that I had to leave. If I didn't leave, then I would
continue on my dark path, and I knew what would happen
next. I would have snuck my dealer into Nick's house and
got back into using. The one thing, outside of painting, that

ANNIE JOCOBY

always helped quell the negative thoughts in my head. Well, that wasn't entirely true – being around Iris and my daughter helped, as well, but I wasn't ready to accept their love again just yet.

If I put it to Iris that it was either visiting Rachael's parents or getting back into dope, perhaps she would've understood. But that still didn't mean that she would've allowed me to leave. She always had my best interests at heart, I knew, and I knew that, from the outsider's perspective, my leaving was absolutely not in my best interest.

I took a deep breath as the plane started to descend. Below me, I saw squares of land and then tiny people, cars and buildings. I got on my cell to call for a limo to meet me, so, when the plane finally landed, there was the car waiting for me with a driver in a limo cap.

"Mr. Gallagher?" the limo driver asked when I got off the plane.

"Yes," I said. "I need you to take me to Brooklyn."

"Yes, sir," he said.

Throughout the ride, the limo driver, John, tried to make small talk. I tried, as politely as I could, to discourage his talk. I wasn't in the mood for talking. I was too busy rehearsing what it was that I had to say to Rachael's parents.

"So, this your first time to New York?" he asked.

"No. Been here before."

"You here for business or pleasure?"

"Neither."

"Nice weather we're having here right now."

"Yeah."

"You going to catch a Yankee's game while you're here?"

"Wasn't planning on it."

"What do you think about that A. Rod business?"

"Not surprised."

And on it went. I wanted to tell the guy that I wasn't interested in talking to him, at all, because he just wasn't getting the hint.

Finally, I got out my headphones. "If you'll excuse me, I need to listen to a podcast for the job I'm going for out here."

"Oh, sure. Sure." And John, mercifully, said nothing more.

I put the headphones in and listened to dead air. I couldn't listen to music or anything else. I had to concentrate on what I would say to the Smyths.

Finally, the limo arrived at the brownstone. "Please wait here," I said. "I'll be right back." Then I went to the door and rang the doorbell. However, because I was appearing on their doorstep unannounced, there was no guarantee that I would be admitted entrance into their home. Maybe nobody was home, and maybe the person who answered the door would slam it in my face. So, the limo driver had to cool his heels until I gave him the signal to go on.

To my delight, a woman answered the door. She was about 55, and had the same cheekbones and blue eyes as Rachael. I had to assume that this was Rachael's mother.

"Uh, Mrs. Smyth?"

She narrowed her eyes. "Who's asking?"

"My name is Ryan. Ryan Gallagher. I, uh, went to school, Harvard, with your daughter, Rachael."

The suspicious look on her face melted, and was replaced by a look of inescapable sadness. She looked down at the ground in front of her, and, when she lifted her head, there were tears in the corner of her eyes. "Rachael. I haven't heard her name mentioned in many a year." Then she looked at me and gestured with her hands to come in. "Come in, come in."

I felt relief flood through me, then I waved John on. I had explained to him, before I got out of the car, that I would call him when I needed him to come back.

I walked into the tiny brownstone that was decorated modernly. Modern art on the walls that was truly magnificent – cubist in detail, contrasting colors and gorgeous lighting. The huge windows streamed sunlight that illuminated the entire room. There was an enormous Ficus tree that was growing in a pot, and various tropical plants that were in other pots that were evidently hand-crafted. There was a bird in a cage that was singing. Iris would've digged this place – she loved birds and she loved modernism.

Thinking of Iris, I smiled. God, I really did love that woman, and there was something about being here that made me realize it anew.

"Uh, have a seat. Have a seat," the woman said, gesturing towards the blue couch with multiple colored pillows.

I sat down.

"Could I get you some tea or wine or anything?"

Wine. It was around noon. I wondered if drinking wine in the middle of the day was something that this woman often did. "Yes, please. Whatever you're drinking."

At that, she went into the kitchen and I heard her pour two glasses of wine. "Here," she said. "I hope you like red."

"I surely do."

She sipped her wine and looked at me quizzically. I knew that I had to come clean, but, where to start?

"Um, I. Is your husband around?" I asked, then immediately felt that was the wrong question to start with . She might think that a) I'm hitting on her or b) I'm an intruder who was trying to determine if she was alone, so that I could rob her.

But, she appeared to think neither of these things. "No. I mean, my husband doesn't live here with me anymore. After Rachael...well, couples can do one of two things when they lose a child. They can either grow stronger or fall apart. We fell apart."

I nodded my head. "Yes, I understand that. I, uh, lost a child as well."

Her face softened as she covered one of my hands with hers. "Oh, I'm very sorry to hear that. May I ask what happened?"

"SIDS," I said.

She nodded. "That must be so difficult. It's bad enough to lose a child when she's just 20, and on the verge of the rest of her life. But to lose an infant, who never got to experience life at all...that's just not fair."

I nodded, feeling the familiar feeling of devastation, grief and loss. Being with this woman was cathartic, I was finding, as I suddenly realized that I had never really processed my emotions about Mia's death. It was something that was so devastating that I covered it up. I was a man, and men weren't supposed to fall apart when they lose their child. They're supposed to be strong and carry on and help the mother through. After all, it was the mother who was supposed to feel the emotions and depression from losing a child, not the father.

Yet I did feel the devastation. I just buried it, like I had so many other things in my life.

"Yes, yes, it was probably the worst thing to happen in my life," I said, honestly.

She nodded. "Let me show you something," she said. "Follow me."

I followed her up the stairs of her brownstone, and she opened up the door to a room. There, in that room, was a young girl's bed. The curtains were pink and filmy, and there was a desk against the wall that had various pencils and pens lying across it. On the wall, there were various medals – cross country medals, and other awards that Rachael had won in writing competitions. There were pictures everywhere – pictures of Rachael's cross country team, and pictures of Rachael and others in various places. Some were her and her friends on a ski trip, others of her at various parties. There was even a picture of her when she was around 12 years old – an old school picture that was blown up and put in a frame. Her blue eyes stared out, and her smile was full of metal braces.

I felt a lump in my throat. It was what I did with Mia's room. I never did touch a single thing in that room until Iris and I moved into a different house. I never told Iris this, but cleaning out Mia's room, which I had to do because we were making the move to the new house, was probably the single hardest thing that I've had to face. I cried like a baby when I put her dresses and shoes into a box that was headed for storage, and her little stuffed animals that went with them. Everything that belonged to Mia was put into a special hermetically sealed storage, and it ripped my heart out to do it. I was depressed for several days after that, not wanting to talk to or see anybody.

But Iris never knew any of this, because she was recovering from what Andrew had done to her at the time, and there was no way that I would dump more grief onto her lap. So, I never said a word to her about my feelings about cleaning out Mia's room.

I suddenly felt myself crying when I was looking in at Rachael's room. The woman put her arm around me. "It's hard, isn't it? I somehow think that maybe you did the same thing with your little girl's room."

"Yes, yes, I did. I did. I had to clean out her room, though, because I was moving to a new place, and that was so difficult." Somehow, my visit to Mrs. Smyth was taking a different turn. It was helping me access my feelings, really access my feelings, about losing Mia. "God, that was so unfair, what happened to Mia. So unfair. She never even got to take her first step. She never got to lose a tooth, and find a quarter under her pillow, or sit on Santa's lap. She never got to have that first crush or first dance or first anything. It was so cruel. Fate was so cruel."

I was really sobbing, now, but I knew that I had to get it together. This visit wasn't about me, and it was never meant to be. It was about making peace with the past and giving Rachael's family a sense of closure.

Yet, I apparently needed closure as well.

Mrs. Smyth put her arms around me, and I could feel her crying as well. I hugged her tightly, my head buried in her shoulder, as the tears fell uncontrollably. I could never access my devastation about all that was taken from Mia when she died the way that she did. I knew that it was unfair, yet I went along and processed it as I did everything else that was bad in my life – it was something that was simply too painful to really examine, so I didn't. I couldn't really open that door of grief, because it might have been the last straw.

Yet, here I was, with this woman I barely knew, accessing how I was feeling about Mia, and feeling the weight of her death slowly being lifted off of my shoulders with every tear that I shed. I clung to this woman tightly, as if she was literally going to save my life.

And, looking back, perhaps she did just that, in her way.

In her quiet way, maybe she did save my life.

Later on that evening, after both of us poured out our endless well of tears, I was finally ready to tell Mrs. Smyth why I came to visit her in the first place.

"Uh, Mrs. Smyth," I said.

"Oh, I haven't gotten around to addressing this 'Mrs. Smyth' business. Please call me Pamela."

"Ok, Pamela. I, uh, there was a reason why I came to visit you. I mean, I did come to visit you because I knew your daughter. But, there's something else."

"Oh?"

"Yes. I, uh, I was responsible for her death."

She barely reacted to this. "In what way, Ryan?"

"She, uh, went to the party with me. I was her companion for the evening, and I should've also been her protector. But, I wasn't that at all. I, uh, had a serious drug problem. I went into the bathroom and got high, and then I not only ignored Rachael's pleas to go home, but I encouraged her to drink even more. If it weren't for me, your daughter would still be alive."

Pamela looked sad, but she shook her head. "You can't blame yourself. I somehow knew that you were here because you blamed yourself for what happened, but you need to stop doing that." She paused for a long time, looking pensively at her drink. "The truth is, Ryan, was that my daughter was an alcoholic and was bent on destruction. What happened at that party would've happened, sooner or later, to her. She was hospitalized several times for acute alcohol poisoning when she was in high school. I almost didn't let her go away to school, because I wanted to have her in my sights at all times. But, that wasn't realistic, so I let her enroll at Harvard. So, you might have thought that you were somehow ruining a pristine girl, and that you somehow forced her to drink so much that she died, but you need to stop thinking that. It was inevitable."

"I don't understand. She acted like she didn't drink at all. She also acted like it was her very first party."

Pamela sighed. "Yes, she always pulled the innocent act with people. She never wanted to admit that she had a problem, so she always acted like she didn't know the first thing about drinking and partying. But, trust me, she did know. She had been drinking since she was 12. Her father got her into it. Please, Ryan, please stop feeling that you were responsible for what happened to her. You're not responsible. She was. She was, dammit."

Her words gave me absolution, in a way, but I didn't feel exactly redeemed. "I appreciate the words, Pamela. I've been carrying around this guilt for all these years, although I haven't exactly acknowledged it to anybody. Except for you, right now. I'm not sure that I feel any less responsible for what happened now then before I met you. So, I still want to apologize for what happened. I, I, I was different then. So different. I was bent on destruction myself. So bent on destruction. Rachael seemed to be a victim of my casualness in how I treated people and life in general."

"I understand that. I know that you've known a great deal of pain. You carry it around with you, and it's evident in everything about you. It's in your eyes, in your stance, in your words. You need to have a lighter load. I hope that my words can give that to you. Whatever it is that has happened in your life that has given you this heavy heart is something that you probably need to come to terms with. But you don't need the death of my daughter on your conscience as well. I hope that I can unburden you about this. I loved my daughter very much. But she had her father's genetics, unfortunately. Brilliant, but a complete alcoholic. Always was."

Then she took another sip of her wine and stared pensively out the window. "I lied to you, when you came in. Sort of. I mean, my husband isn't here, that's true. But the reason why he's not here is because he's homeless. He's one of those guys who hold signs up in the street, begging for excess change. That would've been Rachael's fate if she would've lived. I can almost guarantee it."

At that, I felt immense sadness and regret. Sadness and regret that I would soon be leaving this lovely, and lonely, woman. This woman whose lamentations rival my own. She was one of those people who Thoreau spoke of when he said that most men lead lives of quiet desperation. To tell the truth, I exemplified that quote as well. Quiet desperation. There were bright spots in my life, of course, and Iris and Dalilah had much to do with that. But, inwardly, there was a quiet desperation that was always there, buried beneath the smiles and jokes I told. I tapped into this while I sat there that day with Pamela, whose pain mirrored my own.

And, somehow, that day, I started the process of truly healing.

I stayed the night in the guest bedroom upstairs, and, the next day, I gave Pamela a hug goodbye. "Thank you," I said to her. "You can't know how much you've helped me."

"I'm glad. I see you. I see that you're really a good person. Your pain runs deep, and I see that, too. You don't deserve to live with that dark cloud above your head. You need to let the past go. You can't change it. But it can change you, and not for the better. So, please, let it go. Rachael, Mia, everything that has led to the desperation in your eyes – let it go. Move forward. Regrets serve no purpose in this world. Remember that."

I nodded, then felt the cathartic tears well up in my eyes again. I was ready to return to my beautiful wife and my beautiful daughter. I was ready to own up to my crappy way that I treated the one person who has had my back virtually my entire life. The shooting was the catalyst for all of this, and I started to think that facing death the way that I did at Andrew's hands was the best thing that ever happened to me.

I was ready, but there was one thing that I needed to do before I could face my wife, daughter and best friend with the open heart that I truly needed to let all of them in again.

# Chapter Nineteen

## IRIS

*Shit, shit, shit, shit, shit, shit, shit.* I mean, I had a feeling that Nick was feeling this way. But why did he have to articulate it? Why did he have to say it out loud? As if I didn't have enough to deal with, now I had to deal with the fact that the man that I'm attracted to, who also happens to be my husband's best friend, was telling me that he was falling in love with me.

And I was still living under his roof.

"Nick, why do have to do this to me?"

"I'm sorry, Iris. I just can't stop thinking about you. I wish I felt differently, believe me. I mean, I can't do this to Ryan, but I can't keep it in any longer."

"Well, it can't happen. Ryan is still my husband. I know that it doesn't seem that way right now, and it certainly doesn't feel that way to me, but he's my husband and your best friend. So, please, get back to the office, so that we're not around each other so damned much, and give me and Dalilah some space."

Nick hung his head, evidently embarrassed for putting

his feelings out there. "Sorry, Iris. I…" Then he put my head in his hands and kissed me. I started breathing heavily, unable to push him away. He was intoxicating, and his kiss was tender and gentle. I felt my resolve against him melting away as I put my arms around the back of his neck, letting my tongue explore inside his mouth, as his was mine.

Then he pulled away from me. My heart was in my throat, and I just stood there, mesmerized. I felt the urgent stirring in my nether regions that I hadn't felt in such a long time. It was then that I realized how much I was craving Ryan's affection and love-making.

But I couldn't transpose that urgency and craving to Nick. That would completely destroy everything Ryan and I had worked so hard for.

"I'm so sorry, Iris. I had to do that. I've been wanting to do that pretty much since you and Dalilah arrived here in this house. I'm in love with you, and I don't know what to do about that."

I just stood there, looking at him like an idiot. I could hear my heart pounding in my ears. I could barely catch my breath. I finally said "Uh, I need to go to bed. I, I, think that I need to not be here anymore. I need to find a-a-a hotel until Ryan comes home."

Nick shook his head. "No, you can't do that. I put that out there, but I won't act on it. You'll be ok. If you want, I can bring my bimbos over here."

I nodded my head. "That would actually make me feel better." I felt my hands fly up to my mouth, touching where Nick's soft lips had just met mine. "I really need to go to bed. I'll see you in the morning."

"Ok. Please don't leave. I'm sorry for saying those things to you, and for kissing you like that, but I really want you to stay."

"Ok. I'll stay." I was playing with fire, and I knew it. My resistance to Nick was lowering with every day that Ryan was emotionally distant and Nick was showing his sensitive side. At the same time, I didn't really know what else to do but to stay there with him. I couldn't go to my parents – they didn't have room in their tiny duplex for myself and Dalilah. And going to a hotel was just depressing.

And I really couldn't go home. I didn't even know where home was anymore. Home was not where Ryan almost died and Andrew did die. That place was probably literally haunted. I knew Ryan and I would get a new home as soon as he was back on his feet, but who knew when that would be? Who knew even when he would be coming home? Or if he was coming home?

Once again, my mind wandered into the very worst-case scenario. And that was that Ryan was permanently changed, for the worse, by his near-death experience, and that his feelings for me were gone. I knew that something like that was possible. Perhaps he had taken stock of his life and realized that what he had with me was a chimera, and it evaporated when he came out from under his anesthesia. It just disappeared.

What then? We'd be divorced again, and I'd be raising Dalilah alone. And I couldn't do like before and just refuse to take any money from him. I had to think of my daughter this time.

I never thought I'd be put this position again. The position that I had to think about life without Ryan.

And suddenly I was very, very, very scared.

The next day, though, some very good things happened. Things were finally looking up! One was that I got a call from the prosecutor's office.

"Hello? This is Cindy Johnson."

"Hey, Cindy. What's up?" I was very casual, because, frankly, I no longer cared about Rochelle and her fate. If she walks, great. If she gets life in prison, even better. What happened to me at her hands was such a distant memory, even if the media was still involved. I still got phone calls from various media outlets asking for comments. I had no idea why – I never gave anybody any comment, ever.

Yet they kept trying.

"I wanted to tell you that Rochelle Anderson is going to plead guilty."

"Great. To what?"

"Assault in the second degree."

"Groovy. That means that she'll be out tomorrow, basically, if she gets credit for time served while she was awaiting trial."

"Well, she probably will be out by the end of the year, at any rate. I'm sorry, Iris. I wish the case was stronger."

"Yeah," I said, thinking that I didn't know how much stronger the case could get. But I also knew that, with me and Ryan both being elusive witnesses, and Rochelle having a world-class attorney on retainer, there probably wasn't a whole lot that Cindy could do. "Listen, Cindy, don't sweat it. I couldn't care less about it anymore. That was several lifetimes ago." I wanted to tell her that I'd been raped since then, lived in a drug house, birthed a female Einstein/Degas combination, divorced and reconciled with my husband, almost lost said husband to death and now feared losing him to some unknown force.

I could roll with anything that happened to Rochelle at this point.

"Ok. I was really nervous to call you about this, but I guess you're ok," she said.

"Cindy, I'd be ok if Rochelle never served a day in

ANNIE JOCOBY

prison. I just can't spend mental energy on the matter
anymore. But thanks for letting me know." Then, when I
got off the phone, I realized how much better I felt. I didn't
have to go through the bullshit trial, especially because that
trial would probably have been televised on some obscure
cable station. I really didn't want to deal with that, in the
middle of all the other chaotic crap that was going on in my
life.

So Rochelle pleading was a mixed blessing.

Another mixed blessing arrived in the form of Alexis.
She came to stay with us when she finally got out of her
rehabilitation facility. This turn of events was a very good
thing at this point, because she took Nick's focus off of me
and provided a good distraction for him. Because, even
though Nick and she were on the outs, I figured that they
could at least provide a good sexual outlet for one another.

If only I had one as well.

Alexis arrived with typical fanfare, driving her Porsche.
She had a little dog up front, a Yorkshire terrier with a pink
bow in her hair. When she got out of the car, one could
never guess that she was just released from a mental health
facility, and was dead broke. She carried the latest Hermés
Birken bag, and she was dressed as fashionably as usual with
her Louboutin pumps and designer clothes. She stepped out
of her car, her doggie in her arms.

"Hi, Nick," she said. "Uh, I know that I was supposed
to stay with Ryan and Iris, but I haven't been able to get
ahold of Ryan. Do you know where he is?"

"Oh, geez, Alexis, how long do you got? 'Cause you
missed a lot while you were away."

"What do you mean?"

"Come in with me. I have a lot to tell you. A lot."

Then she finally addressed me. "Hey, Iris. I see you're

here at Nick's house. If I said I wasn't a bit confused, I would be lying."

"Follow Nick into the house," I said. "He'll explain everything."

So, for the next hour, Nick caught Alexis up on what happened.

"Oh, shit," Alexis said. "I really have missed a lot. How are you holding up, Iris?"

"I really don't know just how I feel, to be perfectly honest with you. I'd feel about a million times better if I could talk to Ryan more."

But that was not to be. I tried, and failed, to get in contact with Ryan since he had been gone. And I was feeling more and more uncomfortable as I looked at Nick, and, every time I looked at him, I found that he was already looking at me.

## Chapter Twenty

The next few days were unbearably tense at Nick's house. Alexis continued to stay with us, and I took it upon myself to ensure that she was med compliant, as Nick apparently refused to do so, reasoning that he wasn't her baby-sitter.

However, I had experience with this, as I was always making sure that my own sister was med compliant, so I didn't mind doing this for Alexis.

So, for once, Alexis was not the source of the anxiety. It was Nick, and he was being insufferable to me.

Nick apparently overcompensated for his feelings for me by making me feel like I was a virtual slave in the house. He no longer had the affection that he had for me during the past weeks where we bonded. He went the other way and was cruel, more cruel than he had ever been before. He yelled at me about the slightest things. If I didn't clean the kitchen while I was cooking, I got yelled at. I was berated for forgetting to get the mail from the mailbox, as I was assigned this job when I moved into the house. I went to the store and forgot one item on the list, and I was harangued about this.

"Goddammit, Iris, get your head out of your ass. It clearly says on the list that you were supposed to get Milk Bones for the dogs, yet where are they? Huh? Now, get your ass back to the store and don't come back until you have them. Got that?"

Or it was "you're trying to get all of us sick by getting chicken blood all over the counter, aren't you, Iris? I'll just send you the hospital bill for my salmonella poisoning, k?"

I wanted to protest that I was about the clean up the chicken blood when he stormed into the kitchen to bitch at me about it. But he was on a roll, so I knew that my protestations would fall on deaf ears.

I felt like I was walking on eggshells every single day. And Dalilah was back to her tantrum mode, which made things that much worse. Nick no longer was willing to help me with her, so I held her for hours, walking around the house with her screaming in my ear. I'd bounce her up and down and stroke her back, but nothing eased her screaming and crying.

"Shhh, baby, please calm down. Please, for mommy?"

But nothing could calm her. And she apparently didn't wear out like most infants would. Her capacity for screaming and crying seemed boundless.

*Ryan, where are you? I need you so badly right now.*

Now Alexis was the one who kept me somewhat sane. She was remarkably in good spirits, even though her future was extremely bleak.

So, I found myself wishing that I could be anywhere else but under the same roof with Nick. One small comfort was that the bimbos reappeared, each more stereotypically gorgeous than the last. Beautiful guys appeared as well, sometimes with the bimbos, sometimes by themselves. Nick had a veritable revolving door, apparently not caring one whit about the impressionable 10-month-old prodigy he had under his roof.

I wondered how Alexis felt about Nick's bedroom escapades, so I asked her.

She just shrugged. "It's Nick, what can you say? He's worse than usual, though, because he's hurting. He'd do anything to get his feelings for you out of his system, but it doesn't seem to be working too well."

I found myself curling up into a virtual ball, into the fetal position almost. I tried to will myself not to crack under the strain, but it was becoming more and more difficult to do. These past few weeks, where Ryan was recovering, and shutting me out, I had Nick to bond with. Nick to talk to, Nick to cry to. Now Nick had made it clear that he would no longer be my source of support, and I felt like I was completely, and totally, alone.

To make matters worse, Alexis was apparently clued in to how Nick felt about me. "I know this is hard for you, Iris, being here with a man who is in love with you, while the man that you love is God-knows-where."

"It's repayment for how I treated Ryan after Andrew. Karma. I put him into a state of virtual panic, now it's his turn to do it to me. I hate how this feels, but it's probably comparable to what I did to him."

Then I drew a breath. "How, how, how do you know about how Nick feels about me?"

"It's obvious. So, I asked him, and he told me. He told me that he's never met a woman like you before, and that you're the one he's been waiting for his whole life."

I started to feel the walls close in on me. "What? What does that supposed to mean?"

She shrugged. "He loves that you're devoted to Ryan, ironically enough. He also loves that you're strong enough to get through some of the worst things that a person could experience without going into a rubber room. Most of all, though, he loves your lack of artifice. Nick has never known a woman who hasn't tried to rob him blind, myself included, I'm afraid. He sees that if he had a life with you, he would never have to worry that you're just after him for his money."

I shook my head. "A life with me? Why is he even thinking along those lines? I belong to Ryan, and only Ryan. Yes, it doesn't seem that way right now. I don't even feel that way right now. I feel that Ryan and I are each on one end of a wide chasm, and there isn't a way for us to reach each other. But, regardless, I belong to him, and I always will. Even if I never get to the other edge of the chasm, and we are actually permanently broken, my heart will always belong to him."

"Of course. I know this. But Nick can't help how he feels, so he's just going to keep abusing you. You don't have to take it, you know."

I knew that. Why was I still there? Would it be so bad to stay with my parents, Dalilah and me living together in a 10 x 10 room? It would certainly be better than living here in this beautiful, glorious mansion that had become my prison.

"You're right. I need to leave, and soon."

Just then, the sound of the piano drifted through the open door. It was Nick, pounding on the keys. He was playing a particularly passionate rendition of a Tchaikovsky piano concerto. I always knew how Nick was feeling when he played that piano, as it was always an extension of his emotions. When he was happy, it was light Chopin, Mozart, Beethoven or Bach sonatas. When he was angry and frustrated, he tended towards the Russian composers – Stravinsky, Tchaikovsky and Rachmaninoff. These were complicated pieces, full of passion and angst, and he played them all brilliantly.

Alexis listened for awhile, too. "You know, Nick and Ryan are so goddamned talented. Ryan's paintings always made me cry. And Nick – he's a concert-level pianist without even trying, really. I always admired both of them for their gifts. I wish I had some of my own."

I smiled. "Me too. There really isn't anything that I've mastered in my life. Not like them, anyhow."

Alexis then spontaneously hugged me.

I hugged her back. "What was that for?" I asked with a smile.

"Just for being you. Normal. Not a superachiever. Not rich. Just....normal. And for caring enough to make sure that I stay med compliant. I really couldn't do it without you."

"Well, I certainly have had my experience with med compliance, so it's not a big deal."

"Whatever. I just wanted to say that you're kind of my hero."

I smiled, and knew that she was kinda my hero, as well.

# Chapter Twenty-One

## RYAN

I had just left Pamela's house, and I called the limo to take me over to Nate and Nat's. I had to see them before I left, but I only wanted to stop by. I needed to tell Natalie how sorry I was for all the leading on I did to her during our college years, and I wanted to see for myself that she was happy. So, I had to drop in on the two of them before I headed home.

I was so looking forward to being home. Not just because the love of my life was there, but also because there was something important, so important, that I had to do when I got there. Pamela's words rang in my ears – that regrets served no purpose, and that I had to move forward. I would do that, but only after the last piece of the puzzle was put into place. Then, and only then, would my closure be complete.

But, seeing Nat and Nate would be first.

I got to their apartment and rang the doorbell. As with Pamela, I was taking a chance that nobody would be home.

But, as with Pamela, that fear was unfounded as Nate opened the door.

"Ryan!" he shouted, then enveloped me in a huge bear hug. "Wow, this is a shock. What are you doing here?"

"I was in town for something very important. So, I needed to drop by and see you guys before I left."

"What was so important?"

"Long story."

Nate looked at me skeptically. "There's something up. You don't look so good. You're not...."

"On the smack again? No. I look this way because, I, uh, was shot about a month or so ago. I flatlined on the table, but the surgeons brought me back. I've spent my recovery time obsessing about everything in my life I did wrong. Which brings me here."

"Wait, wait, wait, wait, wait. Shot? What happened?"

So, I told him the story of Andrew.

"Shit. Shit. Shit. Wow." He just stood there, looking at me with his mouth agape.

Then Natalie came in the room, her baby in her arms.

"Ryan, uh, what a surprise."

"Hi, Nat," I said, going over to her and kissing her lightly on the cheek. "How are you?"

"I've been better. Been up for 24 hours with a colicky baby. And you?"

I looked at Nate. "Uh, Nat," he said. "I've got something to tell you." Then he led her away to another room. About ten minutes later, Natalie came bursting through the French doors that led into the living room. "Ryan, are you ok? God, Nate just told me what happened. Are you alright?"

"Yes, yes, yes. Don't worry about me. I'm an old pro in getting shot, you know."

"Don't joke about that. It's not funny. Why are you here? You need to be in bed somewhere, recovering. Why are you here?"

"I really can't go into that. But I needed to see you both before I left. And, Nat, I needed to say something to you that is very serious."

"What's that?"

"I, uh, never treated you very well in college. I used you. You loved me, and I used you. I've come to terms with how I treated you, and it wasn't pretty. I wanted to apologize for that from the bottom of my heart. You didn't deserve the way that I treated you. Nobody did, but you, least of all."

Natalie said nothing, just stood there with tears in her eyes. "Thank you," she said quietly. "Thank you for acknowledging my feelings."

"If it makes you feel any better at all, I always loved you as well. Not like you loved me, of course, but as a close and special friend. I hope that we can always have that with each other."

"Of course," she said. Then she gestured to Nate, and took his hand. "Nate and I are in a really good place right now. We went through about a million hours of marriage counseling, but we're finally rock solid. So, in a weird way, what happened with you and me last year happened for a reason. Nate and I are better than ever."

"I'm glad," I said. "That's all I wanted for you and Nate. To be happy. And, you are. I love you both, so I can't tell you how thrilled I am to see the two of you doing so well."

Nate and Nat both smiled. "Group hug," Nate said, and Natalie put Christopher in his swing, as the three of us embraced for what seemed to be the longest time.

After I left their apartment, my load felt lighter still.

It was now time to face what would be the final piece of the puzzle, so that I could go back and be the husband that my beautiful wife has always deserved.

# Chapter Twenty-Two

I was back in Kansas City, and, as I was getting into my car, my heart was heavy for what was about to happen. I felt panic rising, and I had to talk to myself and tell myself that I was doing the right thing.

I approached the area where I had stored Mia's things. Everything that Alexis and I had bought Mia was in this storage area. I hung my head and called Alexis.

"Hello?" she said.

"Hi. Uh, I need you to meet me at the storage area. Please don't say anything to Nick or Iris."

"Of course. I'll be right there."

Alexis arrived about a half hour later. She just looked at me. "You're ready?"

I nodded. "Yes. Finally."

Then, together, we unlocked the area. I stepped in and fingered everything in there. I took out each dress and held them up to my face. I picked up each stuffed animal and hugged it tightly.

This time, I didn't try to stop the tears. Yes, I was a man, but I had emotions that had to come out.

Alexis stood there. Her tears matched my own.

I smiled, picking up a mobile. "Remember this? We went shopping that one day, and Mia picked this out herself. She was so fascinated by all the colors on this thing."

"Of course. How could I forget?"

I picked up a stuffed animal. "I won this for her at that county fair."

And another stuffed animal. "I think this came from one of those machines in a Chinese restaurant. You know, with the metal claw."

"And the crib," she said. "God, remember how long it took for us to put that thing together?"

"Yeah," I said. "You and I were both ready for a cold brew after that one."

We both laughed.

Alexis and I went through Mia's things, piece by piece, reminiscing about what all these items meant to us. Each of us had vivid memories about everything – where they came from, what we were doing when we bought them, etc.

Then, we both looked at each other. "It's time," I said.

She nodded. "I know."

Then, I got the boxes out of my Escalade, and put each item into them carefully.

We drove along in silence to the Salvation Army. I reached out and held her hand. She was staring out the window, but she looked at me and smiled wanly. "We're doing the right thing."

I said nothing, just looked ahead.

I parked in front of the store. I looked back and saw that Alexis was holding one of the boxes, and stroking her hand on the top of it.

I walked into the store, Alexis right behind me. I addressed the clerk. "Uh, we have some things that we need to donate. Some infant things."

"Ok," he said. "Is that all there is?"

"No," I said, gesturing to Alexis, who was right behind me and carrying a box. "This box needs to go, too. And, if you could get some men out here, there's a lot of furniture in my Escalade as well."

"Great," he said. "I'll go out there with you." Then he called to another guy who was on the floor. "Need some help with a donation, Sal. You busy?"

"No," Sal said. "I'd be glad to help."

Then the four of us worked together to unload everything. The rocking chair, the crib, the chest of drawers, the bookcase and the armoire. It took us about a half hour to unload everything.

"This is mighty fine furniture," Sal said. "Beautiful quality. Some little girl will be lucky to get this stuff."

"Yes, she will," I said. "Please don't overprice it. I want this furniture to go to somebody who is truly needy."

"What would you consider to be overpriced?"

"Over $20 for any one item. That's important. I would appreciate that."

"You got it," he said, as he took out some tape and put $20 on it in black magic marker.

"Thanks," I said.

I got back to the Escalade, where Alexis was waiting for me.

I smiled at her, and she smiled back through her tears.

I took one last look at the Salvation Army's front door. "Goodbye baby Mia," I said, softly. "I love you, and I always will."

And I put the Escalade into gear and headed home.

I was finally free.

# Chapter Twenty-Three

## IRIS

I was in my room, packing my bags. There was absolutely no point in my staying under this roof with Nick even a second longer.

Dalilah was in her playpen, watching every move I was making.

"We go?"

"Yes, we go."

"Where?"

"To nana's house. You want to see nana, don't you?"

"Yes, nana. I want to see nana. Why we leave Uncle Nick?"

"We just can't be here, anymore, that's all. Besides, nana misses you. She talks about you all the time."

"I miss nana. But I miss Uncle Nick, too."

"I know, baby. I know. But we have to go and stay with nana."

I sighed. I wasn't looking forward, at all, to what was about to happen. There was so little room at my parent's townhouse for us. Yet, going to a hotel was way too depressing. I needed to be around people who cared about me. I needed to be able to think, and not stare blankly at sterile hotel walls.

I felt my world falling apart. Aside from the very brief conversation that I had with Ryan, I hadn't talked to him for several days now. And, even before that, I didn't really talk to him. It was me talking, and him ignoring me.

Was I alone again? Would I always be alone? Could I do this – raise Dalilah alone?

I couldn't breathe. I sat down on the bed, and put my head in my hands. I couldn't do this. I just couldn't do this.

Dalilah was looking at me with scared eyes. "Momma?" she said, tentatively. "Momma okay?"

I smiled through the torrent of tears. "Yes, baby," I lied. "Momma ok."

Then, I picked up my suitcase in one arm, and Dalilah in the other, and left through the back door without a word.

# Chapter Twenty-Four

"Hi, mom!" I called, as I came through the door of the townhouse.

"Uh, oh," she said. "What happened now?"

Poor mom. She had whiplash from all the changes that happened as well.

"I don't know, mom. I don't know. I can't even begin to explain what has been going on at Nick's house."

"What's going on? Where's Ryan?"

"I don't know." Then the tears came in a flood. "I don't know, mom, I don't know. I mean, he's okay, I guess, wherever he is. But I don't know where he is. I mean, I talked to him on the phone, briefly, but he gave me no information at all. He could be in Timbuktu right now for all I know."

My mother got quiet, which was unusual for her. "What's going on, Iris? I know that Ryan was home, because you brought him home. But every time I talk to you about him on the phone you always put me off. What's going on between you two?"

I started to hyperventilate a little bit. "I don't know, mom. I think that he doesn't love me anymore."

"Why would you think that?"

"He's just different now, mom. Ever since he was shot, it has been so hard to reach him. I've tried so hard to talk to him and engage in conversation, but he ignores me. He watches television while I'm trying to talk to him. I don't think that he's even watching the television, either. I think that he just wants to shut me out. I don't know what to do."

"Honey," my mother said. "He went through something life-altering. He almost died. Do you understand that? He almost died. Let me repeat that. He.almost.died. He's obviously going through something right now, but you cannot take that personally. I'm quite sure that he didn't magically just fall out of love with you for no reason at all."

"I don't know, mom. It has happened before," I said, thinking about Travis. Travis was a guy that I lived with for two years and thought that I would marry. Then, one day, seemingly out of the blue, he informed me that I had to move out. Later on, much later on, I found out why – he had found somebody else, and, the second I moved out, he moved on with her. And virtually moved in with her, as he started staying with her every single day and night.

"Ryan isn't Travis. He's not some slime who would go behind your back and run around on you. He's a good guy. He wouldn't do to you what Travis did."

"But how do I know? I just don't know, mom. I love him so much, and I think that I would sooner die than lose him again. But I just don't know what to think anymore."

"Don't sit there and think the worst. See what he has to say when he comes back from wherever he is. It all might have a logical explanation."

I took a deep breath. "Thanks, mom. But, I, I, I can't go back to Nick's house."

She narrowed her eyes suspiciously. "And why not?"

"I just can't. Nick is…"

"Nick is what?"

"Nothing, nothing. He just has a lot on his plate, that's all. With his divorce and everything. He's under a lot of stress and he's making more stress for me."

"Well, more stress is not what you need. I don't know where you're going to stay, though."

"In Tad's room." Tad is my nephew, and he used to live there with my parents and my sister, who is his mother. He moved out several years ago, though, so whenever I came home to stay for a little while, I stayed in his tiny room.

"That room doesn't have space for Dalilah's things and your things. Where is the crib going to go?"

"I don't know, mom. I don't know much right now. I only know that I just can't be there with Nick right now. I'm about to go crazy." Then I thought about Alexis. I was leaving her high and dry, and there was the chance that she might slip up in taking her meds and be right back to where she was before. I felt selfish when I thought about that. But, at the same time, I felt that my mental health was rapidly declining, and, soon, I would be no good to her or anybody else.

Thinking about Alexis, I told my mother that "Well, on second thought, I might leave and go back to Nick's in a couple of days. Alexis wasn't there when I left, but, when she gets back, she needs me to make sure that she doesn't slip up in taking her meds. So, I might not be here for as long as I at first thought."

She nodded her head. "Of course, you're welcome to

stay as long as you want. It's just that there isn't a ton of room here, as you know."

Nevertheless, I went into Tad's room and set up Dalilah's crib while she watched me from the playpen. There was just enough room for the crib, and there really wasn't much more room to get around in that space. The crib blocked the entrance to the closet, so I had to get to the closet by going crawling along the bed. Then I opened the tiny closet, and put some of mine and Dalilah's things in there. There wasn't much room in there for any of that, either, and there was no space at all for her little bookshelf.

She sat there in her playpen, looking at me intently, her hand in her mouth. I wondered if she knew my dilemma here – that I couldn't really stay here because it simply wasn't logistically possible.

I laid down on the bed, hoping that Dalilah could keep herself busy with her little puzzles and games, and I could get a little peace and quiet time to rest my aching head. Thankfully, she seemed to be in a quiet mood, so I felt myself falling asleep.

# Chapter Twenty-Five

## RYAN

After Alexis and I were done with giving away baby Mia's things, I decided to take her out to eat, which was something she and I hadn't done in awhile. Just the two of us, anyhow. It was clear that she really needed some kind of comfort and solace, and I felt for her. We weren't married anymore, and I didn't love her like a wife or girlfriend, but I did love her as a friend. How could I not? She saved my life as much as Nick had. It was her idea for me to live with Nick all those years ago, so my getting out of Rochelle's dungeon had a lot to do with her intervention. And she was the only person who really could understand what I was going through, right at that moment, because she, too, was going through the same thing.

So, we found ourselves at a little friendly bistro with an outdoor patio. It was a place that we had discovered many years earlier, and this restaurant had the best Chilean Sea Bass that I had ever tasted. And the wine here was second to none.

We ordered, then I looked at her across the table. She

was back to normal, and she really was very beautiful. Just for a moment, it seemed like old times between us. Then, just as quickly I remembered that, even in the old days, the good days that Alexis and I had were few and far between.

Right now she looked very, very sad.

I put my hand on hers. "You doing okay?"

She nodded weakly. "Yes. But I've been better, to tell you the truth. The reality of my life has been hard to escape lately. I don't have anything, Ryan. And I want a child so desperately. Yet, I can't seem to find a man who wants to stay with me."

"Alexis, I know that things seem bleak right now. But you're beautiful and sweet. If you stay on your meds, then you'll make somebody a happy guy. You have to stay on your meds, though."

"I know. Iris has been helping me with that. So, my chemicals seem to be more in balance. I'm still very depressed, but I think that it's situational more than anything right now."

"Iris has been helping?"

"Yeah. Her sister was bi-polar, as you know, so she knows about keeping somebody med compliant."

I smiled. My Iris. Such a good person with such an enormous heart. How I loved her.

"Do you want to talk about Mia?" I asked Alexis.

"Yes. I mean, I've been through this with my grief counselor. But I still think about her every single day."

"Me too. I don't really let anybody know about that, though."

"Not even Iris?"

"No, not even her. It's something that's so private for me, you know? And I've always felt that I needed to keep a stiff upper lip to the world about how I felt about that. But I

went on a trip to New York, to Brooklyn, and I realized that I didn't need to keep any of that in."

"What happened there?"

"I met a woman who had also lost a child," I told Alexis, not going into how, exactly, that child was lost. "And, I don't know. I had a catharsis there with her. I've turned a corner in my recovery from my shooting, I think. I'm finally ready to let the past go. Iris and Dalilah are my future, and I really need to concentrate on them instead of regrets."

Alexis nodded. "You're very lucky to have people in your life who love you like that."

"Alexis, I love you. I always have, and I probably always will. But as a friend. I realize that you always wished that I would fall in love with you again, but I'm afraid that can't happen."

"Who said anything about my thinking that would happen? I know how you feel about Iris. How you've always felt about her. I don't know exactly why you feel that way, but that's not for me to judge."

I stared at her, wondering if she really felt that way. If she finally accepted that Iris was the love of my life.

"You're going to be ok, right?"

"Sure," she said. But the way that she said that, I doubted it and I immediately assumed that she was lying.

I hoped that I didn't have to worry about her.

When I arrived at Nick's house, he was sunbathing by the pool with two women. They were both topless. They looked up at me, and smiled invitingly.

Nick, however, did not have the same inviting expression on his face.

"Hey, Nick. Where's Iris?"

He shrugged. "Dunno. She apparently left early this morning."

"What? Why did she leave?"

"Dunno."

I looked at the two women. "Care to introduce me to your friends?"

"Yeah. This is Megan and Stephie."

"Hey handsome," one of the women said. She was a typical Nick kind of girl – gorgeous rack, flat stomach, long hair and beautiful face. She turned to Nick. "We need to have him join us tonight. You never told me that your friend was so hot."

Nick just glared at her, then turned to me. "So, I see you're back. Why didn't you tell anybody that you were leaving?"

"Because if I did, I doubt that Iris would've let me. And I had to do what I just did, so I couldn't say anything. But I left a letter for Iris."

"She didn't get any letter. Where did you leave it for her?"

"On her nightstand. I still don't understand how it was that she didn't see it."

"Who knows? Maybe it was intercepted by stalker Tammy. That woman has it bad for you."

"Oh, crap. I'll bet that's what happened. Well, you need to fire her as soon as possible. I can't have women acting like that."

"Women have always acted like that with you. You have something that brings out the crazy, I'll tell you that."

"Whatever. Anyhow, why would Iris leave?"

"I don't know, and I really don't care."

I was suddenly angry with him. "Could I speak with you in private?" I asked him. Nick said nothing, just got up off of his lounger, and the two of us walked back into the house. Once we got into the house, I laid into him. "What

do you mean, you don't care? I guess I shouldn't be surprised, because you never cared about anybody but yourself."

"Oh, now, that's bullshit, and you know that's bullshit."

"When have you ever cared about any woman who was in your life? Now, you had the responsibility for my wife and daughter to be safe here, at your house, and you apparently drove them away and you don't care about that."

"Ryan, I think you need to stop right there. Just stop with the accusations that I don't care about your wife and child."

"Why should I stop? I'm telling you something that you don't want to hear, I know, but you have to hear it. They're gone because of you. She wouldn't just leave unless you drove her to it."

"Ryan, it's not like that."

"Then what is it like? Why would she leave?"

Nick said nothing, just looked down at the floor, his hands in his hair. Then he looked up at me again. "Iris left because of something I said to her."

"And what was that?"

Nick took a deep breath, then looked me in the eye. "I told her that I was in love with her."

# Chapter Twenty-Six

He stunned me with those words. I wasn't prepared for them. Any other words, I would have been prepared for. He could've told me that Iris wasn't around because he killed her and buried her in the garden, and I would've been less surprised then I was right at that moment. "I'm sorry? What did you just say?"

"I'm in love with your wife. I don't know how it happened, or when. I only know that I am completely and consumingly in love with her."

I felt my eyes get wide, and I hyperventilated just a little. "She-she-she doesn't feel the same way. Does she?" I then realized how I had been treating her lately. If she fell in love with Nick, or anybody else, I wouldn't blame her. I had been a total ass to her lately.

"No. In fact she's made it clear that it can never happen, because she's 150% devoted to you. So, no. No, she doesn't feel the same way about me."

I let out my breath in relief. "Oh, thank God. Thank God. Thank God." It was then that I realized that if I lost

Iris, again, I would be so beyond devastated that I probably wouldn't recover.

"Is that all you can say? Thank God she doesn't love me?"

"Nick, no offense, but I'm taking your protestations of love with a grain of salt. Candy and Brandy out there, or whatever their names, are your speed. I think you're infatuated with Iris because she's the one woman you can't have. So, I'm not going to get too concerned about what you think you feel for Iris."

"Oh, really. Really. You think I can't love another person, only myself?"

"Actually, yes."

"I love you. I always have."

"Of course. And I, you. But that's different."

"Not really. Not really that different. So, it's crazy. I'm in love with your wife, but also in love with you. And I can't really have either one of you."

I hesitated. "I feel the same way about you, too, you know. But my life is with Iris. And you really need to find somebody nice like Iris, instead of scraping the bottom of the barrel with these superficial women."

"I don't want somebody like her. I want her."

I sighed. "Nick, please. We've been friends since we were in kindergarten together. Now you're going to possibly ruin everything. Because we can't hang out with you if you're going to make things difficult."

"How will I make anything difficult? I feel a certain way about her, she doesn't feel the same, and that's that. I won't do anything to make things difficult."

I suddenly got an idea. "Nick. What is the most surefire way to get you to lose interest in any one woman?"

"To sleep with her. Which isn't going to happen here, of course."

"Maybe it can."

# Chapter Twenty-Seven

IRIS

For some odd reason, Alexis had been on my mind. I guess because I finally got tired of spending 100% of my mental energy on Ryan, and thinking about Alexis was a little bit less depressing for me. But not much.

And I was remembering why it was that I had so much patience and understanding of Alexis and her situation...

I think that I was eleven years old when it happened. My sister and I always got along, to a certain extent, even though she was always threatening me to make me do what she wanted, when she wanted.

"Let my friend cheat at cards when she comes over."

"No."

"If you don't, I'll run away."

"Ok."

"Do my laundry for me."

"No."

"I'll run away."

"Ok."

Then, one time, I finally kept saying no to something

that she wanted. She then left the car and started walking up the street, like she was going to run away. I started crying hysterically and running after her. "Ok, ok. I'll do it. Just please don't run away."

And, so it went, until I told my mother about Sue's blackmail. That's what finally ended that particular mode of manipulation. But, there were always different methods that she got her way. I was always so gullible, I fell for every one.

But Sue wasn't a particularly bad sister. She wasn't evil. She was simply manipulative.

And, as I soon found out, constantly depressed.

I was angry with her for a long time when I was young. She would blow up over the smallest things – I remember one time I drank some of her milk that she bought from the store. She blew up at this, screaming at the top of her lungs about it. Another time I accidentally spilled an entire soda pop on her lap at a restaurant. She blew up at me right there in the restaurant, screaming at me so that everybody in the restaurant stared in our direction.

But, when I was eleven, things changed. I started to worry about her more than be angry with her.

Because that was the year when she first attempted suicide.

That morning, my mother was making pancakes, which she often does on Sunday mornings. My mother wasn't the greatest cook in the world, but she could make a mean pancake, and the chocolate chip ones were my favorites. That morning she was making both banana pancakes and chocolate chip ones, and my mouth was watering as she took each pancake out of the griddle and on to the plate. I was extremely hungry, so I was impatient to eat my pancakes.

My mother smacked my hand as I tried to steal one off the plate. "You know better than that. Wait your turn," she said. "But go and get your sister. Wake her up and tell her that her favorite pancakes are ready."

"Ok, mom," I said, as I made my way down the hall towards her room. Our house was a tiny ranch-style home that was rented, with worn blue carpeting that had seen better days. I knocked on her door, and she didn't answer. "Sue, get up. Mom's making pancakes." No answer. I knocked some more, then tried to open the door. It was locked from the inside.

Music was playing from the room – Nirvana's *Smells Like Teen Spirit*, which was a new release at that time.

I continued to pound on the door, and there wasn't an answer.

"Mom! Sue's in her room and she's not answering!" I actually didn't think that there was a problem. I just thought that she was being stubborn.

So, my mother got into the act. She started pounding on the door as well. "Sue, get out of that room. Breakfast is ready!"

She finally kicked in the door.

Sue was lying on the bed, her head and her arm draped over the side. Her breathing was extremely slow and uneven. Her face was white as a sheet. My mother rushed over to her, and grabbed her wrist. "Call 911," she said to me. "Now!"

I rushed down the hall and grabbed the phone with shaking hands.

"911 what's your emergency?"

"My sister. Something's wrong with her."

"Ok. We're going to send somebody over there right away."

I ran back into the room. My mother was hunched over my sister, not really knowing what to do. We hadn't yet learned how to perform CPR or mouth to mouth resuscitation, so we were both pretty helpless about what to do in this situation.

"Is she ok? Is she going to be ok?"

My mother was shaking her head. She was holding a plastic container that held my sister's depression medicine in her hand. It was empty. I remembered that this was a new bottle, so she apparently took the entire bottle in one sitting.

I walked over to where they were, and put my head close to my sister's mouth. She was hardly breathing. She breathed once, then her next breath came several seconds later.

Then my mother was crying hysterically. I had no idea what to do. I had never seen my mother cry like that, and I was more alarmed by her reaction than anything else.

*She's going to be ok. She has to be ok. My sister has to be ok.* I suddenly remembered all the fights that we had. All the times that I made her angry or she did the same with me. "Please, make it through. Please. If you do, I'll do anything that you ask me to. I'll clean your room every single day for the rest of your life. I'll even do your laundry. If you wake up, I'll do absolutely anything you want."

The ambulance was soon there, and my sister was loaded on a stretcher. I followed along closely behind her. "Can I go with her in the ambulance?" I asked.

"No, I'm sorry. Medical personnel only."

I nodded my head. "Ok. Thank you."

I went back into the house. My mother was still in Sue's room, clutching one of Sue's stuffed animals. A one-eyed bear named Paddington, after my sister's favorite childhood tale. She was still crying.

"Mom, she's going to be ok," I said, although I wasn't entirely convinced that this was true myself. "She's going to be ok."

She just shook her head, the tears coming down her face. She was mute, though.

Then she wasn't. She started wailing. "Oh, oh, oh. What happened? What happened? Why? Why? Why?"

I was terrified of seeing my mother like this, and terrified that my sister would die. I touched her arm sleeve. "When dad comes home, we'll go to the hospital to see her," I said. My mother didn't drive, then or now. My dad was at work, and wouldn't be home for several hours.

My mother kept crying and wailing. "What went wrong? What did we do wrong?"

I didn't understand myself what went wrong. I had no idea then about chemical imbalances and clinical depression. I only thought that people were depressed and sad because of things that happened to them. To my knowledge, nothing had ever happened to my sister to make her want to do something like this.

My father finally arrived home several hours later. By that time, my mother had finally stopped wailing, and now was sitting in a chair, her hands on the arms of the chair. She wasn't saying a word. I was kneeling down on the floor in front of her, my head in her lap.

I ran to my father. "Dad, you have to take us to the hospital. It's Sue. She's hurt."

"What do you mean, hurt? What happened?"

"She's sick." I didn't know how to explain any of it to him. "She's sick."

"Sick?"

I nodded my head. My mother was still in shock, as she

stared straight ahead at something unknown, while putting a death-grip on the arms of the chair.

My father managed to get my mother out of her chair, and the three of us drove in silence to the hospital. We went to the waiting room, after my father talked to the receptionist about who we were. A few minutes later, a doctor came out to inform us about my sister.

"She's resting comfortably. She's going to be transferred to the psych ward for evaluation."

At that, my mother started crying anew. But now her cry was soft, and she had a wadded up Kleenex that was at her disposal. My father's arm was around her protectively.

My sister stayed in the hospital for a week, and we went to see her every day. She seemed to be getting better. "I' m sorry," she said. "I'm sorry for doing that. I just didn't see any way out."

Out of what? I didn't understand. Our lives with our parents was never perfect, by any stretch of the imagination. There was never enough money for much of anything, and our father was pretty remote. But there wasn't anything that was so bad that dying became preferable to living.

And so it went, for the rest of my life. As I grew older, I became aware of the phenomenon of clinical depression. That sometimes people are just born with a chemical imbalance in their brain that needs to be normalized with meds. I also learned that normalizing anything of the sort was tricky, at best. It was difficult trying to find just the right drugs to work with my sister's brain chemistry, in just the right dose. It was also difficult for a person to stay normal, even once the right combination of drugs are found, because the drugs often stop working. Then it was back to the drawing board.

So my life became a series of incidents that happened

much like the first suicide attempt. She slashed her wrists in the bathtub and almost bled to death before we found her. She took other overdoses of prescription drugs. And she went into the hospital more times than I could count. Her hospitalizations were mainly for depression, but she had her episodes of mania as well. Fortunately, her mania was not as bad as Alexis' mania. It was more non-stop talking and not sleeping, and she would clean her room well into the night. Considering she was the type of person who literally never cleaned her room – she let her laundry pile up for weeks, in trash bags strewn around her room, and magazines and books were piled up everywhere – her cleaning sprees were not entirely unwelcome. She was never hospitalized for mania, but she often was for depression.

So, I understood Alexis. I got where she was coming from, so I naturally had sympathy for her and was drawn to her. She couldn't help any of it. She struggled, just like my sister always did. But she had privilege and money, where my sister never did. Even now, Alexis had Ryan to take care of her. My sister never had even that. My sister was now in her mid-thirties, and she had never lived a day in a home that was not my parents'. And I knew that she probably would never leave home. When my parents passed, I would be expected to take her in. I knew that.

I hoped that Ryan realized that as well.

# Chapter Twenty-Eight

RYAN

Once again, Iris was missing. Although I had a good idea where she was. I figured that the first place that I should look would be her parents' house. That was always where she went when something bad happened. Except for after she was raped, but that was an exception. Besides, she had Dalilah. Iris would never do anything that would jeopardize the life of our daughter, so I knew that she would end up someplace safe.

I got to her parents' townhouse and rang the doorbell.

Her mother answered the door. "Hi, Ryan. Come on in."

"Mom!" Iris was calling. "Who's there?"

"Iris!" I called to her. "It's me."

At that, Iris came bounding down the stairs so fast that she literally fell down them. She slid down the bottom three steps and landed on her rear.

"Iris! Are you ok?" I asked her, going over to where she was laying on the stairs. She was grimacing and holding her elbow.

"Yes, yes." Then she got to her feet and wrapped her arms around me. I did the same with her. I couldn't believe that she was in my arms again. It felt like the longest time since I was able to experience having her in my arms.

"Iris, Iris, beautiful Iris. I love you. I love you so much. I know that this sounds strange, but I missed you these past few weeks. Really missed you."

She was crying softly into my shoulder. "Oh my God. I thought I'd lost you. I was sure of it. I can't believe that you're here."

"I'm here, Iris, and I'm here for good," I said, as I put my hands in her hair and tousled it affectionately. I continued. "I've come to realize something over these past few weeks. And that is that you just never know when you're going to breathe your last. So, I can't have regrets about who I was. It does no good unless you use the regrets as a catalyst to become a better person. And that's what I'm going to do." As I said the words, I thought of Nick. My homecoming and seeing Nick for the first time in a long time did not go the way that I had planned. I wanted to come and see him and make my apologies to him. Unfortunately, I let my temper get in the way of this, and I ended up berating him for losing track of Iris. I would have to rectify that when I got back to talk to him again that evening.

"So, we're going home?" Iris asked me.

"We're not going home, because we don't yet have a home. But I'm going to change this as soon as I can. I'm going to get us another house that's ours. A house that I know we both will love. And then we're going to live in it. Live happily ever after in it, without anybody taking this away from us."

"Oh, thank God."

# Chapter Twenty-Nine

IRIS

Ryan is here! He's finally here! And, for the first time since he was shot, really, I believe that we're going to make it. Not broken, just bent. And I couldn't be happier in this world. He loves me. He still loves me. I decided to let this revelation marinate some in my head. Ryan loves me. Hopefully he never stopped loving me. No matter what had happened in our lives, we always manage to find a way back to each other, and this time was no different.

I suddenly wanted him in a way that I had never before wanted him. It was frustrating not really being able to act on this, as Dalilah was still there in her playpen and my mother was there, as well. Besides, Tad's room was so tiny, and the bed was a small full-size. Therefore, there really wasn't any romantic place for us to get naked and explore each other's bodies.

He kissed me gently and passionately, right there on the stairs. The world faded away as we kissed like this for what seemed like forever. I was captivated and mesmerized by him. I suddenly remembered exactly how much I loved him. I was feeling so far away from him, so disconnected. Now I was feeling connected to him again, for the first time since before he was shot. And this was a feeling unlike any other that I had ever experienced.

He loves me. He still loves me. I looked up at him and felt tears coming to my eyes.

"Are you ok?" Ryan asked me upon seeing my eyes fill up with tears.

"I'm more than ok," I replied. "I thought when you took off like that...I thought that I would lose you completely. That if you didn't leave me for another woman, you might just leave me for some other reason. I couldn't take that, Ryan. Please don't put me through that again. I mean, I know that I put you through it, and maybe this is karma for how I treated you. But, please believe me – I love you, and I don't want to lose you. Ever. So, let me in. You have to tell me when you're going away, because you know how much I worry about you otherwise.

"I know," Ryan said. "honey, I know. I've been beating myself up for my behavior with others, and I really should have been doing the same about my behavior towards you. I love you more than I thought that I could ever love anybody. I only wish that I had a way to express to you the things that I've been feeling and the darkness that was consuming me these past few weeks. The things that I've done in my life have not been pretty, to say the least. I've lived my entire life in self-destruct mode, it seemed, at least until I met you. While I'm not entirely self-destructive right now, the impulse is still there. And I've had to live with the things that I've done. I can try to make amends for them, but I still have to live with them."

"Whatever you've done, it isn't you now. It isn't who you are."

"Don't kid yourself. I struggle every day to not succumb to my demons. It's an internal struggle for the most part. But this shooting has just made it worse. It's opened up the dam of black emotions of who I am and who I was, and I've been trying to repair that dam. I'm still not entirely there, but I feel like I'm enough on the firm path towards healing that I want your love again. If that makes any sense at all."

"I think I know what you're saying. You've gone through a period of self-loathing because of your past. And you've just begun the process of coming to terms with the person that you were and getting some closure on that. You'll have more of an open heart because of this process. Am I close?"

His look of love was back, and I sighed. It had been so long since he had given me that look.

"I love you, you know that? You know me so well. Inside and out. You seem to understand me and know exactly how I'm feeling. I would beg for your forgiveness for how I've been acting, and that's what I need to do. But somehow I have the feeling that you've already forgiven me. That you understand why I did what I did. And I love you so much for that, I can't even express it."

Just then, Dalilah started calling for Ryan. "Daddy! Daddy! Come here!"

Ryan smiled and made his way up the stairs to retrieve our daughter. He came back down with Dalilah in his arms. She was clutching him closely, her legs wiggling excitedly. "Daddy here! Daddy here!"

"What do you say we pack up yours and Dalilah's things and head back to Nick's? I know that it's not quite home, but hopefully Sheila can watch Dalilah for a little bit while you and I make up for some lost time."

I melted some more at his words.

So, we packed up Dalilah's things and my clothes, and left for Nick's. "Bye, mom," I said. "I love you."

"I love you, too," she said. "I enjoyed seeing you, but you're going back where you belong. With your husband."

When Ryan and I got in the Escalade, after putting Dalilah's things away and securing her in the car seat, Ryan took my hand, then put his hands on my face and kissed me passionately. I lost my breath completely. I was always so surprised that it always felt like the first time with him, but that's exactly how it felt. It really felt this way because we hadn't been with one another for so long. I wanted so badly to strip off his clothes and make love to him right there, and truth be told, if we didn't have a precocious 10-month-old in the backseat, that's probably what would've happened. Ryan and I were never concerned about making love in public when we were both really in the mood, and this was definitely one of those times that we were in the mood.

"God, I can't wait to get you alone," he said. "I just can't wait."

"Oh, me too. Me too. Get back to Nick's as soon as you possibly can."

"I will. If Dalilah weren't here, I would be going 90 miles an hour to get you back to Nick's." Then he whispered, knowing that Dalilah understood most of what we said to one another. "I can't wait to feel me inside you."

Just those words made me start to breathe heavily. I swallowed hard, resisting the urge to feel his crotch. No matter, even without my tactile sensation on his groin, his manhood was standing at attention through his pants.

He kissed me passionately once more, then we headed to Nick's.

We got to Nick's, and found the house empty. I would imagine that Nick and Alexis went somewhere together, although that would be surprising. Nick had been making it clear to Alexis that he no longer wanted anything to do with her. I was actually sad for her. I wasn't sure if she saw a future with Nick, but, if she did, it had to be tough to be around the guy. Especially since she was aware of how he was feeling about me.

Ryan took Dalilah to the guest house so that Sheila could watch her. At first, she fussed, but then Ryan told her "Mommy and daddy will be busy for a few hours. But daddy will see you later, and daddy promises to play games with you as much as you want."

That cheered her up considerably. "Ok, daddy. Love you. Bye."

"Love you too, princess," Ryan told her. "See you soon."

"You do realize that you've just committed to about a million hours of Chutes and Ladders, Candyland and Old Maid, don't you?" I teased him.

"Yeah. But trust me, it will be worth it."

And was it.

Ryan and I got into my room, and he immediately put his hands on my shoulders, kissing them lightly. "You are the most remarkable woman," he said. "I don't know how you manage to roll with everything that is thrown at you, but you do. And I love you so much for it. Well, for that and about fifty million other things.

I closed my eyes, reveling in his touch. I realized that it had been weeks now since we made love, but it seemed like years. Eons.

His mouth was making its way down my back. He took my hair and lightly placed it over my shoulder, as his hands worked on massaging my neck, while his mouth made its way to the space between my legs. He licked me slowly there, putting my panties aside with his tongue. I groaned, feeling the extreme jolt course through me while every hair stood up on end. I was breathing heavily, while I felt my nether regions fill up with blood.

Then his hands were lightly cupping my breasts, underneath my dress. He laid me down on the floor, then laid down on top of me from behind. I could feel his manhood poking through his pants as he slowly removed my panties. Then I heard him unbuckle his belt, and pull down my underwear.

Then he slowly entered me from behind.

I groaned as I felt the familiar feeling of fullness and completeness. His face was buried in my neck, as he tongued me lightly. His hands explored my body while he thrust in and out rhythmically. Then he turned my head towards him, and kissed me full on the mouth. His tongue explored inside my mouth, as he slowly and gently thrusted his shaft in and out, in and out. I felt my eyes roll back in my head in ecstasy as I pulled on his hair lightly. We were both silent, as we wanted to enjoy the moment and savor every minute of our lovemaking.

I wanted to have the image in my mind like a photograph. The image of the two of us together after all the time that we couldn't be with each other in this way. I wanted to record the feeling for posterity, because I had found that life never gave you guarantees. There was no guarantee that Ryan and I would make love again after this moment, so I wanted to have a way to feel him inside me always. So, I concentrated on what he was doing and how I was feeling right at that moment. And how I was feeling right then was complete. That was the best word to describe it. Like I had a missing puzzle piece all this time that Ryan was recovering from surgery, and now the puzzle piece was missing no more.

Then I laid on my back and felt his weight on top of me, his hands pulling on my hair. He looked into my eyes as he thrust some more, then he kissed me on the lips hungrily. I had my legs wrapped around him as my hands lightly stroked his back. I grabbed his butt to push him further into me, and I felt him groan and start to shake.

He stayed inside of me for a few minutes, his head on my shoulder. Both of us were breathing heavily. "I don't want to pull out yet. I just want to savor this feeling of being inside you. It's been too long since I have felt this. Way too long. I don't want to ever be away from you again. I don't want to be emotionally away from you, nor physically away from you. I love you so much."

I said nothing, just stroked his back with my hands. Then he was kissing me again, and I felt his hardness grow inside of me some more. "Turns out I don't have to pull out at all," he said, as he started thrusting again. He kissed me passionately on the lips, his tongue slowly exploring inside my mouth. Then he was nibbling on my ears and nipples, as his tongue lightly teased each of my breasts. "Oh, God," he said. "I don't want this to end. Ever. I want to stay like this forever."

"Me too. God, me too." I didn't want to tell him that I was afraid, so afraid, that I would've never gotten the chance to make love with him again. I didn't want to break the mood. "I feel complete again. I was feeling so much like there was something missing from my very soul these past few weeks, so I'm so very happy that I have it back."

"You will have it forever," he said. "That is a promise."

We were like that for several more hours, although Ryan knew that it couldn't last forever. He had to make time for Dalilah, because she was anxious to spend quality time with her daddy. Plus, there was the issue of Nick. Ryan had explained that he and Nick got into an argument when Ryan got home after being away in New York. He didn't say what the fight was about. But he also said that he had something important to say to Nick that evening after dinner.

In other words, we had reality to deal with after we finally got out of that bed. So, we had to savor every second that we were together.

And that's exactly what we did.

# Chapter Thirty

After several hours of lovemaking, Ryan finally said that he needed to see our daughter and bond with her some. I didn't disagree. I knew how much Dalilah was wanting to see him for this long, and how his absence had negatively affected her. She was so perceptive it was almost scary. They say that toddler and babies know more than what they let on. They just can't articulate it. Dalilah, however, not only knew what was going on, but she could articulate it.

And her articulation during Ryan's absence told me that she was very hurt and angry about her father's behavior. So, Ryan had some bonding to do.

So, as promised, Ryan picked Dalilah up from Sheila and made his way to Dalilah's room. I stayed back, figuring that the two of them needed some quality time together. But I walked by the room several times, and the door was open, and I saw the two of them on the floor playing various games and working various puzzles. Dalilah looked extremely happy there next to her daddy, and my heart soared.

Things were going to be going back to normal.

That night, after Dalilah went to bed, I found out what Ryan was going to say to Nick. He, Nick and I all sat in Nick's den, in front of the fire, each of us with a glass of wine. Alexis was also in the den with us, because Ryan wanted her there, as well, although she wasn't drinking. She was trying to make sure that she didn't have any more problems with her meds, and, since alcohol and her medications don't mix well, she had quit drinking for the time being.

"Nick," Ryan said. "I need to say some things to you. I, I, died during surgery. I flatlined, and they brought me back. And it was just like in the movies – I floated above my body and watched the surgeons using the paddles on me. It was a peaceful feeling. It was peace like I've never known it before. When they brought me back, and when I made it through surgery, I was so grateful to be alive. So grateful to be with everybody I loved. But it also made me look at my life. And what I looked at wasn't pretty."

Nick nodded. "You don't have to tell me this, Ryan. I understand everything. I realize that near-death experiences make people take stock of their lives, and I figured that was what you were doing"

"Yes," Ryan said. "But I realized something. I never apologized to you for how I treated you all those years. We just kinda swept it under the rug, and kept going like nothing ever happened. But I wanted to tell you, from the depths of my soul, how sorry I am for how I was to you. I don't know why you remained my friend, but I'm really glad that you did."

"Please. That was years ago. You're so different now. You've been different since you've been clean. It was always the drugs that made you the jerk that you were. I know that."

"Just stop making excuses for me, please. I need to own what I did, and how I treated you. It wasn't right. I really don't know how to make amends to you, though. I can only tell you how sorry I am."

"Apology accepted," Nick said. "Sincerely."

We all drank our wine a bit after that in an awkward silence. The tension was such that it could be cut with a knife. While it was good that Ryan finally apologized for treating Nick like shit, there was still a vibe that was lingering in the air. And things needed to be addressed.

Ryan then said to Nick "And my behavior today was pretty uncalled for. I'm sorry for the things I said to you about the bimbos and how you don't care about anybody but yourself. That's so not true, and I hope that you don't think that I really believe that about you."

"Ryan, it is true," Nick said. "I don't generally care about anybody but myself. And you, of course. I've always cared about you. And your wife."

*Uh oh. Are we going to go there?*

Ryan shook his head. "I don't want to talk about this right now."

"Ok, then when? I thought that you had this great epiphany, which would mean that you aren't going to keep sweeping things under the rug. This is definitely not something that should be swept under the rug. We all need to clear the air and figure out a way to deal with it."

Ryan took a deep sigh. Then he addressed me. "Uh, Nick has told me about his feelings for you. How much do you know about that?"

I felt myself shrinking, and wanting to disappear into the floor. I hung my head, and I could see my glass shaking in my hand. Tears started spilling down my cheeks. I felt ashamed, although I didn't really know why I felt that way. I did nothing wrong. Even in that kiss, it was him kissing me.

But I kissed him back. I didn't push him away from me. In fact, I wrapped my arms around Nick's neck when he was kissing me. *He* pulled away from *me*. Would I have pulled away from him eventually, or would I have just gotten lost in Nick's kiss if he would have kept on going? I didn't know the answer to this, and the fact that I didn't know the answer made me feel tremendously guilty and ashamed.

Ryan immediately put his arm around me. "Beautiful, please don't cry. Nick told me that he's in love with you, but I know that you did nothing wrong."

"But, I did do something wrong. I did."

Ryan looked at me, his expression changed. "What do you mean?"

"Nick, he kissed me. And I…didn't pull away."

Ryan immediately looked at Nick. "Huh. You didn't tell me this pertinent piece of information."

Alexis finally spoke. "Oh, boy. I think maybe I need to leave the room now. I'll be in the theater room if you need me."

"No, Alexis, it's ok," Ryan said. "I'm not going to get angry. I blame myself, completely, for this. Iris would've never kissed Nick back if I wasn't being such a shit to her."

"Well, that's true," I said. "I felt that you were shutting me out, and I was very vulnerable. But I should be stronger than that."

"Beautiful," he said, putting his hand in my hair. "You're one of the strongest people I know. So, you had a moment of weakness. We all do sometimes." Then he turned to Nick. "But, you, Nick, are another story. You knew that Iris was vulnerable, and you apparently took advantage of this."

"Well, the kiss is a part of why we all need to clear the air and find a path forward," Nick said.

"What do you propose?" Ryan asked.

"I don't want either of you angry with me," Nick said. "I can't help how I feel. I, uh, think that maybe if I could get Iris, uh, out of my system, I would be able to ignore my feelings."

*Out of his system? What, exactly, did he mean by that?*

I just looked at the two of them. "What do you mean, Nick?"

Nick and Ryan just exchanged knowing glances.

*Oh, Christ. Not that.* "Hamptons?" I asked.

Ryan nodded. "Don't be angry, Iris. Nick and I have talked about this before. I didn't think that you would be into it, though."

"I, I, I, don't know. I, uh, I need to think about it." I blushed, not wanting to admit that the idea intrigued me more than I could ever let on. I couldn't deny my attraction to Nick. I was never attracted to him before, simply because I found his arrogance off-putting. But I found, over the course of the period of time that Ryan was recovering, Nick's soft side. And Nick was undeniably beautiful, much like Ryan. He was chiseled and smooth, and his face was unbelievably handsome. Piercing blue eyes, sensuous mouth, strong jawline, thick hair. I never really allowed myself to take in his beauty before, especially during the times that he and I bonded. I denied that I even found him attractive.

"You can think about it, Iris. That's really all that I can ask," Ryan said to me.

That night, after Nick and Alexis went to bed, Ryan and

I stayed up in our room. He laid me down on the bed, and then he kissed me, long, slowly, deeply and passionately. All my muscles turned to jelly at his touch. I took a deep breath as his hands worked down to my breast, touching me lightly underneath my top. "Mmmm," he said, as he gently took off my top, and his lips made their way to where his hands had been. He slowly licked my nipples as his hands made their way down my navel and on to my nether regions. "You taste so good," he said, between long and slow licks to my now-hard nipples. He was fingering me gently, while his other hand was caressing my thigh lightly. Then his lips were, once again, on mine. All the while, he was fingering me. Then, he started to gently lick my clavicle, and his hands were exploring the length of my body. He was nibbling on my ear, his breath coming in more forcefully with every passing moment.

I would never get tired of him. Ever. He was such a sensual lover, and every touch was something that conveyed how he felt about me.

He entered me slowly, slowly, filling me up with every additional inch that leisurely made its way inside of me. I threw back my head in absolute ecstasy. Lovemaking with Ryan was always something that was almost cleansing for me. Cleansing because it was a way for me to forget all the bad that was happening in my life and concentrate on the good that was happening right at that very moment. I always orgasmed with him inside of me, because he always knew just how to touch me in just the right areas.

After we leisurely made love like that, exploring each other's bodies with our tongues, for hours, I laid on my stomach and Ryan gently massaged my back and shoulders. There was nothing else that mattered in the world except for his touch.

"Oh, that feels so good," I said, as he laid on top of my back and gently kissed the back of my neck. "Don't stop that."

He didn't stop that, but continued to massage my shoulders and tongue my back and neck. Then I felt his hardness again, and he gently entered me. I immediately orgasmed again. I couldn't get enough of his touch, and feeling him so close to me. He wrapped his arms around me from behind, and thrust hungrily. "I want to be in your ass," he said, and I couldn't think of anything that I wanted more than that right at that moment. I just nodded my head, and I heard him pour some lube on his hand.

He gently put the lube around the opening. It had been a long time since we had done this, but I remembered how much I enjoyed it before. So, I was really looking forward to it this time as well. Then I felt his enormous shaft enter me in my back door, and I felt the feeling of excruciating pain, then the feeling of excruciating pleasure. The feeling of having him in my ass was so pleasurable that it was almost painful in itself. Every nerve in the body was standing on end, and every synapse was firing at once. It was one of the most pleasurable sensory experiences I had ever had, and I started screaming in ecstasy, begging him not to stop anytime soon.

Unfortunately, it all did come to an end, and he pulled out and laid down beside me on the bed. "Mmmm," he said, stroking my back. "The sex was just as good as I remembered it. You know, you may not have suspected this, but all those weeks that I was lying in bed – I thought about sex with you constantly. I have always enjoyed making love to you more than I have ever enjoyed anything in my life. Nothing has even come close. Not even heroin, believe it or not, and, as you know, that rush is one of the most powerful known to man. No, the rush with you is even more amazing than that, and it always has been. Always."

I looked at him, thinking about the afterglow that I was experiencing. And how I was feeling the same way about him. That nothing ever came close to the feeling that I got when he was inside of me. Nothing.

I also started thinking, for the first time in awhile, about how truly lucky I really was to have a guy like him in love with me. Yes, there had been enormous challenges, none of which would've occurred if I had never known him. If I had never known him, I would probably still have the life I had before – plugging away at a two-bit law office, dating jerks and having it go nowhere, and watching a lot of bad television while I ate Duncan Hines frosting straight out of a can. I wouldn't have been raped, I wouldn't have been threatened, I wouldn't have been in a coma, I wouldn't have had my private life splashed to the entire world, and I wouldn't have ended up in a drug house.

I also wouldn't have been with him. And he was the greatest reward. I would gladly experience everything all over again, just to be with him for a split second more. When I almost lost him, I realized this. It was like before, when I thought that I was going to lose my sister – I made a deal with her that if she survived, I would do anything for her. I think that I kept that promise. With Ryan, I would not only do anything for him, but I would experience every tragedy that life could throw at me, as long as I had him by my side to help me through.

I realized that I was just staring at him. He cocked his head at me a little. "What are you thinking, beautiful?"

I just shook my head, as I felt the familiar tears coming to my eyes again. "Just that I love you. And I would do absolutely anything in this world for you. Just that I'm so damned happy to have you back with me. You almost died, and I thought for a few weeks that you would never return to me. Those were the blackest weeks of my life, to tell you the truth. But now you're here. With me. And I never want to experience the feeling that I have had these past few months. Never. I would rather die than live without you. And I would do everything all over again, exactly as what actually happened, if it meant that I got to stay with you forever."

He said nothing, just kissed me again, and I felt his hardness once more. He entered me again, and I once again felt complete and whole. I wanted that feeling to last forever.

It didn't quite last forever, but it did last for the rest of the night.

# Chapter Thirty-One

Several days went by, and there was no more talk of the possible threesome that was proposed to me the other night. And I didn't much want to bring it up.

What was brought up was the possibility that Ryan and I would soon be purchasing yet another house. We started looking at the homes in the Hallbrook area. The homes that we were looking at were $3 million and up.

I just shook my head. No matter how many years I was with Ryan, I still wouldn't get used to this kind of lifestyle. These homes were the homes that I used to drive around and gawk at, knowing that I could never afford one, but knowing that they were damned fun to look at. Now I was the one who people were gawking at, as I walked the dogs around our posh neighborhoods. I was sure I didn't look the part of somebody who would live there, so I figured that the people who drove around in that neighborhood and saw me would assume that I was a nanny or visiting from out of town.

Nick didn't seem to mind us being there. He was nicer

to me these days, probably because Ryan was around. Or maybe it was because he was getting laid again, as I noticed that he and Alexis had started back up.

I worried about Alexis, though. Nick didn't realize how vulnerable she really was, even though she often tried to put on a tough girl act. He was using her, like he used all the women in his life, and I had no idea how Alexis thought about that.

And Nick still stared at me. I would notice it when I would be swimming in the pool. I would come out of the pool to see that he was looking at me. I noticed it when all of us were eating dinner. I'd look over at him, and he would always be looking at me, not saying a word. He didn't try to look away, either. He just kept staring at me. I felt self-conscious about it, not wanting to admit my attraction to him that was still buried deep inside of me.

Maybe I needed to get him out of my system, too.

But Ryan and I were still going at it like teenagers every chance we got. Thank God Dalilah was a baby who always slept through the night. The problem was that I wasn't getting much sleep, because Ryan and I could never get enough of each other, especially now. We'd make love, then say good night to each other. Then I would feel Ryan's hands on my breasts, and, before I knew it, he was kissing me and thrusting into me again. This happened all through the night, it seemed, and we both were getting precious little sleep.

It was all worth it for me, even though I was starting to become dead tired during the day. But Ryan had to return to work, and I wondered how he was able to do complicated financial transactions while running on little to no sleep.

"It's ok, beautiful. Sleep isn't as important to me as

making up for lost time with you," Ryan said, as he made love to me for the fourth time of the night.

Even though Ryan and I were going gangbusters again, though, I still felt tension coming from Nick. I could feel his eyes boring into me as I walked around the house, even when I had Dalilah in my arms. And Alexis told me that, even though she and Nick were having sex again, Nick talked of little else than me.

"It's me he's fucking, but wishing it was you," she said sadly.

I just shook my head. The threeway scenario was still on the table, I knew, even though none of us had spoken a word about it since it was proposed. I was too nervous to bring it up again, and Ryan and Nick didn't either. But the possibility of it was there, and it was like the elephant in the room that nobody would talk about.

Finally, one day, I told Ryan "Ok."

"Ok?"

"Ok. You, me and Nick. Hamptons. One night only."

Ryan smiled. Then he kissed me. "I love you. You don't have to do this."

"I know," I said, not wanting to tell him that my attraction to Nick was strong and I, too, wanted to have him out of my system. "But I'm intrigued."

"You won't be disappointed," he said.

I somehow knew that to be the absolute truth.

# Chapter Thirty-Two

Ryan, Nick and I found ourselves, the very next night, having drinks out on the terrace. Alexis was gone, as she actually had a date with some guy she met on the Internet. Dalilah was spending the evening with Sheila. Sheila was taking her to Baby Gap, then to see a double feature cartoon at the drive-in movies. She had all of Dalilah's things – her favorite blankets and toys, and a bassinet for her SUV. She figured that Dalilah was probably going to fall asleep in the car, and she anticipated that possibility by making sure that Dalilah would be as comfortable as possible.

So, that night was the perfect night.

I couldn't be more nervous, though.

Nick built a fire in the fire pit, and the three of us sat around it. I didn't quite know how to approach any of it. I was so intrigued by it all, but extremely nervous as well. I mean, these two guys were apparently old pros at this sort of thing – they spent an entire summer hooking up this way with Alexis in between them. But I had never done this sort of thing. I hadn't even seen a porn movie about it.

I looked at Ryan and took a deep breath. "So, how does this all work?" I asked.

He just looked at me for a second. "Uh, beautiful, are you familiar with the concept of a safe word?"

I nodded. "Sure. I had a client who was involved in the BDSM lifestyle, so I learned a lot about that."

"Well, we aren't going to be torturing each other or causing pain or anything like that tonight. Of course. But we are going to be exploring uncharted territory. I want to make sure that all of us are completely comfortable with everything that is about to happen. This kind of thing can be very damaging sometimes if everybody is not on the same level. I mean, it's all very erotic and titillating in theory, but who knows how you're going to feel when you see Nick and I going at it, or how I'm going to feel to see you and Nick going at it. So, we need a safe word that we need to call out if things go too far."

I nodded. "Ok. How about mango?"

I looked at Nick and Ryan, and they both nodded their ascent. "Mango it is," Ryan said.

"Mango it is," said Nick.

"So, how does this get started?" I asked. God, I was nervous, but so aroused at the same time. I was definitely going out of my comfort zone, and I also knew that this was going to be a risk for my relationship with Ryan. What if things change between us because of this?

Then I thought my relationship with Ryan was strong enough to handle much, much bigger challenges than this. We had weathered every storm that life could throw at us – from the tiny rainstorms to the Category 5 tornadoes - and still we were desperately and hopelessly in love with each other.

Nick was the one who spoke up first. "I have actually planned this scenario in my head. It's all I've thought about for awhile, to tell you the truth. And I think that we should all smoke a doob and go skinny dipping."

My heart quickened. This was happening. It was going to happen.

I took another sip of wine. My heart was absolutely pounding in my chest. I saw Nick light up the pipe and take an enormous hit, and then Ryan did the same. The pipe came around to me, and I inhaled mightily, and felt the familiar feeling of my lungs burning. I exhaled and coughed for about a half a minute.

"You ok, beautiful?" Ryan asked me, as he put his arm around me.

I said nothing, merely nodded. "I'm ok," I gasped. "Wow. That was some good shit. Where'd you get that?"

Nick shrugged. "I got connections," he said, as he lit the pipe up for another hit. He passed it to Ryan, then to me, and I inhaled more this time. I tried not to cough it all out this time, but it was very difficult.

"I'm sorry," I said. "I'm not used to this."

"Neither are we," Nick said. "I couldn't tell you the last time I spoke with Mary Jane before tonight. You, Ryan?"

Ryan just shook his head. "I think it's been years, my friend."

I said nothing. It hadn't been that long for me, as I smoked pot with my sister from time to time.

"What about you, Iris?" Nick asked me.

"Uh, well, it's been a few months," I said, remembering that I had seen my sister one night while Ryan was recovering. I had asked Sheila to watch Dalilah for the evening, because I wanted to see my family and relax a little bit. The stress was becoming too much for me. My sister had ended up sharing some ganja, and I had to call Daniel to drive me back.

I blushed, and Ryan just looked at me with an amused expression.

"How are you feeling?" he asked, putting his arm around me.

"Buzzed. Extremely buzzed."

"Well, then, we better stop with the pot for now. I don't want you doing things while you're high that you might regret sober."

"No, no, I'm ok," I said. "I'm just very relaxed."

"How relaxed?" he asked.

"Very relaxed," I said.

"Ok. Now, remember the word 'mango.'"

I nodded.

Then Ryan looked at Nick and nodded his head. He was still kneeling next to me while I sat in my chair. I took another sip of wine. Then, I looked up, and Nick was peeling off his clothes. I felt the familiar feeling of flushing and heart palpitations as I saw him, naked, for the first time.

Breathe, Iris, breathe. Nick was beautiful, like the statue of David, with a much larger member. Much larger member. I gasped a little when I got to see him in all his glory.

Either he's a shower, not a grower, or I'm going to be in big trouble. Of course, I was used to such proportions from being with Ryan. Still, I didn't quite imagine Nick would look like that.

Nick dove into the pool and started swimming around. "Come on in," he said, enticingly. "It's heated. And, even it wasn't heated, it will be very soon."

At that, Ryan looked at me. "Remember, mango," he whispered in my ear. Then he peeled off his clothes and dove into the pool as well.

The two guys swam around a little, while I hung back. *Mango, mango, mango, mango* I thought in my head. All I had to do was say one little word, and the three of us would go our separate ways for the evening.

I took a deep breath, and took off my own clothes, leaving my underwear on. I felt extremely self-conscious, even through the influence of the ganja and the wine, but aroused like I had never been in my life. Down below me, in the pool, were two of the most beautiful specimens of men I had ever set my eyes on, and I was soon going to be enjoying both of them.

Even if it was only for one night, how lucky could a girl be?

I dipped my way into the pool, feeling the warm water surrounding me. I self-consciously put my hands over my breasts, wondering if I should call the whole thing off, or pursue this as a fantasy that could come true for the night. Only for the night.

Ryan came up to me, his naked body pressed up against mine. "We have until midnight, beautiful, or even later," he said, referring to the fact that Sheila and Dalilah would be at the drive-in until at least that time. "What would you like to do?"

My heart pounding in my ears, I said, softly "let's go."

At that, Ryan started kissing me while I was in his arms. Then he led me over to where Nick was, and I felt Nick's lips on mine. His kiss was soft and gentle, his lips feathering on mine. I was aware that I had lost my breath, much like when I first kissed Ryan. The word mango no longer was in my thoughts as I felt like devouring the best friend of the man who I loved more than anything in this world.

Ryan whispered in my ears "would you like to take off your underwear, beautiful?"

I nodded and said nothing.

Then Ryan put me up on the side of the pool, and gently brought down my panties. I could feel his tongue gently stroking my vagina. While he was doing this, Nick was above me. "Lay back," he said gently. I obeyed. He sat above my head, and lowered his lips to mine. That feeling was unlike any I had ever experienced. Nick was such a delicious kisser - firm yet gentle, commanding yet tentative. And Ryan's tongue stroking me – oh, there were no words. No words.

My breath started coming rapidly, and I had the most powerful orgasm I had ever had. I moaned in ecstasy as Nick's hands started on my clavicle and worked their way to my naked breasts. I was completely losing myself in the moment.

Then I was being lifted out of the water, and I was being laid down poolside. I could feel Ryan's enormous cock making its way inside of me, and I gasped. I looked above me, and Ryan and Nick were kissing each other. God, this was the most erotic moment of my life. Ryan was thrusting hungrily inside of me, while he was, just as hungrily, devouring the beautiful face of Nick.

Then Ryan and Nick were no longer kissing each other, but Ryan was still thrusting inside of me. Now it was Nick who was kissing me again, his hands running the length of my stomach and landing on my clitoris. He rubbed my clit lightly. His hands and fingers were commanding, just as commanding as he was in his own life.

I could feel Ryan come inside of me.

Nick whispered to me "Can I taste him?" I said nothing, just nodded. So, he flipped me over on my stomach, and I could feel his tongue working its way inside of me. While he was doing this, Ryan was sitting next to me, stroking my hair and my back, and massaging my shoulders.

The sensory overload of that moment was something that made me want to spontaneously combust. I was on my stomach, and Ryan was stroking my back and shoulders, while Nick's tongue was assertively exploring inside of me. Then Ryan was lying next to me, and he started kissing me hungrily on the mouth. Ryan's hand was on his own enormous shaft, so I put my hand on it and stroked him firmly.

Nick laid on top of me, and he whispered "Can I enter you?"

I nodded my head, way too aroused to even try to say no. Then I heard him unwrap a condom and put it on his cock. As his enormous penis entered me, I gasped, then took Ryan's own cock and put it in my mouth. I could hear the sounds of the two of them kissing, and I exploded again.

So far, this was something that I had never experienced, and I was driven to the very height of ecstasy. Then Nick grabbed my hair, pulling my head back while slapping me hard on the ass. I started breathing heavily, the word "mango" running in my head, as he slapped me twice more. But every synapse in my body was firing and every nerve was tingling. Somehow his slapping me just heightened the sensory overload. I felt my entire body shake like an earthquake that I had never, ever, experienced in my life. I had to bite my tongue to keep from screaming in both ecstasy and pain, as he slapped me again and again.

I couldn't scream. We were outdoors still, and, although

Nick's house was extremely private, I still didn't feel comfortable making a lot of noise.

Then Nick brought my head up again, and my mouth was once again on Ryan's shaft. I licked his shaft hungrily, up and down, up and down, while Nick was behind me, urgently pounding me and spanking me at the same time. I was hyperventilating by then, because there was just so much going on, and my body was heating up to an extent that I had never known it before. What were the feelings that were going through my body? Pleasure and pain were mixed in together, so that I didn't really know which was which. I only knew that the pleasure and the pain were both heightened to a degree that I could barely stand it.

Nick was finally spent. I felt him pull out, and I heard him breathing extremely hard, like he had just run a marathon. I was still working on Ryan, though, my hands running the length of his torso, and my fingers massaging his butt opening. I heard him groan. "Stop, beautiful, I want to be inside you again."

So, I laid down on my back, and Ryan was inside of me. I felt him explode inside of me, then he covered my body with his.

I continued to lay on the concrete, completely naked. I looked over at Nick. He was only illuminated by the moonlight, and he was lying next to me. Then he started to stroke my body some more. "Oh, what have we started now?" he asked, as he stroked my breasts and kissed me. Ryan was also next to me, on the other side, and he, too, was stroking and touching me all over. I couldn't stand it anymore. The pleasure was just too intense. I had to come down a little bit.

So, I said "Um, I'm going to go and get some drinks for everybody."

"Sure, beautiful," Ryan said. "We'll be right here."

"Ok," I said, going into the kitchen. I found some vodka and some Blood Mary mix, and put the contents into a glass with some Tabasco and black pepper. I put it all into a plastic glass and took the three drinks outside.

Ryan and Nick were sitting by the side of the pool, and I sat down next to them with the drinks in hand. I realized that my arms and legs were still shaking, and I felt light-headed as I drank my cocktail.

"You ok, beautiful?" Ryan asked me, putting his arm around my naked shoulder. "I didn't hear the safe word, so I guess that you were having a good time."

"You might say that," I said with a smile.

"Good," he said. Then he and Nick met behind me as I sat by the edge of the pool, and I could hear them kissing. "Beautiful," he said. "Tell me that you won't freak out to see Nick and I together."

I was back to reality, brought back by this little interlude. "In what way?"

"What you're thinking," he said.

"No," I said, actually realizing that the prospect was intriguing and titillating to me. "Anything goes tonight, right?"

"Ok," he said, as Nick moved over to Ryan's side. I watched as Nick ran his hands over Ryan's chest and abs, then his head made its way to Ryan's shaft. Ryan groaned as Nick's head bobbed up and down. The sight of these two beautiful men together, one of whom was the love of my life, was strangely erotic to me. I never imagined this sort of thing would be so intriguing.

I made my way over to Ryan, who was obviously getting great pleasure out of what Nick was doing. I started kissing him passionately, my hands running over his chest and abs and into his hair. His breathing was heavy, heavier than anything I had heard from him so far. "Oh, shit," he said, as he evidently climaxed again in Nick's mouth.

Ryan shook his head. "I have to admit it's been awhile since something like this has happened. But that was fucking amazing."

"I'm going to have you return the favor, Ryan, a little later," Nick said. "Right now, though, I say we all take a swim and get into the hot tub and go some more."

So, all of us got into the pool. I floated around the pool a little bit by using some of Nick's noodles. Ryan came up to me and dunked me playfully. When I came up for air, he picked me up and started kissing me again. "God, this has been an amazing night. Thank you so much for being willing to experience this with me. I hope you're having a good time."

"Oh, yes I am. Yes, I am. This has been amazing for me as well."

Nick came up to me. "I'm feeling left out over there," he said, as he put his hands on my bare breasts. He kissed Ryan, then kissed me. I felt aroused again as he continued to slowly roll his tongue around in my mouth. I could taste the Bloody Mary, mixed with Ryan's hot cum, on him in his kiss. Ryan continued to hold me in his arms while Nick continued to kiss and stroke me softly and slowly. Then they were kissing again while Ryan fingered me lightly. I could hear both of their breathing and both of their hearts pounding.

Nick said "what do you say we continue this inside?"

Ryan looked at me. I felt a little like I was having an out-of-body experience. "We have until around midnight," I said. I had asked Sheila to text me before she headed home with Dalilah, so I knew that they wouldn't be home for awhile.

So, all of us headed inside and into Nick's room and his king-sized bed. There, the three of us were intertwined for the next few hours. My connections with Nick had an urgency to it, from both of us, because we both knew that this was the first and last night we would have together. I was able to play out the fantasies that I never really allowed myself to have with him. There was an undercurrent of tremendous attraction to him that I had buried deep within my psyche, and this was playing out between us. And it was so obvious he felt the same way about me.

Yet, this was somehow safe. Ryan was there, and Ryan was approving every move that Nick and I made with each other. If Ryan only said the safe word, the playing would end abruptly. But he never did. He encouraged us to devour one another hungrily, right in front of him. And, as the witching hour was quickly approaching, that was what Nick and I did. We were almost in a frenzy with each other, and also with Ryan in the middle of it all.

Nick was kissing me with an urgent passion. It was as if he had to put all of the past we didn't have, and the future we'd never have, into the present, which was all there was for us. And he took advantage of this present. He entered me again, making sure to use a condom, and the intercourse had the same urgent passion as his kisses. As he thrust inside of me, I stroked Ryan's hard shaft. Then I lay down on my stomach, and put my lips on Ryan's manhood, and my fingers inside his sphincter. He groaned and gave me a mouthful. And, a few minutes later, Nick climaxed as well.

I looked at the clock. It read 11:30. I then looked at Nick. "Uh, I think it's time."

He said nothing, just nodded. "Tonight was amazing. I mean, Ryan and I have done this kind of thing before, but it was never like this. Amazing."

Ryan stroked me, and smoothed back my hair. "I've wanted this to happen for awhile now. I'm just so happy you were open-minded enough to try it."

"Me too," I said. "It was a different experience for me, and it was one of the most erotic evenings of my entire life. Bar none."

"Well, we need to get to our room," Ryan said.

As we left, I gave one last glance back at Nick. He was watching both of us, his expression indiscernible. I hoped this night had the needed effect on both of us – getting each other out of each other's system. Our attraction to each other had no place to go, so we had put it all out there tonight. Of course, the risk was that the night would only result in the two of us wanting each other more. But that didn't matter – I might have been attracted to Nick, but I didn't love him. I only loved Ryan, and the sex between Ryan and me was amazing in and of itself.

I had no need to be with Nick again.

I hoped he felt the same about me.

# Chapter Thirty-Three

I woke up the next day in Ryan's arms. The light was streaming through the window, and Ryan was still fast asleep.

I felt nervous about the previous night. It was all so incredible, so fucking incredible, in the heat of the moment. But it was like how I was in the drug house – the highs that were experienced were out of this world, but the aftermath was more horrible than could be believed. I hoped that the three of us wouldn't have a similar hangover. The whole thing might backfire on all of us, and cause problems that were unforeseen when we all were enjoying ourselves last night.

I nudged Ryan awake.

"Huh," he said, with a start. Then he blinked a few times. "Oh my God. Was last night a dream?"

"No. Not unless we've learned to synchronize our dreams."

"Ok. I thought I had the most amazing and erotic dream, but that really happened, huh?"

"Yeah. You feeling ok about all of that?"

"Of course. You were quite the cuckold. I never knew you had it in you."

I smiled. "I have plenty of surprises. But I can't reveal all at this point. You might get bored with me if you know all there is to know about me."

"Fat chance," he said. Then he lifted up the sheet. "Amazing. Even after all that, I still want you badly." Then he rolled me over on my side, and entered me gently. He wrapped his arms around me while he thrust. "Just a little quickie before we go to breakfast, I promise," he said. I nodded, feeling myself explode again. I thought that I would have been spent after all that happened the night before, but that wasn't the case. In fact, I felt that my orgasm was stronger than usual that morning.

Within a few minutes, I heard him groan, then pull out. Then, he kissed me full on the mouth. "We have to go down and get some breakfast," he said between kisses. "As much as I just want to stay here with you in bed all morning long."

"Oh, me too. Me too."

He kissed me for about fifteen minutes more, then sighed. "Ok, this is the last time, I promise," he said as he entered me again.

I felt a little bit guilty about not going down to breakfast and seeing our daughter, but that was outweighed by the feeling that I was getting with every urgent thrust.

Ryan and I finally made our way to the breakfast table around 10 AM. With a start, Ryan saw a familiar face around the table – his sister, Sarah.

Sarah rose and gave him and me a hug.

"Sarah, what are you doing here?"

"Um, I flew here last night. I couldn't get ahold of you,

227

so I got a hotel room last night, and came in this morning to see you."

"You flew?" Ryan said, more surprised about this tidbit than the fact that she was there at all. "Where's Cori?"

"Gil's watching him."

"I don't understand."

"Sit down," she said.

I looked at Ryan, whose face was suddenly white as a sheet. There was obviously bad news that was being brought, and I silently prayed Maggie was okay.

Ryan took a seat and just sat there and looked at Sarah silently. "Mom?" he said.

"No," Sarah said shaking her head. "Dad."

Ryan took a breath and let it out. Then he looked down at his hands, then back at his sister. "When? How?"

"Yesterday. He…his cancer came back. But he never told anybody. He passed away about seven o'clock last night."

Ryan just nodded. "When…"

"I don't know. I suppose he should be brought here, because this was where he spent most of his life."

I looked at his face, and I think I could read what he was thinking. While we were going at it, his father was breathing his last, and Sarah couldn't get ahold of him to tell him.

Ryan continued to look at his hands. "Thank God we made our peace, huh?" he said. "Thank God for that."

"Yes, that's what I was thinking," Sarah said. "Are you going to be ok?"

Ryan just continued to nod his head. "Yes, yes, of course, of course. Uh, I guess you and I better start making arrangements, huh?"

"That's why I'm here."

I finally chimed in. "Is there anything I can do?"

Ryan shook his head. "I'm uh, sure there is, but I just don't know what it would be just yet."

"I'll do anything that you need me to do," I said. "Anything at all."

Ryan looked at Dalilah, who was sitting in her high chair and eating her breakfast. "Dalilah never got to meet him. Why does that make me sad?"

Sarah took Ryan's hand. "I'm sure you're feeling complicated emotions right now. Do you need to talk about any of them?"

"No, no. I don't know if my emotions are complicated. I mean, that man made my life a living hell. But I forgave him. There were no more words to say." But, at that, he went into Nick's den. "I need to be alone for a second, ok?" he said to nobody in particular.

Nick was sitting there at the table as well, but he was so quiet, I almost didn't notice him.

I needed Nick's guidance on this again, but last night made things very awkward between us, to say the least. "Um, Nick….do you think Ryan's going to be ok?"

"I'd say so. I don't know, though. Ryan had a real love-hate relationship with his father, as you surely know."

I decided to go into the den and see for myself how he was doing.

He was sitting there, motionless, staring at the fireplace that had no fire in it. I sat down and put my hand around his back. He looked at me, smiled wanly, then looked back down at the floor.

He didn't talk for a few minutes. Then he said "it hasn't hit me yet. But it's going to seem weird, you know? My father hasn't been in my life, yet he has always been so ever-present at the same time. He always knew what I was doing, and he was always there to help me. Like a father should.

So, it's strange – in a way, he acted like a father should act. Protective, willing to do anything to help me, even if the help was only coming from afar. Yet, he ruined my entire life as well. I...don't know how to feel about this. What to think about this."

"I understand," I said. "There's probably a part of you that's glad he's gone, but another part of you that just wants your dad. No matter his flaws, he gave you life. So, feel how you feel, but don't try to judge it. Whatever your emotions about this, just know there is no wrong feeling."

"I know," he said. "But, right now, there really isn't time to sit here and ruminate about it. Sarah and I have to plan everything."

"Of course," I said.

At that, Ryan and I left the den and made our way to the kitchen table again to talk to Sarah and make arrangements.

# Chapter Thirty-Four

The next few days were a whirlwind. Benjamin had made out a living will, which specified that he was to be cremated and his ashes scattered in the Atlantic Ocean, off the coast where he made his home in Rhode Island. It turned out that he was very fond of that particular mansion, and it was apparently his favorite home. Yet, Benjamin's life was here, for the most part, and his friends and business associates were all here as well.

So, Sarah and Ryan decided to have a memorial here in Kansas City, then have another service in Rhode Island when Benjamin would be scattered at sea. Benjamin's yacht would be used to scatter his ashes, as the state law specified that such services had to be performed a certain distance from the shore.

I made sure Ryan was feeling mentally ok, but I sensed this was not the case. Dalilah apparently picked up on Ryan's distress as well, as she watched him with her eyes everywhere he went. "Daddy sad?" she asked me.

"Yes, very much so," I said, although I wasn't quite sure exactly how Ryan was feeling.

It turned out that part of his distress was the possibility that some of the people who would be attending the service would be some of the same people who tormented him at the sex parties all those years ago.

"What if I see somebody and I start remembering things again?" he said. Then he shook his head. "I can't think about this," he said. "Not right now. Right now, I have to get through the next week or so."

"I'm right here," I said. "If you feel any kind of anxiety, just let me know."

"Thank God you're here," he said. "I don't know what I would do without you."

"I feel the same," I said.

I helped Ryan write the eulogy, and I was right there when he and Sarah visited the funeral home and had to prepare the service.

The memorial occurred outdoors, and I was half afraid that it would not be well-attended, considering how Benjamin must have alienated a lot of people. That fear was not founded, though, as around 200 people showed up to see Ryan eulogize his father. Several other people spoke about him, as well. They talked about his charitable work and his enormous heart. I learned some things about him I would have never imagined.

I learned he financially supported street kids, and was personally responsible for fifty of these kids being able to pursue a good education at top schools. That his philanthropy extended to many different causes that were disparate – he helped animals, the environment, and people starving in Africa. Other people talked about his stay at the ashram, which was the reason why he was able to turn his life around.

I didn't know the man these people spoke of. I only knew Benjamin tormented my husband, and then was able to get my husband to forgive him. I was surprised that all of these people had such affection for the man, but it seemed they did. They didn't seem to be acting.

Afterward, everybody met at a five star restaurant that was rented out for the occasion. Ryan made his way around and tried to talk to everybody.

I drifted my way around as well. I heard snippets of conversation. "He only had three heirs. They're going to be set for life." And "I know! I didn't know the man they were eulogizing, either. I only knew a misogynistic bastard."

I wanted to go up to these people and scream at them "A man is dead. Dead. Please refrain from making rude comments for just this one day!"

Instead, I bit my tongue and went on.

I drank from the open bar for several hours, not really knowing what to do with myself. Ryan was still making the rounds, then I saw him and Sarah in the corner talking.

Ryan made his way over to me. He took my hands. "Uh, Sarah has to get back to her home soon. So, we scheduled the reading tomorrow. I hope you can be there with me."

I nodded. "Of course. That goes without saying."

The next day, we met with the attorney for Benjamin in a huge downtown high rise. Ryan and Sarah were very quiet. Maggie came in the law office as well. She didn't attend the service, telling Ryan and Sarah she had no desire to have anything to do with Benjamin at all. She never got the chance to make her peace with her ex-husband.

Ryan turned to me. "Uh, you might be shocked a little

at what my father was worth. I just wanted to warn you, in case you feel like freaking out."

"Uh, I wouldn't be freaked out about anything at this point."

How wrong I was.

The lawyer informed Ryan, Maggie and Sarah that Benjamin's will called for the three of them to split his assets three ways in equal measures. He read through the list of Benjamin's property, which included stocks, paintings, coin collections, homes, and savings.

The total value of his assets was valued at $35 billion.

I couldn't help it. My mouth flew open. $35 billion? How much money? Huh?

I heard little else. Suddenly Ryan and I were billionaires. Not merely millionaires, but billionaires. Multi-billionaires at that. Each of the three got around $11 billion in assets. Billion with a B.

After the reading, I sat next to Ryan in silence on the way home in the Escalade. I had to process it all. We were suddenly not just rich, but super-rich, and if it took me awhile to get used to being wealthy, it would take me that much longer to adjust to being super-wealthy.

"What are you thinking, beautiful?"

"Just that none of this seems entirely real. I mean, that much money would never seem real to me. And I used to say you could have too much money and you can also be too intelligent. That excessive money and excessive intelligence causes problems. Now, I have a little girl who is going to have both things, and I worry about how she will adjust."

"I understand. But look at it this way. We have enough money now that we can do absolutely anything we want. We could do a lot of good in the world with this kind of money, even more than the money we already had. The sky's he limit. I always thought that, after my father passes, I would really like to get actively involved with setting a foundation that would be multi-faceted and geared towards improving the welfare of animals around the world."

I looked at him. "That would be the best idea ever. Using this money to really do some good in the world, instead of just possessing it for selfish reasons."

"Of course. There is just no way that I would just want to have this money just sitting in a bank somewhere, not doing anybody any good. You and I could become a team to figure out the best way to use this money."

I smiled. I knew that Ryan wouldn't give all of his father's money away, but I thought he probably would give a great deal of it away at any rate. "That sounds great! We should get on that as soon as we can."

Ryan looked at me, and took my hands. "Things will change now. We need to figure out our future. It's not just finding a new home, but I also need to figure out if I want to continue on at the bank or quit there and spend my time establishing a foundation." Then he paused. "And Nick. I don't really know what will happen with that. I haven't had the chance to really talk to him since that night."

"Yes," I said. "Nick. He hasn't been on my mind, either, lately. For obvious reasons."

I found myself thinking about how our lives would be changing from then on. We would soon be living in a different house, and Nick would no longer be a part of our everyday lives. I had mixed emotions about that, to be perfectly honest. On the one hand, it would be a relief to get some distance from Nick. Ryan and I needed that distance, because Ryan and I had to move forward with our lives together. We had a child to raise, and a future to figure out. And, as much fun as the other night was, it couldn't happen again. I knew that, and I really didn't want it.

I also wondered if Ryan would feel emotional devastation again. After all, even though Benjamin wasn't the best father in the world (what an understatement!), he was still Ryan's father. And they had made their peace with one another in Rhode Island. Ryan forgave him, and even kind of understood him and found a way to love his father again.

But he seemed very serene about everything. "I don't have any regrets," he said. "And, as much as I found that I had loved him towards the end, this was something I was prepared for. My father was lucky to have the extra year or so that he got. I thought for sure he was a goner when I went to see him at his Newport home. But he recovered and was able to have some more time. So, that was a gift for him."

He paused some. "I guess what I'm saying is that I did my grieving about this already. And I'll be okay. As long as you and Dalilah are with me, I'll be okay."

Nick was another story.

"I'm sorry, Iris. I thought I could get you out of my system. But it didn't seem to work. I'm more in love with you than ever," he said, when we finally got a chance to talk to him alone.

*Oh, boy.* "Nick, you're going to be okay," I said. "These past few weeks have been intense, but, soon, Ryan and I won't be here every day, and you can get on with your life. Maybe this was all a sign you're supposed to look past the superficial and find the woman inside. I mean, I'm not a supermodel by any stretch of the imagination. Yet, you had feelings for me. That means that maybe you can look for somebody who isn't as beautiful, but is nice, and will love you for your wonderful qualities."

"Don't kid yourself. You are beautiful," he said. "I didn't think that at first, but I completely think that now. Your beauty is in your strength and your vulnerability. It's in your complete guilelessness. It's in your loyalty and devotion. It's in everything about you."

Ryan was actually in the room with us while all this was going on. "I really don't know what to say," he said. "This is the first time you haven't lost interest in a woman you'd slept with. My luck, the first woman is my wife."

So I guessed there might continue to be some kind of strain on Ryan and Nick's friendship, and my friendship with Nick as well. But that seemed to be a small problem, considering that my future with Ryan was appearing to be smooth sailing from there on out. There weren't any kind of threats on the horizon. Andrew was dead. Rochelle was still out there, which sucked, but I somehow didn't think she would continue to be a problem. I'd recovered from my traumas and Ryan seemed to be on the mend from his emotional issues as well. Dalilah would be a handful, I knew, but also knew she had the potential to be amazing. Ryan and I had to look for ways to nurture her talents and intelligence so she would end up reaching the potential given at her birth. If Ryan and I could only have some uninterrupted time where we could just move forward, we would be unstoppable.

Absolutely unstoppable.

So, Ryan and I made plans for our new home, and made plans for our future. I didn't know what the future would hold at that time. I only knew that, for the first time, there was a light at the end of the tunnel.

I could breathe for the first time in I didn't know how long.

There was one thing I learned, really learned, in my

relationship with Ryan. And that was that I no longer thought that people had it made, while others struggled. I realized everybody struggled with the same types of issues. Alexis struggled with mental illness and loneliness. Maggie did as well. Nick also struggled with loneliness, and he also had the added pressure of being extraordinarily handsome and rich, which, ironically, lured the exactly wrong type of woman into his life. Ryan struggled with his demons and his past. Natalie struggled with insecurities. I did as well. It was remarkable how much we were all the same, and I felt, perhaps for the first time, that I really belonged in Ryan's world. Yes, I wasn't as beautiful as them, nor as rich. But that was all superficial stuff that really doesn't matter in the end.

In the end, it really only mattered who you were inside. I know that's a cliché, but things are cliché for a reason – clichés are generally true. I always was under the illusion that beauty and wealth equals a great life, and now I know that's not true. That doesn't mean wealthy and beautiful people can't have a great life, though. It just means that it's not guaranteed.

So, even though Ryan and I were catapulted into the pantheon of the super-rich in one fell swoop, I hoped nothing would really change. I hoped that I wouldn't change, and I prayed that Ryan wouldn't change either. And I really hoped that Dalilah wouldn't grow up spoiled and bratty. I hoped we could just find happiness, the same as people around the world find it – through their relationships, friendships, family and work. There no longer was the illusion that simply being wealthy would mean we would be happy. We had to make our own happiness, whether we had $13 billion dollars in the bank, or $13 in the bank.

I suddenly realized that it was the end of illusions.

# Epilogue

## IRIS

## Five Years Later

"Hey, Sammy, how're you doing?" I said. "I was wondering where you are with our suppliers?" There was a shipment of vaccines that were due any day now, and there were 100 dogs in desperate need of them.

"They should be in tomorrow around 5 PM," Sammy said. "I know how important it is that we get those in as soon as possible, so I put a rush order on them."

"Thanks," I said. There was so much to do. Running an animal sanctuary was hard work, much harder than I ever could have imagined. It was stressful and heart-breaking. It was also the most rewarding thing that I had ever done in my life. Bar none. It was a beautiful thing to have the money to really fund something like this properly. You could get so much done with the right cash flow, I was finding.

We had started out, five years ago, small. Ryan and I got all the necessary permits to open up an animal shelter that took in dogs and cats. Neither of us had much experience in this sort of thing. I mean, I did pit bull rescues when Ryan and I had met, and continued to do this, periodically, for years. But that was my extent of knowing about how to run an animal shelter. Ryan had no experience at all in that sort of thing. So, there was a steep learning curve, I was finding. But it helped that we had the money to hire the best talent there was. We found an executive director with 30 years experience. Our fund-raisers were second to none. Our veterinarians were also top-notch. Most importantly, we were able to find people who had on-the-ground experience running a shelter.

And our dogs and cats were in the lap of luxury. No cement pens and small cages for them. With help from a socialization expert, we were able to group animals in large rooms that were outfitted with toys, blankets and cushions. These dogs had each other, and that was important. Dogs are pack animals, and we acknowledged that. We also gave each of these dogs love and exercise – we did it, we found volunteers to do this, and also hired quite a few full-time employees dedicated to giving the dogs the proper care and love they deserved.

After about a year of running the shelter full-time, we decided to branch out into a sanctuary that would take in all kinds of different animals. We bought several acres of land, and we took in everything from llamas and goats to horses and cows. We also took in wild animals. Whenever there was a case of horses neglected and starving, we were one of the first people contacted. If there was an injured deer, she was brought to us. If there was a pit bull ring busted, the dogs were brought to us. We were busy making sure that as many animals as possible were rehabilitated and either returned to the wild or given a loving home. Some just became full-time residents, for whatever reason – perhaps they were too old for most people, or perhaps they were in need of socialization.

And, as promised by Ryan, all those years ago, Polly the horse came to live at our sanctuary full-time. She was just as beautiful as ever, and she seemed to remember me. Ryan bought himself a horse as well, and Dalilah got her own pony. Horseback riding became something we enjoyed as a family, and we tried to go out on trails at least once a week.

Life was wonderful. We were running the sanctuary full-time, and Ryan decided that there was a need to branch out. After all, there were animals all over the world that were neglected and abused, and they needed our help. We had the money to make a difference. Not many people could say that. So, Ryan developed an international foundation dedicated to helping animals around the world. Part of the foundation was devoted to lobbying efforts on behalf of factory farm animals. This part of the foundation was dedicated to trying to influence legislation that affected animals. Part of the foundation was dedicated to research that would alleviate the pressures that farmers had, so that there would be a possibility that food could be raised in a much more ethical manner, while still affording a profit to the farmers who raised the food. Part of the foundation was simply supplying grant funding to organizations geared towards helping animals. And part of the foundation was focused upon pushing for international treaties that would require that animals have more protections in other countries. And another part of the foundation was strictly PR. That part of the foundation was focused upon getting the word out about the plight of research animals, factory farm livestock and the like.

Of course, our lives were not completely focused around animals. It was just a passion that we were able to develop, because we had a never-ending spigot of money that would help us really make a difference in the world.

And, of course, we had to walk the walk, so we became vegans and gave up any kind of animal products around the home. That was challenging at first, but I found a great vegan chef who taught us how to get proper nutrition and make everything taste great. I learned from her enough that I became a pretty good vegan cook myself, so myself, Ryan and Dalilah always had delicious and nutritious food on the table.

But our passions were not just for our animals – all of our animals – but also for each other. I was right five years ago – Ryan and I had gone through fire. Through some of the worst things that could possibly happen to anybody. And it didn't break us, although I often thought, while I was in the thick of it, that it would. Actually, looking back, I realized that all of our trials strengthened us. We knew that we could get through the worst things that life could throw at us, come what may. Because of this, little problems that cropped up were just that – little problems. We had our everyday quarrels and disagreements, then would realize that if everything that happened to us didn't break us, nothing would.

And it also helped us, because it made us realize that life was so very fleeting. Ryan almost died, and so did I. If the bullet had landed a millimeter to the left or the right, then he probably wouldn't be here. And, if he was here, he would be permanently in a wheelchair. But he was alive and he was perfectly healthy, so he was eternally grateful, and so was I. But, because we were faced with the ephemeral nature of life, we knew that we had to savor every single moment with each other, because we knew, probably more than most people, that every moment with each other could be our last.

So, we savored every moment with each other. Our passion for each other never dimmed even one iota. We had been together for over seven years at this point, and we loved each other more today than we did yesterday, and would love each other even more tomorrow. It was kind of crazy that we were able to find one another and stay together despite the odds, but we were both so glad that we did.

And Dalilah was living up to her potential so far. She took after her father – she was just under six years old, and she already had read several books that were at a college level. She wasn't quite reading Proust, but she was reading Dickens and even Tolstoy. Even so, some of her favorite books were *Harry Potter* and *Twilight*. And her artwork was amazingly sophisticated. She really was a prodigy in that area. Her work had a sophistication well beyond her years. Ryan was able to teach her the art fundamentals and techniques, and she took to them like a Golden Retriever to lake water. She had studied some of the genres, and was able to come up with a fusion that was distinctively hers. A little bit cubism, a little bit impressionism, and a lot surrealism. I couldn't believe my eyes when she created her little masterpieces. A future Van Gogh, I thought.

And she was just as strong-willed as I thought she would be. There was no telling her what to do. She had a mind of her own, and she had her own thoughts. I found myself wishing that she was just a normal child – learning to read, making friends in school, having sleepovers and generally being a kid. Dalilah didn't have too much trouble fitting in at school, though. She was in a very exclusive private school that was extremely rigorous, so she was stimulated as much as possible. The teachers had suggested that she skip some grades, but Dalilah refused to even consider it.

"No, mom. I won't do it. I have friends in my class, and they won't talk to me if I skip ahead. Anyhow, I don't really want to be around older kids. They're bigger than me and they already have their cliques. So, if you really want me to be a social pariah, go ahead and skip me ahead. But if you want me to be a happy, well-adjusted child, then I suggest that you leave me exactly where I am."

I was the lawyer, yet she was the skilled debater.

I just sighed. "But, Dalilah, aren't you a little bored? Most of those kids are just learning to read, and you're already on the classics."

Dalilah just shrugged. "Yeah, it's boring. But my gifted and talented courses are challenging enough. There are other kids in there who are almost at my level. And, if you think about it, school doesn't really mean that much to me, academically-wise. It's most important for my social well-being, and, socially, I'm doing very well. So, please, mom, please leave me where I am."

So, Dalilah stayed right where she was – she was six years old and still in the first grade. She was exactly where she wanted to be, and I had a feeling that she would be calling the shots on her life for the rest of our lives.

And Nick – well, that was another story for another day. He finally fell out of love with me, thank God, and he became our greatest asset and friend. And he finally found somebody to love. Somebody real who loved him for him, and not for his pocketbook. He was happier than I had ever seen him. His man-whore ways were gone. The woman was so not like his usual bimbos, and she gave him a hard time when he first tried to pursue her. But he won out in the end, and won her heart.

Even Alexis was doing well. She was able to stay on her meds and was stable ever since her stay in the mental hospital more than five years ago. She also was able to finally give up the illegal drugs that had haunted her life. Ryan helped her overcome all of her demons, and gave her money to live on for a few years. But she was doing so much better that she was able to find another law job, albeit at a much smaller salary than before, so she no longer had to rely upon Ryan. She had to learn how to live like a normal person, which meant that her standards were lowered quite a bit. Her new job had a wonderful perk, however – she met somebody there who she promptly fell in love with, and they started living happily together within a few months of meeting.

That person was a woman, which surprised Alexis as much as it did everybody else.

Alexis and her girlfriend, Anna, even made plans to be married. So, there was an invitation that came in the mail announcing this ceremony. I was excited to meet Anna, as was Ryan. We were even more excited to find out that Alexis and Anna were in the process of adopting a child from Russia. Alexis had found out what all of us had – that love was the only thing in life that mattered. Once she figured that out, she was able to find peace and no longer had the need to overspend.

As for Natalie – she and Nate were on their third child. Natalie had long since quit her job at Goldman Sachs to become a full-time mom. We went to visit them at least twice a year, in their new house in Connecticut, and there no longer was the undercurrent of tension. Natalie loved Nate and now merely saw Ryan as a really good friend. We were actually able to laugh about all that happened before with Natalie and the pregnancy issue. I never thought that was possible, but it was.

All in all, we were happy. Really, really happy. Yes, we were literally billionaires. Just one of our Rembrandt paintings that was inherited from Benjamin would give us enough money to live on for about 1,000 lifetimes. But that didn't matter. We didn't live like billionaires. We lived well, but we didn't sit around and just try to amass more money. We made a difference in the lives of these animals, and we made a difference in the lives of each other and our friends.

This was our story. Nothing was ever perfect in life, but, all in all, it came damned close.

# More by Annie Jocoby

**She has never been kissed. He has kissed half of Manhattan.**

When the shy, traumatized grad student catches the eye of New York's most notorious billionaire playboy, sparks fly—but old wounds threaten to tear them apart before they've even begun.

Turn the page for a free preview…

# Broken: Chapter One

## SCOTTY

"Scotty Marie!" the woman cried in the bar where I worked. She was slovenly dressed, her tie-dyed A-Shirt barely covering her 280 lb girth. She was evidently on her 800th vodka tonic of the evening, for her words were slurred, and she was swaying. She leaned on the bar, apparently trying to stop herself from falling. "Scotty Marie, I'm talking to you! Don't ignore me!!!"

Lane, the other bartender on duty that night, gave me a sympathetic look and motioned to the irate woman. "You better tend to her. You know she won't leave on her own."

I sighed. It was happening more and more frequently these days.

"Mom," I said to the woman. "You have to leave. I'm working here."

"You have to come home. I can't handle Aaron on my own."

I rolled my eyes. Aaron was my 2-year-old brother. I was 23 years old my mother was 38, having gotten knocked up by yet another of her one-night stands. She probably never even got this particular trick's name.

"Mother, I have to work." I wanted to tell her she made her bed, she better lie in it, but there wouldn't be any reasoning with her right this very minute. Her eyes were bloodshot, and she reeked, absolutely reeked, of Popov Vodka. Since she drank so much of the stuff, she had to buy the cheapest. I felt this particular brand was how I always imagined rubbing alcohol to taste, but it was like water to her by now.

Lane leaned over to me. "Scotty, your mother is here. Where is your brother right now?"

I felt immediately embarrassed. I couldn't tell him that Aaron was probably unattended right that very minute. Because that would certainly make me look bad for not calling the authorities and getting Aaron taken away from Mom. How could I tell him I was terrified I'd get custody of the kid? Not that I didn't love him, but I was busy all the time between going to school and working here, and if I got custody of Aaron, that would be the very end of my dreams for myself. And God knew I didn't have the resources to care for him.

Of course, Aaron would be better off in foster care than being with my mother. Theoretically. However, having been in foster homes periodically throughout my childhood, I knew it was hit or miss. Sometimes literally hit or miss because some of those homes involved me missing getting hit only because I ducked. Other times, I didn't duck fast enough, and, sure enough, I got hit.

Not to mention the home where I wasn't hit but was hit on, despite the fact I was only 13 at the time. And that pervert was a well-respected Wall Street trader.

Aaron was stuck between Scylla and Charybdis right at that moment.

Lane was looking at me. "You gotta go home," he said, having surmised from my silence the situation. "Your two-year-old brother can't be home alone."

I looked at my bleary-eyed mother desperately. No way could I afford to leave. I needed this shift. My checking account was on the verge of becoming overdrawn as it was. I had written some checks that would bounce unless I put the money from my shift into my account ASAP. And, unfortunately, that wouldn't be the first time. Three checks bouncing, $35 over-draft charges apiece, and suddenly, I wouldn't be able to make rent.

Because I constantly lived on the edge, any minor blip meant I'd become homeless again. And going home to watch Aaron instead of working the bar on a busy Saturday night would be one of those blips. I didn't work at the most popular bar in New York City, but I could still count on at least $400 in tips on a Saturday night, and, without that $400, the little rock would become an avalanche. I had a roommate, Jack, but he was in the same boat as me and couldn't spot me when I was short.

Then I heard a familiar voice. "Ms. James," the voice addressed me. I turned around, startled, and then saw who was calling to me. It was Professor O'Hara, the adjunct instructor in two of my architectural design courses at Columbia. He wasn't a full-time professor — I think he just taught a couple of courses. His full-time job was as the newest senior partner of the largest architectural firm in town. I understood he was new to the city, having come from a large firm in the Midwest somewhere. St. Louis, maybe? At any rate, I thought he lived in Missouri some-where before coming to New York.

My heart quickened. I had a mad, mad, mad crush on this guy, as did virtually everybody else I knew. He was, for lack of a better word, beautiful. And it helped that he was young and hip. Not for him a suit and tie — he taught our classes in casual jeans and button-downs, and he always looked just a bit like an English rocker. Or a male model. Certainly not a stuffy professor type. And I knew his work and admired his cutting-edge sensibilities with the buildings he designed. They were very signature, and his name was associated with many major projects around the world. Plus, from what I understood, he got his Bachelor's at Harvard and his Ph.D. at Oxford, so his educational credentials were more than intimidating.

"Hi, Professor O'Hara," I said. "What can I get you?" I peeked with a side-eye at my mother, who was still leaning on the bar, looking like she was about to hurl or hit me. I had no idea which would happen, as these events had always been so frequent in my life. She narrowed her eyes and looked to launch into another tirade. I felt like sinking into the floor in embarrassment and shame that my gorgeous professor would be privy to my dysfunctional life.

He motioned me closer and whispered in my ear. "You need some help?"

I felt myself blushing. "What do you mean?"

"I couldn't help but overhear. It sounds like there is a bit of a quandary you're in tonight."

"Oh, that," I said, waving my hand toward my mother in a dismissive way. "That's uh-"

"A big deal. You have a two-year-old that's unattended in your mother's house?"

I felt a bit stunned. I didn't even realize he was in the bar, let alone heard all of what was happening. "Well, yes, uh-"

At that, he was on his phone. "What's your mother's address?""

I hesitantly gave him the address.

He nodded. "Charisse," he said. "I've got a situation. You free to sit tonight?" He paused for a bit, looked at me, and nodded his head. Then he gave her the address. Then, addressing me after he got off the phone, he said, "I've got it covered."

I shook my head. "How is she going to get in the place? I'm pretty sure it's locked up tight."

"You got keys?" he asked.

At that, I dug into my purse beneath the bar. I handed him the keys to my mother's house. "Here," I said. "I'll pay you-"

He shook his head and took the keys. "Don't worry about it. I'll be back with these keys within the hour."

And, just like that, he was gone.

I was shaking now, with humiliation and rage at my mother. More people were streaming in the door, and crowds were forming around the bar. In the middle of it stood my incoherent mother. She now had her head on the bar and looked close to passing out. What was I going to do with her?

As if in answer, a man entered the bar and put his arm around her. "You need to come with me," he said.

I looked at him. "Who are you?"

"I'm Mr. O'Hara's driver," he said. "He asked me to come in here and give your mother a ride home."

I looked at my mom, hoping against hope she wouldn't make a scene and protest. But she was past that by then. She'd gone past her loud and screaming stage and into her incoherent stage, so she docilely let him lead her out of the bar.

I shook my head but didn't have a second to contemplate what had just happened because the bar was full of people, and I had to start rolling. People were already shouting and waving their glasses in the air. I felt shaken, but I trudged on and then addressed Lane while the two of us were passing one another to get various glasses and liquors.

"Sorry about that, Lane," I said. "That won't happen again," I said as I opened up a carton of cream and poured it into a glass with some vodka and Kahlua for a customer's White Russian.

"Sure," he said, scooping some ice into a glass and pouring rum and coke into it. "Let's hope not. Your mother is a piece of work."

"Ya think?" Then I turned to another customer and pointed to him. He shouted, "Tanqueray and tonic," and pointed to his glass. I grabbed the Tanqueray, poured it with some tonic, and shot it to him.

This continued as more and more people rushed in. In the back of my mind, I looked forward to seeing Professor O'Hara again and then shook my head. *Hot for the teacher? Aren't you just a bit old for that?* Actually, I never liked that particular song. A better song for the situation would be The Police's *Don't Stand So Close to Me.* I started singing the lyrics to this song softly to myself while I poured another drink and then smiled.

I caught my breath about an hour later when I spotted him again. Then I felt my spirits fall upon seeing he wasn't alone. He had on his arm a runway model I recognized from Fashion Week last year. Her face was also plastered on advertisements all over the city and in every magazine you could think of. The woman was at least six feet tall, only a couple inches shorter than Professor O'Hara, yet she

ANNIE JOCOBY

couldn't weigh more than 130 lbs. With a short blonde bob, cheekbones that could cut glass, enormous blue eyes, legs a colt would admire, and an impressive rack, she had the kind of physical perfection that was truly wondrous to behold in real life. I bit my lip, knowing this would be the kind of woman a guy like Professor O'Hara would date.

I immediately felt embarrassed for fantasizing about him.

He finally reached the bar, his arm still around his supermodel. "Your mother and brother are okay," he said. "Your mother is passed out on her couch, and I called a nanny I know to watch your little brother."

I nodded. "Thanks," I said, then shot a look over to a guy frantically waving his glass in the air. "I owe you."

Professor O'Hara just shook his head and then disappeared into the crowd.

I took a deep breath and continued my work.

I didn't see Professor O'Hara for the rest of the night, much as I wanted to. I scanned the crowd several times, but it seemed he'd completely left. *It's just as well. Like he would ever look at somebody like you. Drunk-ass mother and you're a broke student. To say he's way out of your league is overstating the matter.*

Of course, I was working on my master's in architecture, so that was something. I was proud of myself for this, as I never got even a modicum of support from anybody except for Jack, my roommate. At one point, I was living in an abandoned car, having sneaked away from the Wall Street trader. Nobody could find me for a year, which meant I'd also dropped out of school. Still, I was able to make up my missed classes and graduate on time, and at the top of my class at that.

Finally, the 3 AM last call arrived. I leaned against the bar, feeling exhausted and happy. I knew I'd made enough money to cover my floating checks, so there was a keen sense of relief there. After cleaning up my areas and doing my side work, I headed home, grabbed my ratty winter coat and hat, and headed to the subway station three blocks from the bar.

I finally got home around 4:30. My roommate, Jack, was still awake. He had one of his boyfriends over, and they were sprawled on the couch and watching a slasher pic.

"Scotch," he said, calling me by his special nickname for me. "Would you like a cocktail, love?"

"Oh, God, yes," I said, even though it was 4:30, and I really needed to be getting to bed. I was too wound, however, to sleep. "What are you watching?" I asked as Jack paused the movie to get up to make me a rum and seven. I sat on the floor, and Jack's sometime boyfriend, Rob, affectionately tousled my hair.

"One of the *Final Destination* movies. Not sure which. They all look the same after a little while," Rob said in his way-gay voice. Jack didn't usually like the twinks because Jack wasn't exactly a man's man himself, and he always said he wanted his men to balance him out, but apparently, he made an exception for this one.

"They do," I said, accepting my cocktail from Jack. "So, I guess I get the couch tonight, huh?" Jack got the bed whenever he had somebody over, which was often. Since I never had anybody over, I ended up sleeping on the hide-a-bed more often than not.

"Do you mind?" Jack asked. "I hate to ask that. You'll get the real bed tomorrow night, I promise."

I shrugged my shoulders. I lived in a car for a year. Anything beat that.

"Thanks, love. You're as adorable as ever," he said.

The three of us finished the movie around 6 AM, at

which point Jack and Rob finally retired to the bedroom. I pulled out the bed and fell asleep, still fully clothed.

I could sleep in a little because Jack and Rob, thankfully, only emerged from the bedroom around noon. Over breakfast, I told them about my night.

"So my mom comes in drunk off her ass again. Of course. And you'll never guess who came to my rescue."

"Who?" Jack was interested in this.

"You remember me telling you about my professor?"

"The hot one?"

"The smoking hot one," I said with a giggle. "Oh, lord, I'm quite sure he got an eyeful and an earful from dear Ms. James. I hope she wasn't too much in rare form last night."

"You know she was," Jack said. "Bitch don't know how to act differently." Jack poured me another glass of orange juice. "So, how did he come to your rescue?"

"He hired a nanny to go and watch Aaron and sent a driver to drive her drunk ass back to her hovel." I shook my head. "What a guy, huh?"

"Uh-huh. Just don't go fantasizing about Professor O'Dreamboat."

"I'm not," I said, immediately feeling embarrassed. I took another sip of orange juice and dug into my French toast. "So, what're you guys doing today?" I hoped they were going somewhere. I really needed some personal time.

"Catching some movies at the film festival they're having in midtown. You wanna come with?"

"No, thanks. I really need to decompress. This is my only day off. Besides, I need to do some studying." God knew I was way behind on that.

But I didn't end up studying. I ended up watching shows on television and zoning out on the couch. This was usually my stress reaction, and the entire events of the previous evening had me feeling way overburdened. I ended up dozing on the couch.

At about 3 PM, however, I heard my door buzz.

"Hello?" I said into the receiver. "May I help you?"

"Ms. James?" a familiar voice questioned me. "This is Professor O'Hara. Can I come up?"

*What the hell?* "Yeah, come on up," I said, buzzing him, and then looked around the room. The apartment was neat enough, but I felt even more embarrassed about the size of it. Living in Manhattan was ridiculously expensive. He had to understand that. Even so, I imagined he might be appalled by my hovel.

He appeared at my door a few minutes later. My breath caught upon looking at him. Dressed in a leather jacket, scarf, white button down and jeans, he looked the part of a male model who somehow managed to become one of the world's premiere architects. His eyes were so blue I couldn't stand to look at them for more than two seconds before I looked away with shyness.

"Come in," I said. "Sit down. Can I fix you a drink?"

"No, I can't stay," he said. "My girlfriend is in the car downstairs."

"You have a car?" I said, feeling my heart sink when he referred to the coltish supermodel as his "girlfriend." "You're the only person I know who has a car." I went to the fridge to find him bottled water, even though he said he couldn't stay. That was the least I could do.

He smiled, showing his dimples. I felt my knees turning to jelly, and I saw my hand shaking as I handed him my proffering of water. He opened it up and drank it politely. "I just wanted to make sure you're okay. I didn't get to see you much last night. Penelope didn't want to stay."

I felt a little stunned. Nobody had ever gone out of their

way to help me like this. "Yes, thanks so much for last night."

He waved his hand dismissively. "Well, we were in the neighborhood so...." At that, I heard a loud sound of a car honking. He shrugged. "Double parked. I'll see you tomorrow."

And, just like that, he was gone.

# Broken: Chapter Two

## NICK

I made my way back to my car after seeing Scotty, my student. I felt bad for her, having seen the effect of dysfunctional parents upon Ryan, my best friend and sometime lover back in the day.

I got into the car. Penelope had a disinterested look on her beautiful face. She raised a single eyebrow. "You see your lackey?" she asked, then brought out a compact mirror and looked into it. "I really need to get more highlights," she said with a note of disgust. She fluffed her hair up a little and then pursed her lips. She looked like a parakeet flirting with her reflection. The parakeets had an excuse, though- they thought their reflection was another bird. Penelope was just a narcissist.

"Yeah, I saw her. She seemed okay."

Penelope wasn't listening to me, though. She was too busy looking in the mirror. I reached over and grabbed the mirror out of her hand.

She narrowed her eyes, said nothing, and just brought another mirror out of her purse.

I sighed. It wasn't worth fighting about.

"So, I was thinking of asking Scotty if she'd like to intern at my office," I said.

This got Penelope's attention. "Like hell, you will."

I raised both of my eyebrows. "I wasn't aware I had to get your permission to do this."

"Listen, buddy. Don't ever think I can't snap my fingers and be with anybody in this city. You piss me off, and you'll see what happens."

At that, I stopped the car in the middle of the busy Manhattan street. "Get out," I ordered her. "NOW."

The look on her face was priceless as she stepped out of my car and made her way to the sidewalk. She was immediately on her phone and hailing a cab simultaneously.

I shook my head. Somehow women like Penelope were losing their hold on my attention. It was almost as if Iris broke some kind of fever I had, a fever that actually drew me to these narcissistic bimbos in the first place. Penelope wasn't even particularly good in bed. Narcissistic people usually weren't. Alexis was the exception, but she really wasn't narcissistic as much she was just plumb crazy.

Iris had managed to penetrate my armor, and I didn't like it. It was time to put my wall up again. So, I backed up the car and motioned to Penelope. "Get in," I ordered. To my surprise, she got back into the car without a word of protest. She looked at me expectantly. "Let's get one thing straight," I said, "if I want to offer Scotty an internship, I'm going to. I won't have you or anybody else dictating anything in my life. We clear?"

She said nothing, just nodded her head.

"Good. Now let's go to my home."

And we headed to my loft in Tribeca, Penelope not saying another word.

# Broken: Chapter Three

## SCOTTY

Monday evening, after my night design course, Professor O'Hara asked to speak to me.

"Ms. James," he called to me as I was packing up my backpack. I turned my head. I was still so mortified about how he had to help me with my mom, and his short visit to my place didn't dim this mortification one bit. I spent the entire class that evening studiously avoiding his eyes.

"Yes, Professor?"

"I was wondering if you could meet me in my office tomorrow."

"What time?" I asked, thinking I'd have to fit the visit between studying, going to class, and my night shift at the bar tomorrow night, which would start at 4 PM.

"What's good for you?"

"No later than two," I said. That would give me time to take the subway home, change and shower and get to the bar on time, assuming that this wasn't a long meeting.

"Two it is then," he said.

Which was how I found myself going to his office at two

o'clock that Tuesday. I had no idea why he wanted to see me. I hoped the incident with my mom and brother wouldn't rear its ugly head. I really wanted to put that entire thing behind me.

I took a deep breath as I made my way to his office. I knocked lightly on the door, which was open.

"Come in," he said, and I entered his enormous office. I was stunned he could have such a beautiful place here on campus, considering he was only an adjunct professor. High ceilings and floor-to-ceiling windows that looked out on the bustling city.

He had an amazing and modern taste in decor. A glass desk wrapped around one of the walls, and a leather sofa with chrome feet was on another wall. His floors were hardwood, with an enormous throw-rug in multiple colors and patterns covering much of the area. A Kandinsky painting was on one of the walls, a piece of artwork typical for the artist - it was abstract, a riotous melange of color and form. I somehow knew this about him; he preferred edgy and contemporary because the buildings he designed all had a certain contemporary and edgy flair.

My heart was pounding as I approached one of his ergonomic chairs. He looked at me, and my heart was pounding even more. Those eyes, those beautiful blue eyes….so bright and so…haunted? Was I interpreting them correctly? I shook my head, shaking off my woman's intuition in the process.

I took a deep breath. "You wanted to see me?"

"Yes. Do you mind if I call you Scotia?" Which was my given name.

I shook my head. "Actually, everybody just calls me Scotty."

He smiled, his dimples reappearing. I wanted to melt

after seeing those dimples. His teeth were absolutely perfect, and his smile lit up the entire room.

"Ok, Scotty," he said. "Let's get down to brass tacks. I asked you here because I was wondering where you wanted to go with your career. You have some real talent, and my firm is looking for an intern."

My mouth dropped open. The top architectural firm in New York City, one of the top ten in the world, and I was getting the chance to intern with them?

My mouth ran before my brain could catch up. "What's the catch?" Then I immediately felt embarrassed. "I mean-"

But Professor O'Hara was smiling. "No catch. I just see some real potential with you, that's all."

I wasn't prepared for this, somehow. And I really didn't know where I would ever fit it in. A full load of graduate architectural classes, working part-time...I barely had a chance to sleep as it was. And there was, in the back of my mind, the thought that this was possibly a pity offer. Although I didn't quite know how he could've convinced his partners to hire me out of pity.

"Professor O'Hara," I began.

"Please, call me Nick."

That didn't seem right, calling him by his first name. I never called a professor by his first name. But I obliged anyway. "Nick. That's such a wonderful offer, but I don't have the time to fit something like that in."

He nodded. "Well, there'll be pay, of course. In exchange for 20 hours a week at the firm, we can pay you $40,000 a year."

$40,000 a year? I made about that working 30 hours a week at the bar. And this position, unlike my bartending position, would actually give me a great deal of professional development.

"Uh," I began.

He interrupted. "Scotty. I get the feeling you don't believe in yourself." He didn't elaborate on this comment but just sat there, looking at me. His body language and expression were no longer inviting. He looked annoyed, and his arms were crossed in front of him.

"No, it's not that. It's just, well, there are so many other talented students out there. I was just wondering if, you know, this has something to do with my home life."

He raised one eyebrow. "What, you think I would stick my neck out for you because your mother is a drunk, and your brother probably needs to be in foster care?" Then he snorted. "Somehow, I get the feeling you not only don't believe in yourself, but you also don't believe in me."

This conversation was taking a turn for the surreal. I never imagined I'd be having such a talk with my professor. "It's not that," I said, feeling my defensive hackles rising.

"Then what is it?"

I wanted to tell him I didn't feel I was worthy. I wanted to be honest. Being a foster kid, off and on, for most of my life instilled a general sense of unworthiness in me, as did my verbally abusive mother, who always told me I'd never amount to anything. But I was too embarrassed to admit to this. So I just said, "I don't want to work for your firm. It's not the direction I want to go."

"Really. Not the direction you want to go." This was not a question but a very skeptical statement. "Not the direction you want to go."

"Right. I was thinking more along the lines of a firm with more of a classical aesthetic."

"Scotty. I've seen your designs. You're a perfect fit."

"I just don't want to," I said, well aware of how unprofessional I was sounding. "Can I go? I'm going to be late for my shift." I desperately looked at the clock on the wall. It read 2:30. I would be cutting it close as it was.

He said nothing but just waved his hand dismissively.

He looked pissed.

At that, I left.

**Grab your copy...**
**vinci-books.com/broken**